all fired up

A Barefoot by Moonlight Mystery-Romance

by
Carmine Valentine

Other Stories by Carmine Valentine

This book is dedicated to my children
Jace Marius Anderson and Marci Ash Anderson.
Love you both with all my heart.

Chapter 1

It was her experience that if she wanted a light to turn green at an intersection, Marianne would only need to reach for her lipstick. Sure enough, she'd never get the glossy pink to her lips before things were in motion again. Sometimes it worked to her advantage and sometimes it didn't.

When it worked, she considered it lipstick magic.

It was her modern day take on what her grandmother used to tell her.

Find something to occupy your time and what you're waiting for will happen before you know it.

Marianne had just boarded the ferry bound for the San Juan Islands. She was ready to try some lipstick magic to get the vessel in motion. At this rate, the sun would be down before she pulled into the dark driveway of her new home on Orcas Island, a home that was turning out to have far more shadows in the night than she'd anticipated. And she was having a hard time remembering if she'd left a light on to welcome her home.

She pulled down the visor mirror and twisted up the slender pink tube. In that moment, not only did she get a reminder in the mirror that her self-attempt at hair coloring out of a box had brought out more of the red in her hair than the blonde, and quite unevenly, but the magic didn't happen.

A warning yell from the deckhand yanked her attention to the rear fender of the black-as-night motorcycle she was about to crunch. She stood on the brakes so hard that her gold hoop earrings swayed wildly against the side of her neck. Another inch and the heavy-duty front grill protector on her Land Rover would have done more than just press into the black duffel bag strapped to the back of the motorcycle.

How she'd managed to forget to put her vehicle in park was beyond her; too much on her mind perhaps. Now she was about to take the heat. A tall, lean man in a black Kevlar jacket turned from where he stood near the safety chain strung across the opening of the ferry. Behind him, the waters of Rosario Strait looked cold and choppy with a gray sky above.

One look at the straight line to his mouth and the unyielding jawline and the silver lipstick tube fell from her hands. He looked like the dangerous pirates in the romance novels she wrote. And just as handsome with the black bandana he wore on top his head. Only her fictional pirates didn't sport aviator glasses hiding death rays. She felt it all the same, right through the windshield.

Like her fictional heroines, she didn't run. Didn't mean her pulse didn't race as she fought the urge to bolt from her vehicle. With her imagination always at work, she had to consider how to defend herself, if said pirate loved his motorcycle so much that he'd take revenge. Unlike her heroines, she didn't keep a dagger hidden in a corseted bodice. She had nothing in the form of defense, except a semi-decent swing with a five-iron and that was three years ago when she'd given up golf along with her last boyfriend.

She let go of the steering wheel long enough to lock the doors as the man approached.

He rapped on the offending grill protector, not that he needed to get her attention. He had it.

"Back it up, slowly," he said. Along with the command came another death ray.

She did as he'd instructed, watching the rearview mirror to make sure she didn't hit the car behind her. This time she put the vehicle in park and set the emergency brake, all with the deckhand in her side vision shaking his head like he hadn't seen enough stupid things today.

Knowing she had to do the right thing, she got out of her vehicle.

"I'm truly sorry. Any damage?" she said to the pirate biker.

Peace wasn't to be made so easily. He ignored her as he inspected the motorcycle by first testing the stability of the kickstand and then running his hand over the rear fender. Only then did he unstrap his duffel bag as if that was the signal to the Motorcycle Gods that all was good and no lightning bolts were needed to strike down an inept mortal driver.

There wasn't much standing room in between the tightly-packed lanes of vehicles. It was even more obvious that she was in the way when he took her by the upper arms and bodily moved her to one side so that he could pass. The biker who was going to hold a grudge over a gentle nudge to his motorcycle favored one leg as he walked toward the stairwell.

"Sensitive," she said, thinking that the hottest looking man she'd seen in a long while was out of hearing range.

He wasn't.

The pirate biker stopped dead in his tracks, his head turned slightly as if his radar had picked-up on an anomaly.

If his tactic was to intimidate without straining a muscle, it worked. She was back in her vehicle in two seconds flat and locking the doors, again, only to see that she hadn't been worth his time. He was out of sight up the stairwell.

She'd give the biker a head start, in finding a seat on the passenger deck.

Lipstick was good for other things besides getting traffic lights to change and seaworthy vessels to begin moving. Sometimes, it was simply a woman's body armor. It wasn't an easy task applying it to her lips. Her hand shook from her near-death experience.

From the back seat, she retrieved her handbag. It felt heavier than when she'd moved it there to make room in the passenger seat for her friend, whose expensive perfume still lingered in the air.

She should have known that Fiona was up to something when she'd spent too much time fussing with whose shopping bag was whose when she'd dropped her off at her home in the Magnolia neighborhood of Seattle.

With her hand in the tote-style handbag, Marianne's fingers closed around a hard, cold object leaving no doubt as to what it was her friend had left behind. She'd shared enough of the mysterious happenings in her new home with Fiona that she should have expected something like this. One of Fiona's predominate traits was her protective nature.

Marianne stared down at the diminutive gun she held. It was very tempting to walk back to the stern and throw her friend's idea of protection into the ferry's frothy wake. But she knew the history of the Lady Derringer and it held great sentimental value to her friend. Only now it was in Marianne's possession and she wasn't sure how to handle the situation.

Fact was, she wouldn't be in this situation, handgun in her lap and a dangerous-looking biker she now had to avoid, if she hadn't pulled the short straw this year resulting in this becoming her turn to accept the writing group's dare; that they select the location of her next novel. The stipulation being that she had to live in that location for a short period. It was a game they played that had worked quite well for the other writers and produced some of their best work.

Marianne wasn't so sure she'd have the same luck. The group had selected Orcas Island, her hometown. She had only herself to blame. She had once told the group that she would never move back to the San Juan Islands. The group felt that the conflict of returning home would be great for writing. If only they'd met her grandfather, first. But on the other hand, she hadn't seen her younger sister in a while. So, after convincing herself that time would fly by, she'd accepted the dare.

Time wasn't flying by.

She was two weeks in, and it wasn't the homecoming she'd envisioned. The air between her and her sister Missy was chilly, to put it mildly. She would far prefer traveling in the opposite direction, back to downtown Seattle and her loft-style condominium overlooking Elliott Bay.

Instead, she was returning to a second home that she'd purchased at auction, on impulse. What had she been thinking? The dare had only required that she lived in the location for her next book. Not buy real estate as an investment.

As a young girl, she had always dreamt of living in the quaintly, beautiful Perrigo Mansion that looked like something right out of a fairy tale. Decades later, it still had that charm. It also had chilling drafts, broken faucets, and creaky floors.

And too many noises in the dead of night.

Then there was the note that she'd found tied to the front gate last week. She'd yet to decide if the tone was threatening or just unfriendly. Either way, one thing was clear. It hadn't been delivered by any welcoming committee.

The ferry began to pull away from the dock. She felt drawn to look two lanes over to her right to a black Suburban. The sky had darkened since boarding and, although the car deck had lighting, it wasn't so easy to see into the interior of the vehicles. She couldn't tell if the man in the driver's seat sat facing forward or looked in her direction.

Her cell phone rang, playing a little Beethoven Tune of *Für Elise*.

"Hello?" she felt she needed to whisper.

"For a minute, I thought I'd dialed a hot sex number," her friend Fiona said.

"Girlfriend," Marianne began sweetly, "you are in so much trouble."

"You found it. Good! There's a box of bullets in your handbag, as well."

"I don't need a gun for protection."

"Quit being a ninny. You can't kill anyone with it. Just aim for their kneecaps. You don't know what you're dealing with, yet. My great auntie's gun may come in handy. Which brings me to say, again, please take the note to the sheriff."

"I'll think about it." Marianne tried to get a better look at the driver in the Suburban.

"You sound distracted. What's going on? Did something else happen?"

"I'm on the ferry. I think there's a weirdo a few cars over. I can feel him staring at me."

"Don't look at him, for God's sake! Or better yet, do look. Be aggressive. Walk over there and ask the creep if he wrote the note."

"You're not helpful."

"I'm kidding. Besides, the group and I have been texting about you and we're worried. The more we think about it, the note read like it was meant for someone else. *'There's traitor in your blood*,'" Fiona quoted the note. "What is that supposed to mean?"

"I'm just as baffled. However, you all don't need to worry. I truly appreciate your concern, but I can take care of myself."

"This is not something to handle on your own, Marianne. Receiving an anonymous note, such as this one, is threatening. What are you planning to do? Wait until he's standing over your bed in the middle of the night before calling the sheriff? That might be a tad too late, my dear."

"It's not going to come to that."

"How do you know it hasn't already? What about those muddy footprints in the hallway?"

"They could have been mine. I was out in the yard that day."

"Are you certain? I thought you said the footprints were larger than yours."

The reminder sent a chill up her spine. "I don't remember what I said, Fiona." She let out a sigh. "Here's why I don't want to go to the sheriff, if I can help it. I went to school with the dispatcher who is the biggest gossiper on the island. Far too many residents didn't hold back telling me that I was getting in over my head buying Perrigo Mansion. I don't want them to think they were probably right. Besides, now that I think about it," and she knew that she was looking for the quickest fix by pinning this on the suspect easiest to pin this on, "I may know who this is and she's really not a threat." If indeed her growing suspicions were correct.

"Dish. Who do you think is the intruder?"

"The eccentric old lady who used to live in the mansion."

"She doesn't sound like the type to leave a note. I thought you said she doesn't hesitate to get in your face and tell you what she thinks. Besides, why would she be talking about 'traitor in your blood'? I thought you barely knew this woman."

"She knows my family. She and my grandpa went to school together here on the island." Marianne thought of old Gilly and realized that an obvious physical limitation might remove her as a suspect. Just as quickly as her hopes of solving this mystery had soared, they plummeted. "Now that I think more about it, there's a good chance it wasn't her. She's short. I even had trouble reaching the note."

"It must be a man, or a really tall, mean chick." Her friend's shiver was palpable through the cellphone. "Promise me that you'll keep your cellphone on you at all times, in case you need to call for help?"

"I promise."

"Now tell me, my dear city girl, how's the re-acclimation going back in your hometown?"

"Wouldn't be so bad if my sister would talk to me."

"Ah, yes. Otherwise you could have stayed with her instead of sinking money into a distressed relic."

"Perrigo Mansion has potential. Besides, Missy would invite Attila the Hun to sleep over before she'd invite me. Then there's her boyfriend who I like to avoid. He thinks he's every woman's dream."

It wasn't unusual for Fiona to stray towards her next question. "Have you heard from your brother, lately?"

"He's a hard one to pin down. He always drops in unexpectedly."

"I'd sure like to be there when he does," Fiona sighed. Her friend had met her brother only once. Ever since, she'd been trying to find a way to meet him again, however subtle her attempts. "Can I give you a bit more advice?" She didn't wait for Marianne's go-ahead. "You know what I always say about the best way to deal with any form of stress or craziness going on in one's life. You need to put just two things together."

Although Marianne rolled her eyes at her friend's go-to fix-all, her body responded otherwise and her heart rate increased. It wasn't like she hadn't thought about her friend's remedy before. She just wasn't sure she could be as casual about it as Fiona.

Her long-time friend went on with her sell, "It takes your mind off your troubles long enough to gain a different perspective. Sometimes you realize that the problem just isn't yours. Trust me, Marianne. It works."

Truth was, Marianne's fictional heroines seemed to have no problem sliding between the satin sheets with pirates they barely knew.

Fiona laughed. "You're considering, aren't you?"

"No!"

"Liar." There was a smile in her voice. "Call me when you get home so that I know you made it safely."

"Yes, ma'am."

Not a second later, the dome light came on in the bad-vibe vehicle and she cringed at its occupant.

Her sister's boyfriend, Gerald Cain, lowered his window as he smiled in a manner that she'd seen him work on several of the women on the island. She struggled with whether it was her duty to let her sister know how *friendly* her boyfriend was with the female population.

She would have preferred to ignore the man living with her sister. However, politeness had her lowering the window to cold air and the noise from the ferry's engines.

"Fancy meeting you here," Gerald said.

"How are you this evening?" she replied.

"I'm all fine and dandy." He brushed his sun-bleached hair out of his eyes. The sleeves of his white sweater were pushed up past his elbows to bunch over his biceps making them appear bigger. This wasn't the first time he'd displayed his beach tan and muscular arms.

"New car?" Marianne asked.

"Isn't she sweet? Just picked her up last week."

She smiled politely, wishing he'd kept his older model Saab with black exhaust trailing because it was easier to see coming, giving her time to go in another direction.

"What brings you off the island?" Gerald said. "Lunch date in Seattle?"

The back of her neck tingled. She hadn't told anyone where she was going today.

"I didn't go that far." She felt zero guilt lying to the man talking like he knew her intimately.

It creeped her out that his smile remained frozen on his face even though it felt like there was no longer a smile in his eyes. She thought for a moment that their chat was over.

"Don't you want to know what I was doing today?"

"Not really," she said through the tight smile she held in place. Her finger hovered on the window control.

He told her anyway. "I just got back from scouting out new business in estate sales and antiques. My uncle and I are starting to specialize in that area. We help people figure out what they should and shouldn't hang on to."

This wasn't the first time Gerald had hinted at the antiques inside of Marianne's new home.

Something about his tone made her wish that the dark-haired pirate was standing between her and the Suburban. She wasn't too surprised by his next approach.

"A woman living alone should have a man checking on her from time to time."

She knew where that was going and stopped him. "Thanks for your concern. I'm fine on my own."

The window was halfway up when he brought up her elderly neighbor's name, a woman who was also the unhappy former owner of Perrigo Mansion.

"Gilly mentioned that there may be more to the set besides the ruby and diamond opera glasses we sold for her recently online. If you come upon them, it would sure help her in her dire situation."

At first, she wasn't sure that she'd heard him correctly. Marianne had a knack for details and she didn't recall seeing any opera glasses on the inventory list that came with the mansion. Even if it was an item that was missed, and ended up leaving with Gilly, all the better. If she could help Gilly additionally by getting her to take more antiques to sell, she would do so. Just not with Gerald's help.

She waved goodbye as she powered up the window.

With more incentive than ever before, she was out of her vehicle and heading for the stairs. Cold wind blew through the car deck, whipping at her hair, and tugging on her coattails. Out through the wide opening at the stern, the ferry's white frothy wake left a trail as they drew farther and farther from the mainland.

A fragment of nostalgia hit her, a feeling from long ago when she was returning from camp and longing for Orcas Island with her grandmother's oatmeal raisin cookies and warm hugs and a bedroom shared with her little sister where they had matching blue and white quilts on their beds. Where had that feeling come from and so out of nowhere? Seattle was home now. Not Orcas Island.

The sound of her heels echoed hollowly as she hurried up the narrow set of stairs. She pushed in through the heavy steel door to the crowded passenger area only to find a long line at the concession stand where she'd hoped to buy a decent cup of coffee. From where she stood, a vacant seat did not look promising.

Keeping her fingers crossed that she wouldn't have to return to the car deck for the crossing, and possibly be subjected to more of Gerald's attentions, she made her way through the seating area.

She came upon what appeared to be an unoccupied booth in the forward section. Until she saw a man's long denim-clad legs stretched out, his head back against the seat where the last of the sun's golden rays came in through the window and fell across his cheekbones.

The pirate-biker looked peaceful enough in sleep, completely throwing her off as to how this could possibly be the same man who'd sent her death rays. Instead of the sexy don't-make-me-kill-you look, she now saw a man who was sexy and approachable and maybe stayed in touch with his mother. The things a little nap and a kiss from the setting sun could do for a pirate.

Struggling not to be led in by the half-moon of his dark lashes, that lay innocently against his cheekbones, making a woman wonder what he dreamt of, she allowed her curiosity to roam. A faint white scar resided just beneath his chin, not quite covered by the stubble along his dark unshaven jaw. A rebel rouser scar or one earned while defending a woman's honor? She gave her head a shake to snap out of this transfixion that had come over her, and got back to the business-at-hand. She needed a place to sit.

His long legs and the duffel bag on the floor blocked access to the opposite bench seat. Both deterrents sent a clear 'not sharing' signal. In the open side pocket of the bag, a folded map and an eyeglass case were visible.

There were some decisions in life that she was more than willing to think twice about, even as Fiona's love advice cooed to her in her head. Another look over her shoulder did nothing more than to confirm that he was it for a bench buddy. However, looking away proved to be bad timing. The rough water in the channel caused the floor to roll just enough to send her off balance on her high heels.

She fell forward over the bag and right on top of its owner.

Strong hands locked onto either side of her ribcage.

Through the disarray of her wind-blown hair that had fallen across her eyes, she saw only his mouth, inches below her own.

A highly precarious position to be in, and all she could think of was that Fiona would give her a perfect score for ingenuity.

"I didn't plan this," she said as her heart thumped an unusual rhythm against her ribcage.

"I was hoping this was an improvement on your apology," he replied, still with his focus on what was before him.

As his breath moved the silky fabric of her blouse, going right through the thin material, the thought occurred to her that she should get off this man's lap.

She'd blame her next words on Fiona's love coaching working on her sublimely. "Does this mean I'm forgiven?"

Thick black lashes slowly fanned up until a pair of dark blue eyes locked onto her own. He looked warmly amused, and more, making her aware of the heat from his hands where they held her, as well as the warmth of his thigh where her hip rested. A slow bone melt had begun.

"Would you mind letting go?" she said.

"You first."

To her embarrassment, her hands were attached to his biceps, like she was on a hot date.

"I'm sure we can work this out," he said.

"I would hope so." Her face grew warmer. "We are, after all, adults."

His voice deepened. "That, we are."

She released her grip and he did his part.

Back on her feet, she promptly spun around to straighten her clothes, sending another look around for any place else to sit.

It grew worse. Her handbag was no longer on her arm.

"Looking for this?"

The leather handbag lay upside down on the floor between them. As he made to pick it up off the floor, the Lady Derringer tumbled out. Their heads nearly butted together in their grab for the handgun. He proved to have a faster response time and her hand closed over his.

"Is it loaded?" he said. "I'm asking for my own benefit."

"Of course, it's not loaded." *Smart-ass,* she wanted to add but was more concerned as to whether she'd alarmed any of the passengers by the sight of a gun.

"Open your handbag and I'll drop it in and no one will be the wiser," he said.

The handgun made it successfully back into its hiding place. Her next move didn't exactly reward him for his assistance. As she stood and turned toward the opposite seat, her handbag swung wide. The accidental smack of hard object to kneecap brought a flat-out curse from the biker.

"Christ!" He was tight-lipped with a hand over his left knee, looking more like a man trying to pretend it hadn't hurt.

"I'm so sorry." She'd truly meant it as he'd grown pale beneath his healthy color.

"It's nothing," he said through gritted teeth. Yet his pointed look told her that she was the reason for the bottle of over-the-counter pain relievers he'd pulled from his jacket pocket. He popped the lid off with practiced ease and tossed a few tablets back to swallow them dry.

With the air between them distinctively cooler, he resumed his nap, or at least that's how it appeared. He was relaxed in the same manner as when she'd landed on him. And that was that, apparently.

However, she couldn't get comfortable just yet. Unless she was mistaken, that was Fiona's box of ammo that was now sharing the side pocket with his map.

Chapter 2

Her opportunity would come soon enough. She'd give his pain medication time to work and then test his mood.

Two strikes against her with this bad-boy stranger. She seriously doubted that the unavoidable look down her blouse had balanced the score. Perhaps it would have been wiser to stay in her vehicle. However, she wasn't about to retreat because that wasn't an out she'd give her fictional heroines. She'd get those bullets back. She just didn't know how, yet.

She pulled a fashion magazine from her handbag and idly flipped through the pages while trying not to look at her handsome bench buddy. If she had a measuring tape, the biker would easily hit the six-foot mark. When she'd had her hand over his on the gun, she'd noticed scars across his knuckles and his pinky finger was crooked, like it had been broken at one time. Her guess was bar fights.

This wouldn't be the first time that she was guilty of unfair stereotyping. However, in this case, it was necessary. Otherwise, her thoughts kept wandering back to how it felt to have his hands on her and whether she'd imagined that he'd brushed his thumbs ever so slightly near the swell of her breasts when setting her back on her feet.

She used the magazine to fan her warm face and neck. This was going to be a long crossing.

To pass the time, she read the magazine front to back and then back to front. A check of the time on her cellphone showed that they were only halfway to Orcas Island. She was running out of ways to keep her mind off the pirate biker, even going as far as to have pulled all the perfume advertisement cards from the pages of the magazine to rub along the tender spot of her wrists.

Suddenly her bench buddy stirred.

In the next moment, he was smoothly on his feet, even with the care he took with his leg.

From behind the magazine, she discreetly watched as he used his boot to guide the duffel bag against the seat he'd occupied, moving it farther from her reach.

With that tended to, he said, "Watch my gear for me? You do owe me." He added a wink as he walked away.

His limp was more noticeable than before. She tried not to feel guilty and tried not to like this unexpected charm.

How easy he had made this for her. Keeping one eye on the biker now at the concession stand, she reached out with the toe of her polished boot to try and hook the strap on the bag to drag it closer. She missed the first time and her second attempt ended up being more of a kick, with her boot connecting with a hard object.

Curious, she gave the bag another kick.

Whatever it was, it was solid, like metal. All that kicking proved to be time wasted. Just as she leaned forward to reach for the far pocket, he turned away from the counter, pocketing his change.

She quickly turned to the window and saw, not the pink-tinged sky silhouetting darkened islands, but the reflection of a woman looking wide-eyed and unsure about another night in a big house with mysterious sounds.

Maybe she should call her brother.

Maybe she should have done a better job of tucking in her silky blouse. Her eyes were drawn to the rest of her appearance, like her hair mussed from the wind. Dangerous biker to avoid or not, she couldn't believe she looked like this.

Just as she tucked a loose strand of hair behind her ear, she noticed her reflection was not alone.

The biker stood behind her holding two cups of coffee.

"Truce?" he said.

***

Bad coffee in a Styrofoam cup; Jack Sanders wasn't sure it would work on this stiff and untrusting figure of the most attractive woman who'd fallen into his lap in a long time. He took his seat again, sipping from the hot beverage while sending casual glances to the woman who'd been kicking his duffel bag.

The long drive up the Interstate had tested his rehabbed knee and not in a good way, putting Jack in a bad mood because he needed to be in top shape the following week.

The nap and pain relievers had helped. As did thinking about what the redhead would look like wearing nothing at all.

He hadn't planned to go there, but he'd needed the distraction, and it was hard not to fantasize with the way she kept flipping her thick, wavy hair over her shoulder and playing with the buttons on her silky blouse, like she couldn't decide whether to unbutton one or not.

Jack glanced out the window. One week was the maximum time he'd allotted for checking out the island and the property left to him by his grandfather.

He thought about his grandmother's reaction the day of the funeral. She'd been stunned and then angry that her husband had property on Orcas Island. She hadn't wanted Jack to travel to Washington State, telling him, almost begging him, to let a realtor handle it all.

His mother was just as eager for him to sell the property and buy something in Portland close to her, believing that his injury spelled the end of his army career.

That wasn't his plan, despite the advice from his friend and sports physician, Maxwell, whose text message this morning hadn't set well with him. He'd been expecting his friend to be more supportive of his plan to return to his unit. His thumb hovered over the delete button as he read the text message again.

You asked for my professional advice. Well here it is. Your x-rays look like shit. Don't fight the medical discharge.

All it's going to take is one time for your knee to fail on a mission and you could get yourself killed not to mention others. I'm telling you as a friend, time to get out while you're still in one piece. What is it you tell your men? Suck it up and move on.

Jack deleted the message then slipped his cellphone into the same jacket pocket as his airplane ticket to Virginia where he was scheduled for a physical evaluation. He'd pass. He had to. Then he'd be back doing what he did best.

The woman who'd landed on him had provided, for now, the distraction he'd needed to ignore the little voice in his head that might agree with Maxwell.

His seat companion sat with her back to the corner where the cushioned seat and large window met.

She was stylishly dressed wearing a tan suede coat that complimented her coloring along with the fringed light blue scarf around her shoulders. The coat had fallen open to reveal a nice shape beneath the drape of a cream blouse and slender jeans that flared out over fashionable boots.

He hadn't had a view this nice in a long time. A woman who'd felt good in his hands, and with a pair of blue eyes he wouldn't mind getting lost in during his short stay. Now she sat as far away from him as she could. It bothered him that that bothered him.

Jack's career didn't lend well to the type of relationship his best friend, Maxwell, had with his long-time lady. He envied his friend, however, the decision of career over that of making time for a relationship was his own. Yet the woman sitting across from him had given him a glimpse of something that he couldn't quite put his finger on. The saying 'two ships passing in

21

the night' came to mind. Two ships could at least have a conversation to pass the time.

"Visiting or do you live on one of the islands?" He sat casually, waiting to see if she would answer him or ignore him.

***

"I live in the area," Marianne replied.

Unless he had reason to leave his seat again, she might as well say goodbye to the box of bullets.

She'd considered telling him of where her box of ammo had landed. What were the chances this man might think she'd dropped them there on purpose, as an excuse to continue to engage with him? She'd eat the Styrofoam cup before giving his ego that reward.

The Lady Derringer was now destined to be a dead weight in her handbag. The best it would serve her, now, would be to just throw it at any intruder, or the note writer, if they were to show themselves.

He moved and she jumped, coming close to spilling the hot beverage. She felt foolish, then, as he'd done nothing more dangerous than lean forward with a hand outstretched.

"Jack Sanders," said the biker pirate.

"Gigi Divine." It was out before she could take it back, using the name of the heroine in her latest manuscript. She tugged her hand free and wished for a million miles between them. Just because he looked like Gigi Divine's hero didn't mean she needed to be the heroine.

"Where are you staying on Orcas Island?" he said.

"I never said I was going there."

He looked amused. "You might want to let your vehicle know. It's in the lane bound for Orcas Island."

His observation of this fact irked her. She shoved the magazine into her handbag. "Maybe I'm in the wrong lane."

"Good thing I'm not parked behind you."

She sent him a phony smile and pointedly looked out the window hoping he'd get the hint and wishing she didn't like that he was flirting with her.

The ferry slowly passed evergreen-covered islands that looked tranquil in the dusk with warm, golden lights in the windows of the homes tucked along the shore.

"I bet you never get tired of this view," he said.

It sounded like another truce. One difficult to not accept. And her grandmother had raised her with good manners.

"No, I don't," she said.

"I've been told that San Juan Island is the one worth visiting, that I shouldn't even bother with Orcas Island."

His eyes briefly glanced to her ankles then her waist before making eye contact again. Flattering. Dangerous. She drew in a steadying breath and tried to stay focused on making this just idle chit-chat.

"It depends on what you're looking for. In my opinion, Orcas Island has more to offer. It's the only island in this cluster of islands with several mountains worth hiking. The view from Mount Constitution is breathtaking. And there is a cove popular for its level of privacy, if you're into that sort of thing."

"What sort of thing?" He smiled as he sipped from his coffee. When she didn't reply, he nicely changed the subject, much to her relief. "The reason I asked where you might be staying is because I'm looking for lodging and I was hoping that you could recommend a place."

A safer topic, or was it? Suddenly the unknown returned to hover at the back of her mind. What if all these questions had a purpose? Her heart gave a little leap of alarm. What if this man had left the note at her gate and now he was just playing with her? Or was she just on edge because he was dangerously attractive and she'd never met anyone like him before? Regardless, the last thing she was about to do was to help him find a place to rest his head for the night.

"I could recommend a few places, although, you may be out of luck." She set the coffee she'd barely touched on the windowsill. "It's the start of whale watching season." She crossed her fingers and hoped that he'd strike out finding any vacancies on her island.

"What do you know about the Heron Inn at Deer Harbor?"

She caught her breath. "You can't stay there."

"Why not?"

The excuses came rapid fire. "It's been closed for decades. The roof's about to fall in. It's barely clinging to the side of the hill."

"I'm adventurous."

She surged on with every conceivable reason as to why he shouldn't visit the old inn, "It's infested with rats and there's black mold everywhere. If the place burned down tomorrow, I'd be saved from another night of listening to some teenager's loud music. I suggest you try San Juan Island for lodging."

"I take it you live near the old inn?"

The moments ticked by as she realized how clever he was. What all had she revealed as she'd babbled on about the island? Had she told him enough to lead him to the window above her kitchen sink that no amount of hammering and W-D 40 could get it closed?

"Maybe we'll run into each other during my stay."

"I doubt that will happen. I don't frequent biker bars." She hadn't meant to say that. At least not aloud. Judging others and making assumptions based on their attire or lifestyle was a bad habit she'd picked up from her grandpa who thought that long hair on a man automatically made them a lazy hippy. "I mean, I'm very busy. I don't go out much."

He appeared unfazed. "Do you commute to the mainland?"

"I'm not a commuter. I'm doing time, so to speak."

He raised one eyebrow.

"Not that kind of time," she quickly added. "I meant that I'm living on the island temporarily. Hopefully the fastest few months known to man."

"Not liking island living?"

She kept it simple. "Already had my fill."

"Is it the people or lack of malls?"

The ding took a moment to recover from and she probably deserved it.

"Since we're stereotyping," he added.

She should have hit him harder with her handbag. "For the record, you're not even close."

"My apologies."

Like a chess move, he'd put her in her place. She could be a grownup about this. "I have a question for you," she said.

"Ask me anything," he said.

"Where are you from?"

"I'm up from Portland."

"Why are you visiting Orcas?"

"I never said I was."

Man, he was good at this. She shrugged her indifference.

"What do you do to keep busy on the island?" he asked.

"I give tours," she said. "I start by telling visitors not to talk to bikers on the ferry and to stay away from the Heron Inn."

He laughed. It was a nice sound and she struggled not to smile as the air warmed between them once again.

"I'm a writer," she finally gave it up.

"Really?" He seemed impressed. "What genre."

"Romance."

"Interesting," he said after a moment of watching her. "What do you do when you're not writing, if it's okay for me to ask?"

"Something I never thought I'd be doing. I fixed a drippy faucet and changed out a lock, for starters."

"I'm impressed. However, I can't picture you wearing a tool belt."

It was posed innocently enough, yet she had to bite her tongue to keep from asking what the smiling Jack Sanders did picture her wearing.

Suddenly, the ferry's speed decreased. Recognizing the lights of Orcas Village where the ferry would dock, and thanking the Good-Timing Gods, she snatched up her handbag. In that instant, a plan fell into place as to how she could retrieve her box of ammunition.

It was very easy to make it look like an accident, dropping her handbag on top of his duffel bag.

Jack made a move to assist.

"I've got it," she said.

To a passerby, it might appear that she intentionally gave the man in her booth a look down her blouse, a clever move her heroine Gigi would do in a heartbeat to distract the pirate.

Jack looked where she wanted him to look as she blindly slipped her hand into the side pocket and stood, a smooth two-second maneuver she would have been proud of, if it had worked.

"Goodnight," she said and walked away, hoping she never saw him again. That would be the only way she might avoid explaining why she had something in her pocket that wasn't hers.

Chapter 3

She sat in the driver's seat fanning her face with the photo she hadn't meant to take. When she'd stuck her hand into the pocket of his duffel bag, it had all been instinctive; grab and go.

The car deck hummed with engines starting up as the deckhands dropped the heavy chain across the opening and pulled the blocks out from the tires of the cars at the front of the line.

When Jack came into view on the car deck, there went her hopes that his destination was one of the other islands and that it was he who'd parked in the wrong lane.

Pretending interest in checking messages on her cellphone, she covertly watched as he snapped on his helmet and secured his duffel bag to the back of his motorcycle.

Seeing that she had a few minutes before vehicles would begin disembarking, and curious about the photo, of which she expected to see a hot babe smiling invitations, she turned on the light feature on her cellphone to use as a flashlight.

The black and white photo was from another era and it held a familiar landmark. Standing on the front steps of the old Victorian-style inn, named for the species of bird that nested nearby, was a group of five young adults smiling at the camera.

In the center of the group was a tall, dark-haired man. The woman on his left wore a slim-fitting suit. She had her arm hooked possessively through the man's as she smiled shyly at the camera. The other woman wore a bomber jacket over pants that belled out over her shoes. A hat sat jauntily on her white corkscrew hair. She smiled flirtatiously at the camera.

Directly behind the trio stood the other two men in the group, their faces shadowed by the veranda's overhang.

It began to sink in that Jack's interest in the old inn was a reality and not just him making small talk. It also increased the likelihood that Orcas Island might not be a brief visit for him.

The car deck suddenly rumbled with the growl of a powerful engine. Jack disembarked onto the island and up the hill, his single headlight sending a swath of light ahead on the dark road.

How he came to be in possession of a photo of the old inn was curious indeed. The fact that the photo held a familiar face was as well.

A piercing whistle snapped her head up.

"Let's go!" The deckhand pointed toward the taillights that she needed to follow.

The photograph went onto the seat beside her and she put her attention to maneuvering off the ferry and onto the dock that accessed Orcas Village. The center lane of cars had disembarked first and she followed, gunning the Land Rover up the hill and under the white banner across the road welcoming visitors to a busy weekend of festivals and events for the start of whale watching season.

She spared a glance up at the landmark Orcas Hotel to see if she could see the taillight of a motorcycle traveler looking for lodging. She was out of luck.

Ahead of her, a long string of red taillights followed Orcas Road toward Eastsound, the commercial center of the island. It was hard to tell if a motorcycle rode in the pack.

She turned on her signal and slowed to take a left onto Deer Harbor Road. As she made the turn under a streetlight, she glanced to the rearview mirror. A black Suburban made the turn as well.

An uncomfortable feeling came over her. Gerald lived with Missy and their home was on the north end of the island past the airport. Before she let paranoia rule tonight, she allowed for the possibility that he was merely taking a faster route home rather than follow behind all the slow ferry traffic. If that were the case, he'd be taking the turn coming up onto Crow Valley Road.

She didn't have the opportunity to see if Gerald did just that. He was too far back, and as she continued toward her own home, both the shadows of tall fir trees and the many curves in the road made it impossible to see if his vehicle still followed. She decided to find out.

She turned onto Cormorant Bay Road and quickly pulled a three-point turn to return to the stop sign. She cut her headlights and the dark closed in as she waited.

A small car went by followed by two more heading for Deer Harbor. After a few more minutes, with no dark-colored Suburban appearing, she turned her headlights back on and made the last leg home, with repeated glances to the rearview mirror.

In another mile, the marina came into view; the soft, welcoming lights of the quiet harbor where her grandpa had kept a boat for all the time that she'd known him up until he'd sold it.

Her headlights gleamed off the reflectors on the white fence that marked the entrance to the private lane she shared with one other home. She made the turn and eased her vehicle carefully along the pothole-riddled, dirt road and under the branches of the ancient gnarled oak tree.

Grassy lawn, once meticulously maintained in bygone days, spread out on her left toward the quiet harbor, looking darkish green in the dusk. Moonlight reflected off the water and rigging clanged against ships' masts.

She cracked her window to let in the fresh, sea air.

The sound of waves slapping against the shoreline never failed to ease her to sleep at night. That same gentle sound acted as the antidote to the more unpleasant part of the last hour. Although she was temporarily rid of Gerald Cain, her sister was not. What Missy saw in the jerk, she could not understand.

The rambler on her right was her closest neighbor. It was a rental home owned by the sheriff and currently occupied by the former owner of Perrigo Mansion. From what Marianne had learned so far, information shared by residents she'd met in town, the sheriff was not charging Gilly Bullock any rent due to her financial circumstances and until a social worker could complete the process of finding assistance for the elderly woman.

Between caring neighbors and various groups on the island, weekly food boxes were left on the front porch. Marianne was discovering the level of appreciation that Gilly had for these food boxes. What didn't suit the old woman's taste, ended up tossed at Marianne's front gate or into the overgrown lilac trees and rhododendrons bordering the rental house.

Marianne was surprised that any neighbor would willingly approach Gilly's home. She'd found out already just what kind of welcome they might receive. And it wasn't just the message that the driftwood scarecrows delivered as they stood guard in the front yard. At night, their shadows stretched long and threateningly as if they reached for the wrought iron gate that marked the entrance to Marianne's property.

She was almost to her gate when suddenly an animal ran out into the road.

Marianne stood on the brakes.

The orange tabby cat arched his back and golden eyes flashed in the beam of her headlights. She set the parking brake and stepped from the vehicle. The night air was cool and condensation rolled in white waves across the warm hood of her vehicle.

"Pete, what are you doing out?"

Gilly's cat sat down in the dirt road taking advantage of the headlights and began to clean his fur. She approached the unpredictable animal that generally remained inside due to the fact that Pete was a declawed rescue cat and an easier catch for raccoons, if they dared to take on his personality.

"Here, kitty, kitty, kitty."

The self-absorbed grooming continued as if she wasn't there.

"Come on, baby. Don't want the mean raccoons to get you." She bent down to gingerly stroke the cat's head.

He purred and stretched out in the road as if he enjoyed the attention. She hadn't seen this side of him before.

"You are a nice kitty behind that snobby attitude." She picked him up and carried him to her vehicle, keeping him on her lap as she backed up the few feet to Gilly's driveway.

She made the mistake of thinking that he might like his tummy tickled. With a hiss, Pete sank his teeth into her hand.

"You freaking, crazy cat!"

It was a tense moment. She was afraid to move. Pete looked like he was just waiting for her to give him a reason to thrash with what he had for back claws.

She slowly turned into Gilly's weed-strewn driveway and maneuvered as close to the front steps as she could without knocking over the driftwood scarecrow that leaned over the pavers. Wind tossed the scarecrow's seaweed hair about and its many necklaces made of tin cans and seashells clanked together like a warning.

The front door flew open. A small woman in baggy jeans, big rubber boots, and the gray and white Native American designed sweater she always wore stood in the doorway with a solid hold on a heavy shotgun. Pulled yarn from holes in both elbows of the sleeves dangled beneath her arm.

The effect of hair and fibers moving about her frame in the wind, backlit from the light inside, resembled that of the unwelcoming sculptures in her front yard. Her neighbor's halo of corkscrew white hair flew about in the wind.

"If you're the tax man," Gilly called out in her gravelly voice, "I'd advise you to think twice before stepping out of your vehicle."

Marianne opened her door and called out, "Don't shoot. I have your cat."

The barrel of the shotgun lowered. "Make it fast," grumbled the cat's owner.

Holding Pete as if he were a ticking time bomb, she slid out from the driver's seat and made her way to the front steps.

Trying to avoid the strands of scarecrow seaweed-hair blowing about, Marianne bent down to set the cat on the lower porch step. He held on like a lichen to a rock.

"Please call your cat," she said.

"Pete, bite her finger off and get in here."

Miraculously, she was left with all fingers intact as the cat shot past his owner's legs and in through the open door. Something fell from Gilly's hand and rolled to a stop at the toe of Marianne's boot.

The ring's large stone of translucent yellow caught the porch light and gleamed against the roughened boards of the porch.

"You're going to lose this, sooner or later. Why don't you wear it around your neck instead?"

The ring was snatched from her hand.

"It belongs on my finger," Gilly said. "What would you know about that; a single woman at your age, something must be wrong with you."

The temptation to stick her tongue out at the old woman's back just about won.

"You still got a good pair of eyes?" Gilly said gruffly over her shoulder.

"Why?" Marianne asked warily as she reluctantly followed her inside to where the dimly lit home smelled of wood smoke, stale air, and something more overpowering than the drying seaweed and beach finds her neighbor collected.

"Shut the door before the cat gets out again."

Taking one last breath of fresh air, she did.

The desk lamp gleamed off the barrel of the shotgun where it had been returned to rest against the wall between the door and the window.

Pete was licking something. Her head swiveled toward the sound about the same time her nose sensed the offending smell that wasn't present on her last visit.

The orange tabby was on top of the desk beneath the window eating out of a familiar blue baking dish. Her jaw dropped at the sight of the cat enjoying the casserole meant as a neighborly gesture. He apparently had been offered the entire dish. The noodle mixture had yellowed and crusted. Pete didn't seem to mind. He purred as he ate.

"I thought you said that you liked tuna casserole," Marianne said.

"I do." Gilly lowered herself tiredly onto the sagging sofa and pulled a crocheted afghan over her lap. "I don't recall asking you to bake me one." She pointed toward the dining table. "Go take a look at that."

The clock from the wall sat on the table next to a newspaper with drying kelp.

"It's a clock."

"Brilliant, Numbskull. Make your young eyes useful. I got the old battery out and I can't tell which end of the new battery has the plus sign on it." Even with the eyeglasses on her nose, Gilly still squinted at the jigsaw puzzle spread out on the coffee table.

As Marianne decided whether she dared to touch the grimy old clock, her neighbor continued to test her patience.

"Is your grandfather dead yet?" Gilly said.

The new battery slid easily into place at the back of the clock.

"No, he is not. I'd be happy to tell him you were asking after him."

A puzzle piece was snapped into its spot. "Don't bother. If I cared how Ed Dunaway was doing, I'd go see myself."

Ten weeks to go: an eternity living next to cranky Gilly. A woman who never failed to let Marianne know of her displeasure that she now owned her former home. So much displeasure. Nah. She stopped where that was going and reminded herself again that Gilly didn't seem capable and wasn't tall enough to tie the note at the height she'd found it on her gate.

"Have you seen any strange cars coming down the lane in the past few weeks?" Marianne asked.

"Just yours."

"Please, Gilly, have you seen anyone nosing around?

Another puzzle piece found a home before Gilly replied, "Only that blue Ford with all the bumper stickers that has to turn around in my driveway."

"That's Eleanor, the mail carrier."

"Yup."

"That's not a strange car."

"Is to me."

Marianne counted to ten. "Would you do me a favor? Let me know if you see anyone near my gate who looks suspicious."

The clock's place on the wall wasn't hard to find. A dark circular pattern stood out where sun and time had faded the wood paneling.

"Go home to the home that shouldn't belong to you," Gilly said. "Hope you're keeping nice and warm while I'm barely able to pay my bills."

It wouldn't do any good to remind Gilly that she didn't have any bills to pay. The sheriff's generosity went as far as to cover monthly utility services. Marianne was sympathetic to a person's need to feel independent, the very reason she tried once again to invite Gilly to take any antiques that either meant the most to her or that she could possibly sell.

"If you'd like to come over tomorrow and go through the rooms with me," she began.

"Not interested," Gilly said without looking up from the puzzle.

Marianne braved on. "Gerald Cain asked me if there was more to the set that matched the opera glasses that he sold for you. If there are, you can have them to sell as well. Just tell me where they are and I'll bring them over. Although, my advice is to find someone else to sell them for you."

Gilly's head snapped up. "I told him there was nothing more!" There was a look of panic in her eyes. Then she looked like she'd said too much. "Don't you be talking to him about me, ever!"

"I'm just trying to help."

"You're snooping into my business is what you're doing. I never told you that I sold anything and you shouldn't be listening to the gossip from others. For the last time. I don't want your charity." Gilly looked like she'd fight every inch of the way to her grave. And when she got there, who would pay their respects?

Marianne thought of the black and white photo and how Jack had come to have it in his possession.

"Are you expecting any visitors? Family, maybe, who are still living?" She cringed, thinking she might have left that latter part unsaid.

Her neighbor looked taken off guard. "Why are you asking?"

"Just curious that's all."

You'd think that Marianne was the crazy one by the look on Gilly's face. "Don't you have someplace else to be?" she said.

The cat jumped up to sit on his owner's lap. In his eyes was the same message.

Marianne let herself out. The scarecrows' clamshell features frowned at her as she passed. She drew the collar of her coat up as she climbed behind the wheel, turning on the wipers to clear away the light rain beading on the windshield.

The dome light aided in her inspection of the damage done by the psycho cat. He'd left enough to remember him by; several marks were turning purple.

Thankfully, there was no broken skin. She'd live a happy life not to see either cat or owner again.

She drove through her gate not looking forward to what she might find, muddy footprints in her hallway or any sign that she'd had an uninvited guest, again. Although at the back of her mind was the suspicion that it might be Gilly just based on the size of the rubber boots on her feet. In fact, she hoped it was her neighbor taking things, despite her prideful declaration that she didn't want anything. Gilly was a far better intruder to deal with than the unknown. She just wished she had proof.

***

Later that evening, Marianne stood at the big window that overlooked the backyard. She held a hot mug of cocoa between her hands. Across the smooth water of the small harbor, a hillside dense with evergreen trees towered over the shore. Warm, golden lights gleamed from the few homes perched way up on top of the hill. Halfway down the hillside, moonlight reflected off the upper windows of the old inn that faced her home.

Would Jack need the photo to find his inn and the people in the photo? He might not. All he had to do was describe the inn to a local and he'd be pointed right to it.

She thought, then, that perhaps she should have done a better job of warning Gilly that someone might be looking for her.

Or maybe Jack was the one in danger should he step foot on her neighbor's property.

Chapter 4

The next morning, the sun peeked through the overcast and shone through the library window where Marianne sat at the desk she'd designated as her writing spot.

However, a designated writing spot didn't necessarily mean there'd be productivity.

Her latest manuscript with marked changes was doing nothing more than making itself useful as an oversized coaster for her coffee mug.

The antique suitcase under the desk that held writing props currently did better service as a foot rest.

A fire burned in the fireplace and the table lamps were turned on to combat the dismal skies outside. She eventually pushed the laptop away and took another look at the mysterious note.

Taking the magnifying glass from the desk drawer, she examined the handwriting. Her guess was that the writer of the note was right-handed and they'd used inexpensive notepaper. That was the extent of her analysis. She wrote romance novels not detective novels.

The magnifying glass was of better use getting a closer look at how her hand was healing up this morning. Last night, she'd carefully washed and applied disinfectant to her souvenir from the cat. Only faint purple markings remained and she'd live to see Pete another day. As for the note, she needed an expert opinion.

Her brother answered on the first ring.

"Dunaway," his deep voice always gave Marianne immediate reassurance. She could tell by her brother's tone when he might have his feet up and a beer in his hand versus when he was in the field on a case. As a Special Agent for the FBI, Ian had met his fair share of criminal minds.

"It's me. Got a second?" Marianne said.

"You have two minutes. Everything okay with Grandpa and kid sister?"

Ian had left home long before Marianne. He'd remained close with his siblings, his frank and practical manner, and natural sense of fairness making him the peacekeeper in the family. To Marianne, he was her rock. However, to the women he left in his wake, it was said that a wild stallion was easier to capture than the handsome Ian Dunaway.

"Grandpa is still his cranky, critical-self, a reminder of why I left right out of high school. He receives great care at the assisted living center, but he still finds things to complain about." Marianne paused. "It's a good thing we moved him there when we did. He's declining, Ian, and he looks so frail. As for our little sister, it's kind of hard to reconnect with her when she'll hardly talk to me. She won't reply to my text messages and her voicemail box is full so I can't even leave a message. And I met the boyfriend."

"Yeah, I met him, too" Ian said dryly. "He's a sneaky one, watch out for him."

"What does Missy see in him?"

"Hell, I don't know. He's got the moves and women fall for him."

"He reminds me of that California beach bum who charmed his way into marrying wealthy women only to skip town with their bank accounts. I wish Missy could see past that fake smile of his and dump him."

"Me, too. Just not sure why she hasn't done that already." Ian changed the subject. "You regret buying the big mansion, yet?"

"Don't tell anyone, but, yes. God, what was I thinking? It's falling apart!" She looked around the room. The home's age showed in the jagged cracks that ran along the alcove ceiling and in the fact that the large marble fireplace did little to heat the room, instead the flames fought to stay alive against the downward drafts.

"Hey, I told you it was going to require a lot of work."

"I know." She sighed. "Sometimes I get impulsive."

"You can always sell it."

"True." Her eyes returned to the fireplace mantle. Something didn't look right. Marianne could have sworn that she'd moved the red Venetian glass collection, that had taken up too much room on the mantle, into the dining room to pack up with other nick-knacks. Yet, one small, red bird remained on the mantle.

43

"Sis, I'm going to have to go."

"Ian, wait. Since moving in, strange things have been happening."

"Like what?"

Marianne picked up the glass bird. Maybe she had overlooked this one. What she hadn't overlooked or imagined, were the notes. "Someone left a note on my gate. It wasn't very friendly."

"What did the note say?"

"That I have traitor in my blood."

Her brother was silent for a moment. "Are you sure the note was meant for you?"

"I assumed it was, since—"

Ian cut her off. "We're on the move. I'll call you back."

"Bye," she said to the dial tone, and sat back down at the desk.

Her eyes fell on the old photograph. She was still, fairly, certain that the woman in the trousers was Gilly. Using the magnifying glass, she took a closer look at the two men in the back row.

The stance of the man with jet black hair was familiar in the way that one of his shoulders dropped lower than the other. More so was the hawk-like nose.

She pulled the lamp closer to throw additional light onto the photo. Perhaps it wasn't only Gilly who might expect a visit from Jack Sanders up from Portland. At the same time, she'd recognized the second familiar face in the photo, she noticed another detail. The young man standing directly behind the girl in the bomber jacket had his hand resting possessively on her hip.

Her cell phone began playing Beethoven. She didn't recognize the caller I.D.

"Hello?"

"Marianne Dunaway?" a woman's voice asked.

"Yes?"

"This is Lynn from the assisted living center."

***

Once her heart had returned to its normal pace, as Lynn explained that there was no emergency, just a matter of an unpaid bill, Marianne jumped in her vehicle and made the twenty-minute drive to the north end of the island where Missy lived.

The winding country road along pastures, eggs-for-sale signs, newborn lambs in fields, and having to wait patiently as a doe and her fawn crossed the road, helped somewhat in calming her frustration with what she could only see as her sister's irresponsibility.

Fishing Bay came into sight and the road dipped down as she came around the corner and had a view of the town of Eastsound and the tourist traffic already crawling through town on this Saturday morning.

As soon as the slowing cars ahead of her made their turn towards the shops and restaurants, she put the peddle down and skirted town, taking Lovers Lane as a time saver. She was soon slowing her speed through a residential area that ran parallel to the beach.

To her relief, there was no black Suburban in the driveway of the white shingled house that had always reminded her of a sea captain's home. The only car in the driveway was their grandpa's old blue Buick that Missy now drove.

A white picket fence surrounded the property. A flag pole took center stage in the small front yard. Marianne pulled into the narrow driveway and parked behind the Buick. The backyard faced North Beach where a crumbling cement seawall and storm-tossed driftwood divided the yard from the pebbled beach.

Small pieces of driftwood and sun-bleached clamshells littered the stubby grass, left behind by stormy waves on a high tide. The same storms left short, gray reeds that were even more difficult to clean up afterwards. A chore their grandfather would give to them. Her grandmother had called these broken reed sections smoking sticks because they'd pretended they were cigars when they were kids.

When her grandmother was alive, the gardens were colorful with orange and yellow nasturtiums, wild pink roses, and lavender that had once grown along the picket fence. For several years after their grandmother's passing, Missy had kept up the gardens. Now they were weed-choked and getting to the back porch involved sidestepping patches of mud and several places where a car's ashtray had been dumped alongside the driveway.

On the beach side, waves beat against the shore. The wind and a splattering of rain hit her in the face as she climbed the worn back steps. On her last visit, she'd noticed that the windows were dingy with sea salt and dirt. Due to her sister's habit of being a meticulous housekeeper, she'd expected them to be cleaned by now. They were not, making it appear that the jars of sea glass that sat on the inside windowsill were just as dirty.

The tip of her nose felt cold and her fingertips as well. She knocked on the wood frame of the screen door and hoped she didn't have to wait long. The cold wind went right through the suede coat that she wore. Even the black cashmere sweater underneath and slim-fitting jeans tucked into riding boots didn't help to keep her warm. She cinched the belt tighter, turned up the collar of her coat, and pounded again with her gloved fist, all on an empty stomach and needing a second cup of coffee.

The trip from her vehicle to the back porch had resulted in mud clinging to the toes and heels of her polished boots. A boot cleaner next to the back door brought back memories of her grandmother wiping off her garden shoes. The worn-down bristles did little to remove the mud on narrow heels.

The back door opened.

Her younger sister stood there in a light blue, kitten-print bathrobe, a Christmas present Marianne had sent years ago. Missy's short, dark hair looked flattened from a pillow and she had puffy circles beneath blue eyes smeared with yesterday's mascara. She looked more like a twelve-year old than an adult in her late twenties with the freckles across her small nose and naturally pink lips in a pale face. Light glinted off the tiny, diamond piercing in her nose.

"What do you want?" Missy said. The screen door remained shut between them.

"When did you get your nose pierced?"

Her sister rolled her eyes. "This is why you got me out of bed?"

"I drove over here because you were not answering your phone."

"So?"

"The assisted living center is trying to get ahold of you. You forgot to pay Grandpa's bill for the month."

At first, Missy wore a blank look. Then a deep flush rode up her neck. "I paid it. In fact, I know I did. Gerald took it over there for me..." her voice trailed off.

"They didn't get it. You need to call them." Marianne shivered. "Do you have any coffee?" She knew her chances were slim, but if coffee as an ice breaker could work for the man on the ferry.

"I'm out of coffee," was the cold reply.

There was a time when that screen door didn't stand between them. It appeared it wasn't going to open for her anytime soon.

Marianne tried again, saying, "Ian told me that you're considering going to nursing school."

"When did he tell you that?"

She quickly searched her memory archives. "Recently?"

"Try five years ago," Missy said. "Are we done with the reunion? I want to go back to bed." The door began to shut.

"I saw Gerald on the ferry last night coming back from Anacortes."

"So?"

"He asked if I'd had a nice day in Seattle." Marianne paused, wondering if she was making too much of nothing. "I never told anyone where I was going. I just had this strange feeling that he may have followed me off the island."

If it wasn't for the nervous way that Missy swallowed, Marianne would have thought she was simply boring her sister.

"Sounds to me like it was all coincidence," her sister finally said.

"I don't think it was. He followed me home for a few miles. Or does he usually cut over to Crow Valley Road to avoid ferry traffic?"

"Did you see him take that road?"

"No. But I also didn't see him continue on to Deer Harbor."

"You're certain?" The look on her sister's face was now an anxious one as she looked over her shoulder to the large picture window in the living room that had a partial view of the driveway.

"Missy, what do you see in Gerald? He's not good enough for you. I think you should call the bank to see if he cashed the check for himself."

The door slammed shut in her face.

She was so focused on avoiding the patches of mud on the way back to her vehicle that she didn't hear her sister's approach. Suddenly a hand shoved her between the shoulder blades.

"Think you can do a better job taking care of Grandpa's finances?"

Out in the daylight, the dark circles under Missy's eyes looked more like the remnants of bruising and her face looked thinner.

"I didn't say that," Marianne said.

In her sister's arms was an old, black leather briefcase where the color had rubbed off on the rounded corners. Marianne recognized it as the one their grandpa had owned for as long she could remember. Its home had always been in the roll-top desk where he'd kept his pipe. She thought for a moment that Missy was going to hit her with it, but she'd only swung the bulky briefcase up to push into Marianne's arms.

"It's your turn." On her return to the back steps, her sister walked oddly as she clutched at her side. She hadn't even bothered to put shoes on her feet.

"Are you hurt?" Marianne asked.

"I fell." That she was in some pain was obvious. She looked out of breath and bit down on her lip as she used the hand railing. "Aren't you busy enough making Royce miserable?"

"Who's Royce?" Marianne gave the inside of the briefcase a quick look. Her grandpa's worn gray checkbook, copies of tax returns, and unopened bills made up the weight of the contents.

Missy wasn't moving up the back stairs very fast.

"You don't look okay," Marianne said.

"Jeez! Back off!" Missy took a moment to catch her breath then shifted the topic back to Marianne's offense. "Royce is the teenager who was minding his own business until you called the sheriff on him."

"That scrawny kid partying in the old inn is trespassing. His music blares across the water and in through my bedroom window." She looked around for a means to clean the mud off her boots before climbing into her vehicle.

"He fits in around here better than you. He's working for Gerald's uncle if you're feeling big enough to apologize."

The clump of weeds near the back tire did a better job of removing mud than the worn boot cleaner on the back porch.

"Why should I apologize?" Marianne was growing frustrated with getting nowhere in making peace with her sister.

"Because not everybody's got it good like you." The cold air off the water was nothing compared to her sister's chilling glare from the porch.

"It seems to me, Missy, that I can't say or do anything right in your eyes." She opened the car door and tossed the briefcase into the back seat before slamming the door shut. "What's going on? We used to share everything. Now you've got this frick'n wall up between us!"

The wind blew her sister's dark hair around her pale face. Marianne's outburst was futile. The wall was still there.

"I'm not surprised someone left you a note. You're not exactly making a lot of friends since you returned."

"How do you know about the note?" Marianne asked in puzzlement.

"Eleanor was talking about it in town.

To say she was dumbfounded was an understatement. "That's an invasion of privacy!"

"Welcome back to the island."

***

She backed out of the driveway so roughly that she bounced through potholes before speeding away with gravel sputtering out from the back tires. She hit auto dial on her Bluetooth.

"About time you called," Fiona answered. "You were supposed to check in last night. I've been worried."

"I'm getting off this island today! I'm quitting this dare-where-you-write. I've had it!"

"What's going on? Did you get another note?"

"No, it's Missy. I can't get through to her. She's mad at me for something and I don't know what it is. And she's acting strange. I think it has something to do with her creep for a boyfriend. On top of that, I'm dealing with the crabby old lady next door. There's no way I'm going to get any writing done with all the shit going on since I arrived."

"Are you driving?"

"I'm on Bluetooth." She reached for her Kate Spade sunglasses as the sun moved out from behind gray clouds.

"Pull over and let's talk this out."

A small rabbit suddenly ran out from under a split rail fence and into her path. She hit the brakes sending her handbag to the floor and the small gun spilled out once again.

She pulled to the shoulder along the fence and stopped. Off to her right was the airfield where a small plane taxied in the distance preparing for takeoff.

"Take a couple of deep breaths," her friend said. "You're not thinking with your writing head. This is actually some pretty good drama for a story."

"Maybe you're genre, not mine. I need to fix this, Fiona, so that I can get something else done."

"I told you to take the notes to the sheriff. As for your neighbor, stay away from her."

"Easier said than done. She's got a way of making me feel badly for her situation."

"Well, hopefully these three months will go by fast. Now as for your sister, I can relate. When my older sister moved away to the East Coast, she made new friends and I felt that she forgot about me. It wasn't until we dealt with aging parents that we began to grow close again."

"Whose side are you on?" Marianne said. She cracked the window to let in fresh air and let out the old pipe smell coming from the briefcase.

"Yours. Look on the bright side, this could turn out to be a bonding experience for you and your sister."

"I seriously doubt that."

Fiona laughed, then continued with the pep talk.

"There has to be something good that's happened in your first few weeks."

A vehicle sped by, its tires spraying up water from the wet roadway and sending the smell of musty rain into the air. A black motorcycle came over the rise from town heading her way.

She held her breath until the rider was close enough to recognize a more sedate model of motorcycle whose very large rider showed a preference for a stuffed Garfield toy as his travel companion.

Her heart rate slowly returned to normal. Not without her realizing that the thought of Jack had been all that was on her mind for a moment, or two, giving her a nice break from her other problems. Maybe Fiona was right.

"I did meet someone yesterday. On the ferry."

"Please tell me that you're not talking about the weirdo?"

"No. The weirdo turned out to be my sister's loser boyfriend. It was after I was done talking to you. I went upstairs to the passenger area. We shared a booth."

"What's his name?" Fiona sounded very interested.

"Jack. You won't believe how I really met him. I rear-ended his motorcycle on the ferry."

"And you're still alive?" Fiona exclaimed.

Marianne found herself smiling as she remembered how Jack had given her a lethal look at first only to be looking at her quite differently after she'd landed on his lap.

"Yes. Luckily, there was no damage. I believe all is forgiven."

"Is he good looking?"

"Very. Tall, dark, and sexy."

Her friend practically purred. "When are you going to see him again?"

"We didn't exactly get to the point of exchanging phone numbers. We just shared a booth, that's all. Besides, he's not my type."

"I hope not. Your type bores both you and me."

"That's not true!" Marianne defended her taste in men. "I've dated some very nice men."

"Men you have no trouble leaving behind. This Jack guy is different. I can tell that you like him and that you're interested. I can tell because you said that you 'met someone'. That's not what you say when someone doesn't interest and excite you. I think you hope to see him again, despite him not being 'your type'." There was a knowing smile in her friend's voice.

"Are you done trying to read between the lines?" Marianne said.

"Tell me something," Fiona went on, "Has 'your type' ever thrown you over their shoulder and hauled you off to their man cave and done things to you that you will never forget?"

Marianne's pulse leaped as Fiona described one of her own fantasies. Or maybe it was every woman's fantasy.

"Well?" Fiona demanded.

"Has that happened to you?"

"No," Fiona sounded disappointed.

The thought of Jack doing as Fiona described had her body threatening to convince her that perhaps she should break out of her pattern of dating the same type of men; someone her grandmother would have set her up with saying, 'now there's a nice man your grandfather would approve of'.

She'd never felt this level of attraction before. She had to be careful. The thought of the photo came to mind and thoughts of romance went right out the window, her type or not. Jack's charm and questions could have ulterior motives.

"It would probably be best if I didn't see him again. I'm not sure I should trust him due to the circumstances."

"What? No! No circumstances. This is the first man who's piqued your interest in eons. Go buy a bottle of wine and find that man!"

"I can't, Fiona. It's complicated. Besides, I just had this feeling from talking with him that he's from a different world, like he's seen some bad things, dangerous things. And he's bold. Like he'll go after what he wants, no hesitation."

"Can I have him?"

Marianne laughed. She ended the call and the annoying handgun went into the glove box. Despite the cold, the window had to stay down and the heat off.

There was no other option while the smelly briefcase road shotgun.

Chapter 5

The old Heron Inn looked far better in the photo. A photo he no longer had in his possession. Thanks to a redhead who'd walked off with the photo half-sticking out of her coat pocket, leaving him with a box of bullets that weren't his size at all. He could have easily walked up to her vehicle and asked for his photo back before leaving the ferry. It was a risk, parting with the photo, and one his mother wouldn't have appreciated. A crazy risk that he took on impulse in hopes of seeing the redhead, again.

He sat on his motorcycle staring up at his inheritance.

Weeds grew from the gutters and green moss covered the roof. The chimney leaned and shutters hung askew at the windows. It was doubtful that the rooms inside were in any better condition, which was a concern. He'd been fortunate to find a vacancy at a bed-n-breakfast last night due to a cancellation. Now it appeared that his plan to bunk in his own accommodations wasn't going to be as appealing as he'd hoped.

There certainly wouldn't be a sofa to sit on because it was tossed on its side in a patch of ferns along with a kitchen stove.

The inn wore a dark stain of maroon. Jack imagined that on this hillside covered in trees the inn would be almost impossible to see at night. The front yard consisted only of a small parking area off to his left that would accommodate three vehicles, maybe four. Jack took a guess that this would be the number of rooms the inn had to offer.

The crescent-shaped drive was partially hidden from the road by large rhododendrons and the fat trunk of a cedar tree. The overgrowth of vegetation was the reason he'd almost missed the driveway. As he'd rode in under the low-hanging bows of the cedar tree, the inn's three-story turret had towered up in front of him, built as it was on a narrow strip of land running parallel to the street. Leaving his motorcycle, he set out to see what exactly his grandfather had left him.

Under his feet, a thick layer of pine needles covered the gravel drive. The air smelled fresh and clean, a mix of rain, pine, and sea. Ferns grew densely up against the foundation, their vivid green fronds still wet from last night's rain.

The veranda led around to the water side and a view he wasn't expecting. Through the bows of fir and cedar trees, there was a harbor below with a busy marina. Farther out were more islands.

If it wasn't for the occasional car passing by on the road, the otherwise quietness gave the impression that he had the hillside to himself, with only the wind stirring the tree branches. He was curious as to how close Gigi Divine might live, if she could hear teenagers partying in his old inn.

Walking to the center of the veranda, he tried the French double doors. The door knob came off in his hand. He was about to step inside when a reflection in the large bay window caught his attention. He turned back around to the view.

From the railing, the hillside fell steeply below. A fir tree grew so close to the railing that a squirrel used a branch as a private lane from the tree to the deck. He scurried out of Jack's way.

Pushing the branch aside, Jack had an unobstructed view of a large home across the short span of water at the back of the harbor. Graced by oak and willow trees, it wasn't just any house. He didn't know how he'd missed seeing the structure when he'd rode over the bridge, other than he was too intent on looking for an old growth cedar tree with a clamshell decoration on its trunk that was in the shape of a heart. The landmark and directions had been provided by the owners of last night's accommodations.

Sitting on a small spit of land, the pale-yellow home was more the size of a mansion with a widow's walk, chimney pipes dotted along the roofline, balconies off some of the upper rooms, and a wrap-a-round veranda for those hot summer days.

Over the roof of the mansion, a smaller structure could be seen. It sat not far from the front gates of the mansion. Smoke curled up from its chimney. A straight, dirt lane shot from the gate to the country road.

From the angle of how the inn faced directly toward the mansion, and based on the information she'd given up, Jack was willing to bet that Gigi, if that was her real name, lived in one of the two homes. His own home inspection could wait. She had something that belonged to him.

Down the hill and back over the bridge, he'd found the private lane easy enough. The road dead-ended at a pair of wrought iron gates that stood open. In contrast to the disrepair of the property, the welcome sign on the gate looked, fairly, new. The oval-shaped sign boasted a colorful painting of a rabbit wearing a wreath of pink and yellow daisies. Flowing script across the top of the sign sent a cheery, "*Welcome Friends*," message.

This close, the mansion looked more like an old hotel, giving Jack hope that a vacancy might await. Despite the cool response she'd given him when he'd inquired about the island's lodgings, he ventured forth and followed the moss-covered pavers up to the front door.

Birds chirped in the low branches of shrubbery and a small brown rabbit suddenly darted across the patch of grass in the front yard. A Romeo-and-Juliet style balcony jutted out over the front step. Ivy climbed up the two roman-style pillars supporting the balcony. A pair of large urns standing to either side of the front door held fresh soil and red and yellow primroses. A stone rabbit sat at the base. The doormat repeated the same message as the sign on the gate.

He pressed the doorbell and doubted anyone inside would respond as a bee buzzed louder than the doorbell did. When there was no response to his knock, he walked around to the back door on the harbor side.

Beneath the giant willow tree, a pair of blue-gray, weather-worn Adirondack chairs faced the water and the narrow strip of sandy beach. A split rail fence lay broken across the sand. One of the few fence posts still standing bore a '*Private Beach*' sign. In contrast to the friendly rabbit sign out front, this worn sign sent an entirely different message.

The mansion had this narrow end of the harbor to itself with only the bridge traffic to disturb any solitude. A small orchard provided some measure of privacy between the property and the road accessing the bridge.

A pair of hikers caught his eye. He followed their movement until they stepped onto a narrow footbridge that ran alongside the concrete bridge and sat lower to the water.

Jack returned to looking for the owner of the mansion. On the veranda, summer furniture was pushed up against the side of the house to protect it from the elements. The red-painted flooring of the veranda looked freshly swept. Through the window in the door he saw an outdated, yet, tidy kitchen. A yellow coffee mug and matching plate were upside down in the dish rack. Near the wood burning stove, a leather armchair looked inviting. A pair of women's black riding boots leaned against the ottoman.

There was no response to his knock.

He next investigated the smaller house outside the gate where gray smoke came from the chimney and followed the wind current. The front yard was home to a small army of scarecrow figures made of driftwood.

Gravel crunched under his boots as he walked up the short driveway to the front steps. The windows were covered with closed drapes. The '*Get Lost*' sign tacked to the porch post had him slowing his approach.

The front door cracked open a few inches and the long barrel of a shotgun emerged. Due to the darkened interior of the home, he could not see clearly the figure of the person holding the shotgun.

"Stop right there," the voice was shaky and raspy, the pitch making it difficult to guess at the gender.

"I'm looking for accommodations," Jack said. "Do you know when the owner of the hotel will return?"

"That's no hotel and neither is my place. Now tell me what part of 'get lost' don't you understand?"

He began to back away when suddenly he stepped on an object that rolled out from under him. Jack went down hard on his back.

"Christ!" he exclaimed, grabbing at his knee that had twisted going down.

"Quit lollygagging and get off my property!"

Jack slowly got to his feet, gritting his teeth as he put weight on his knee. Right next to his boot was a can of baked beans with a dent in the side from the heel of his boot.

"Keep going!" yelled the owner of the shotgun.

"I'm going!" Jack said, kicking the can of beans out of his way. He limped over to his motorcycle as the door to the rambler slammed shut.

His cellphone vibrated in his pocket. It was a text message from Maxwell. With his knee hurting like blazes, Jack read the message.

"You talk some sense into yourself yet?"

With a curse, he deleted the message.

Determined to have something go his way today, he started up his motorcycle with more revving than was necessary and roared back over the bridge and up the hill. However, he would soon learn that disappointment for Jack wasn't over for today.

***

The front door to his inn opened with one push of his hand. His nose immediately wrinkled as he was greeted with the smells of damp and mustiness. Water dripped somewhere.

Through the archway on his left, a big puddle of water glistened in the middle of a room where a bulb-less chandelier hung from the ceiling and wallpaper peeled away from the walls.

In the office behind the registration counter, he found signs that he might not be the only one looking for shelter. Under a brown tarp, in the only dry corner of the office, he discovered a sleeping bag and a beat-up red cooler.

The rest of the tour of the downstairs rooms sent a few rats out from under wooden crates and startled a bird from behind tattered drapes. That the inn might have potential as a fixer-upper to a buyer was a short-lived hope. The kitchen was the deal breaker of all deal breakers with its sagging ceilings, ripped out plumbing, and graffiti on the cupboard doors. Jack had seen enough.

***

With a hot latte in one hand and a bag of donuts within reach, Marianne took a scenic drive to help put perspective on her troubles with her sister. The perspective didn't happen, but her tummy did get its breakfast.

Of course, Fiona would have told her that the reason perspective didn't fall into place was because she was doing this all wrong. However, when neither preferred selection of man and wine were seeming to come together in a compatible pairing, one had to default to the next best thing. Sugared donuts.

Now that she'd cooled off, she was circling back to town to take care of a few errands.

Familiar with driving the road with pastures on one side and Turtleback Mountain on the other, and the matter of the missing check for the assisted living center on her mind, Marianne didn't bother to slow for the Y in the road. Seeing no cars approaching, she sped through the stop sign toward town.

A heartbeat later she heard the deep, vibrating rumble of a motorized beast.

A black motorcycle rode her tail. He flashed his single headlight.

Even as she tried to convince herself that there could be more than one motorcycle like Jack's on the island, as she'd discovered earlier, a little voice told her that that wasn't going to be her luck today.

This rider had no stuffed toy keeping him company.

He kept right up with her, such that his presence on her bumper quickly got under her skin. She purposely reduced her speed.

Suddenly he swung around to pass. Marianne kept her eyes on the road ahead, seeing enough in her peripheral vision. Aviator sunglasses and a set jaw gave as good of a dark look as any she'd ever received.

He accelerated ahead, sweeping in front of her with a graceful and expert changing of lanes before roaring away and disappearing around the corner. Only then did she let out the breath she'd held.

What man would let a driver off the hook with two attempts at taking out his motorcycle?

Although she felt a bit ridiculous with her over-the-top evasion tactics, she drove around to the north side of town and came in from that direction, all while keeping her eyes peeled for a motorcycle.

It didn't matter what street you drove through town, there was always a glimpse of the bay and today the sun sparkled off the blue-green water.

She slowed as she approached the first commercial building and pulled over onto a gravel parking strip, deciding that a few minutes staying out of sight wouldn't hurt. If she was lucky, maybe Jack was only doing a bit of sightseeing before catching a ferry.

She glanced over to the business she'd parked in front of and realized that she'd landed in enemy territory.

Swan's Pawn Shop, the place her grandpa had warned her away from for as long as she could remember. She didn't know why he didn't like Harold Swan. Asking had only brought an angry frown to her grandpa's face and when he was displeased with her, the cold shoulder generally followed. And now the nephew of the enemy was living in Ed Dunaway's home. The only good she saw in a man slipping into dementia was that he might be spared some of the things in life that could otherwise burn a hole through your heart.

A three-sided corral in front held a grouping of miniature windmills for the garden. From the eaves of the shop, windsocks in the shape of black and white orca whales flapped and snapped in the wind.

If Gerald were here, she wouldn't hesitate to go in and ask him about the check he was supposed to have delivered by now. As luck would have it, or not, the black Suburban was nowhere in sight.

She drummed her fingers on the steering wheel. Missy's words came back to her regarding the teenager's situation and how Marianne had it better than most.

There were times when a woman had to cross enemy lines.

The bell above the shop door jingled as she stepped inside. The store was divided into two sections by a separation of old and new. The new was everything from windbreakers to mugs to stuffed toys, all with pictures of orca whales.

The opposite side of the store was burdened under the weight of everything second-hand from kitchenware to fishing gear and tools. The smell of silk-screened T-shirts clashed with items that had been in a basement far too long.

A counter sectioned off the back of the store. Behind a cash register, the bent frame of Harold Swan attended to the task of counting money. He was the same age as her grandpa. Either good genes or shear stubbornness had him upright, and, still, keeping a business running at the age of ninety.

His movements were slow as he made an entry in a black journal, set down the pen, and zipped closed the banking bag he held. Only then did he give his customer his attention.

"How are you, Mr. Swan?" she said.

Harold Swan was soft spoken and his words always carefully chosen, giving Marianne the impression that he was trying to trick her into saying something she otherwise would have kept to herself. He wiped his nose with a handkerchief and tucked it into his back pocket.

"Gerald said you might be in with more of Gilly's antiques." He moved aside a pile of sweatshirts and souvenirs to clear space on the glass-topped counter.

Seeing that she was empty-handed, he went as far as to peer over the counter to see if by chance she had set anything on the floor.

"I'm not here on Gilly's behalf."

He blinked his eyes rapidly for a moment, making her feel like she'd stunned him with bad news.

"I stopped by to speak with Royce," she said.

"You won't find him here," he said. "Fired him last week. He's a no-good kid."

In the past, the same description had been used by Harold Swan to describe just about every young person on the island, including Marianne and her brother. It wasn't so much the memory that pinged at her core, it was the guilt that suddenly swept over her for having judged just like this man.

"Most people are good people," she said, knowing that saying it wasn't even close to gaining redemption for how she'd stereotyped a few times in her life. Maybe more than a few times. "Do you know where I can find him?"

"Can't help you there." He turned away to take a cardboard box from a shelf.

She was at the door, looking out the window first to make sure there wasn't a black motorcycle in sight, when Mr. Swan had more to say.

"Tell me something, Ms. Dunaway. I've always been curious where Ed got all that money to send you and your brother off to college. 'Because, I don't recall the boat charter business doing so good during those years."

This was more than Mr. Swan usually said at one time. He wasn't looking at her expectantly for an answer. Yet, even as he removed handfuls of candy bars from the box to add to a display, she knew that he waited.

"Grandpa didn't pay for our education, Mr. Swan. My brother and I took out student loans." His prying bothered her. "Why do you need to know?"

"Just answers a question we all had, that's all. Doesn't resolve our suspicions." His tone left speculation hanging consciously in the air. He continued focusing on his candy arranging.

Even as she responded, she knew he was baiting her. "What suspicions?"

The bell above the door jingled and a woman entered carrying a microwave. Unlike what Marianne had received in greeting, the shop owner smiled at his new customer with a flash of yellowed and crooked teeth and didn't give another look to the granddaughter of Ed Dunaway.

Chapter 6

Jack stepped out of the hardware store with the plastic sheeting and duct tape that he'd purchased. Despite the rain showers, the town was busy.

Pedestrians packed the sidewalks and traffic inched through town. Everywhere he looked there was an orca whale theme going on. Either in the form of stuffed toys in shop windows, posters advertising whale watching tours, or vehicles driving past with miniature whale windsocks fluttering from the car's antennas.

The aroma of freshly roasted coffee beans coming from one of the shops, and that of baking bread from another, teased his appetite.

An attractive woman in jeans and a tan, hip-length coat caught his eye. He recognized the wavy hair and long legs of Gigi Divine. So intent was she on where she was going, that she nearly bumped into a baby stroller. She waived an apology to the parents and kept going, her attention never deviating from her mission. About the same time that he looked farther down her path of travel, she attempted to hail someone.

A thin-framed youth with brown hair to his collar stopped and turned around. He took one look at her and made a sharp left onto a side street. She was right on his tail.

Jack secured his purchases into one of his saddlebags. Drivers who couldn't watch out for motorcycles were at the top of his list of pet peeves. A nice ass in a pair of jeans wasn't going to get her off the hook. Jack set off on foot to have a word with Ms. Divine.

The teenager was nowhere to be seen when Jack came around the corner onto the next street. He caught sight of Gigi's coat as she disappeared around the side of a low, brown building with neon beer signs in the windows. Unlike the typical bad guy that he trailed in his line of work, the only danger in following her was that he had to dodge a family van and a group of bicyclists that zoomed by all in a row in their matching yellow jerseys.

It took a few minutes for his eyes to adjust to the darker interior of the tavern. Conversation hummed and pool balls hit together over in the far corner. The pine-paneled walls held a collection of maps, framed posters, and several big screen televisions with both basketball and baseball games airing. A railing divided the bar seating from the tables and booths.

A slender woman with long, black hair to her waist and wearing a figure-hugging, band T-shirt moved swiftly past him carrying a tray of appetizing-looking baskets of fish-n-chips.

"All I've got is seating at the bar right now," she said.

He nodded his thanks and strode across to an empty barstool.

It didn't take him long to find his seating companion from the ferry. She stood near the swinging door into the kitchen, having cornered the teenager who was attempting to slip a black apron over his head, only to get the buckle on the apron caught in one of the many braided leather and rope bracelets that he wore.

"What'll you have?" The bartender approached, slinging a white towel over his shoulder. He wore a black shirt and his thinning hair was pulled into a ponytail.

"Budweiser," Jack said.

Light amber liquid filled a tall schooner. "Someone joining you?"

The bartender's observation of where Jack's attention had landed since walking into the bar had him thinking twice about why he'd followed her, putting perspective on what exactly he was doing. Had he really chased her down to lecture her on how she should be more observant of motorcycles? Or was he just looking for an excuse to talk with her again?

Jack tried to shut out the sound of her voice from the end of the bar and put his attention to the blackboard attached to the wall between two sets of mirrored shelving.

"No one's joining me. I'll take a bowl of your chowder."

"You got it." The beer was set before him. "Visiting?"

"Checking on a piece of property I recently acquired."

"Where's your property?"

"Deer Harbor."

The bartender nodded, as if familiar. Until he looked puzzled. "I have family out there and my aunt knows everyone's business. I don't recall her mentioning that there was any other property selling, other than the old mansion that was auctioned off not too long ago because the previous owner couldn't pay off the back taxes."

"The Heron Inn," Jack supplied.

The bartender shook his head in disbelief. "This is a first; something happening out there that my aunt didn't know about." He chuckled. "You plan on selling, or fixing her up?"

"Sell, as fast as I can."

His lunch was set before him, along with a slice of toasted and buttered French bread. "If you're in need of a realtor, there's a display of business cards over by the juke box."

Jack nodded his thanks as he dipped his spoon into the aromatic, creamy chowder that wasn't in short supply of chunks of red potatoes with the skin still on, chopped clams, and celery.

"Or," the bartender had more to say, "you could ask the gal you've got your eye on if she'd be interested in buying your property. That's Marianne Dunaway, the new owner of the mansion." The bartender nudged his head toward the redhead. "There're a lot of rumors going around as to why she'd want that monstrosity. My guess is that she's buying property to flip it. There's a lot of that going on nowadays.

Raised voices came from the end of the bar. The bartender picked up the remote control and increased the volume on the television above the bar. When his tactic didn't catch the attention of the two having words, he said, "Excuse me," tossed the towel over his shoulder, and moved off to attend to the disturbance.

Jack watched the action in the reflection in the mirror behind the shelves of liquor. He had his confirmation of who lived in the mansion. He was a little disappointed that her real name wasn't Gigi. It had made for a nice fantasy.

"I told you, I didn't see a thing from up there," the teenager said.

"What's the problem here?" the bartender said.

His busboy shifted uncomfortably from foot to foot. "She doesn't believe me." He then pushed through the double doors to the kitchen without a look back.

The bartender crooked a finger at the redhead. She approached the bar, tucking her hair behind her ear and looking embarrassed. They spoke for a few moments before she nodded her head in understanding.

Jack had his head over his chowder when another reflection in the mirror caught his eye. A man had stepped out of the restrooms. He had a medium build and blonde hair falling across his forehead. His eyes fell on the activity at the bar and he zeroed in on the redhead.

"Darlin', seems fate has us running into each other, again." The man pushed the sleeves of his navy-blue sweater up past his elbows. "Let me buy you a drink."

"No thank you, but I will take the check to the assisted living center and deliver it myself," she said.

The man stiffened. His neck turned a blotchy red. "Did Missy send you after me?"

"No, she did not."

"They have it," he said through tight lips.

"Apparently, they don't. That's why they called me."

"Maybe someone over there is lying," he said.

Even from where Jack sat, it was evident the man was covering his ass. The guy wasn't a novice. He knew when being pissed wasn't to his advantage. He switched back to charm, as bad as it was.

To Jack's enjoyment, red wasn't so easily charmed by the sleaze-ball.

"This won't happen, again," she said. "I'm taking over our grandpa's finances. I've got his checkbook now." She made to step around him.

The man whipped out his arm and hooked it around her waist. "Whoa there, darlin'. Let's go talk about this over that drink."

Jack was off the stool before he realized what he was doing. He stopped halfway down the length of the bar. "I can tell from here that the lady doesn't want your company. I'd think it would be fairly obvious from where you're standing." Appreciation wasn't coming from the redhead. "Unless, you want this guy's company?" Jack said.

"Hey, back off, Gladiator." The man sized up Jack.

A throat cleared behind Jack. "Gentlemen?" the bartender said.

The one in the middle had the final say. "You, quit hitting on me," she said to the blonde man. Jack received his own reprimand. "You'd better not be following me."

To receive the same as the sleaze-ball rubbed Jack the wrong way. "Look, Red, if I was following you, it would at least be safer than being in front of you, as has been my experience."

The look she sent him could have stopped lava from flowing.

"Don't you have something of mine you need to return?" he said.

Her hesitation was as good as an admittance of guilt. However, his only reward was to watch her backside as she left the bar, giving the tavern door a hard push that sent blinding daylight in from outside.

"How do you know her?" the blonde-haired man said accusingly.

Jack wasn't about to share that information. Before he could even tell the guy to get lost, the tavern door suddenly whipped open and the redhead stormed back in.

It was evident who was under attack when she came to a stop, still riled up, just inches from Jack.

"This," she pointed to her hair, "is not red. It's strawberry blonde."

With that, she pivoted around and pushed out through the door.

"Even I knew she was a strawberry blonde," said the annoyance at his elbow.

Jack sent the man a cold look. "You're standing too close."

When the teenager came through the swinging doors carrying an empty tub to collect dishes, he stopped cold when his eyes fell on the man who had taken Jack's advice and moved off to take a seat in the family dining section. The teen did an abrupt pivot on his heels and slipped back into the kitchen.

The bartender didn't miss a thing. "I don't know what's going on," he said, lowering his voice as he nudged his chin toward the far corner, "but ever since Harold Swan's nephew arrived on the island about a year ago, there's been nothing but one degree of trouble or the other. Or more trouble, I should say. The Swan family name, in these parts, is one you want to watch out for, if you're planning on sticking around."

Wishing his inheritance had put him on a different island, Jack took a long drink from the cold beer. He had to get his mind off Strawberry. "What sort of trouble?" he asked the bartender.

"Sheriff says I have no hard evidence, but the crime rate has gone up in my opinion. My 'till's been robbed and so has our tip jar and about a half-dozen homes on the island." He sent a look toward the door to the kitchen where his busboy had yet to make another appearance. "I suspect he's also a relentless con man. He's got young Royce there dodging him for reasons I've yet to get out of the boy, other than it could have something to do with the fact that Royce worked for Gerald up until last week. Add to that, you saw him just hit on Marianne and yet he's the boyfriend of her sister." The bartender shook his head in disgust, continuing to keep his words only for Jack, "I'll tell you this much, Gerald Cain can't leave this island soon enough."

The bartender then switched topics as smoothly as he slapped the towel down and started polishing the bar. "What's an old inn cost these days?" he said.

As a rule, Jack only shared personal information with a few people in his life. But he was here to sell, and if talking helped. "I inherited it from my grandfather."

The bar towel stopped moving. "You inherited it?" He leaned closer to Jack and lowered his voice again. "You're a Bullock?"

Jack paused in pulling his wallet from his jacket pocket. "No," he replied. "My grandfather's last name was Smith."

The bartender looked puzzled. "I was under the impression that the inn remained in the Bullock family all this time."

"Not sure who the prior owner was. It's been in my grandfather's name for over thirty years." Jack could feel the bartender staring at him. He looked up. "What?"

"Not sure we're speaking of the same piece of property."

"It's up on the hill overlooking the marina. The old growth cedar has clamshells nailed onto its trunk in the shape of a heart," Jack said.

"This is getting odd," the bartender said after a moment. "I'm fairly certain that property has never had any other owner than the Bullock family. They couldn't have left it to the daughter because she would have sold it to save the home she lost. They had to have left it to their son Albert. However, it's possible he may have sold it to your grandfather, unbeknownst to anyone."

Gears began moving around in Jack's head, an instinct when he was on assignment and clues began to show themselves and he would systematically sort through them. Only thing was that this wasn't an assignment, just a trip to check out a piece of property he'd inherited. Still, the gears were now up and running.

"My grandfather's name was Albert. Albert Smith," Jack said.

The baseball team on the television scored a home run in the time it took the bartender to say next what he wanted to say.

"Any chance your grandfather changed his name?"

Jack wasn't sure he liked the bartender's speculation. "I'm not related to the Bullocks."

"Probably all just a coincidence, the two having the same first name. However, I'd keep a low profile. Speculation alone could throw up road blocks for you on this island."

"I take it the Bullock name isn't a favorite around here?" Jack said.

There was a spark of excitement in dark eyes beneath bushy, black eyebrows. "I've heard enough gossip to be able to tell you this much. Albert Bullock was born and raised on this island. Shortly after he returned from the war and became engaged to Louise, the FBI came looking for him and a few of his friends. What he did after that made him a few enemies."

Jack slowly set down his now empty beer glass. "His wife's name was Louise?"

"Yup." The bartender nodded. Then understanding dawned on his face. "Let me guess. Your grandmother's name was Louise?"

Jack nodded. "She's still living."

"You by chance have a photo of your grandfather? Not that I'd recognize him, as all this was long before I moved to Orcas. There is someone on the island who might, though. That is, if you're looking to sort this all out."

"I have a photo, just not on me." Jack looked over his shoulder to where the troublesome woman had exited. He wasn't leaving the island without the old black and white photo. His grandfather had been camera shy, his mother only now realizing how few photos she had of her father to remember him by.

The older man dropped his voice even lower. "I'll tell you what I do know. Albert and Louise Bullock were last seen heading for the Canadian border and there isn't a single person on this island who would welcome them back."

The waitress stepped up to the far end of the bar. "Pop, I need three fish-n-chips and two ales."

The bartender introduced Jack to the waitress. "This is my daughter, Julia. She takes care of this place better than I ever could." He smiled fondly at the waitress and told her that Jack was the new owner of the old Heron Inn.

"You've got your work cut out for you," Julia said with a warm smile. She picked up her tray with the drink order and returned to her customers.

"If you're interested in learning more about the prior owners of your inn," the bartender said, "the best source of information on what happened back then is with our town historian. Most days he hangs out at the Banner, our local newspaper office over at Deer Harbor. Something else that might interest you. The mansion that Marianne now owns was previously in the Bullock family. Perrigo Mansion is where Albert and his sister were raised."

Jack slowly stood, giving his knee a moment before he added more weight. "Is this sister still on the island?"

"Yup. She's the only woman on the island who opens her door with a shotgun pointed at you." He grinned and extended his hand to Jack. "I'm Tom Harris. I own this watering hole. Welcome to the island."

Chapter 7

Ed Dunaway's room at the assisted living center looked out over the Deer Harbor Marina. Today, as always, he sat close to the window in a wingback chair wearing his navy, terrycloth bathrobe over a pair of striped pajamas. Suede slippers covered his feet. On his blanketed lap sat an open journal.

Marianne dropped her coat and handbag on the hospital bed. "How are you today, Grandpa?"

The hawk-like nose turned slowly toward her as he lowered a pair of binoculars.

"Marianne," he said in greeting, recognizing her today. On her last visit, she'd had to remind him several times that she was not a new nurse.

His voice was thin and weak, like the eighty-five-pound frame of this man who'd once had a muscular build from a lifetime of work on a boat. His hair was now snow white and thinning. Ice blue eyes that were once sharp and bright were now, on most days, just tired and confused.

She kissed his unshaven face of white whiskers, patting the bony hand that held tight to a pencil. It was her grandpa's belief that he needed to keep mentally busy to hang onto what was left of his memory and reasoning skills. He did this by noting the activity outside his window, whether it was boats coming and going from the marina or a tourist carelessly discarding litter on the small beach below. He even documented the hourly changes in the weather.

In the margin of the open journal, her name was penciled in with 'granddaughter' noted in brackets. Only it wasn't his handwriting.

It made her throat burn to see the reality, that someone she loved was forgetting her more, and more, as each day passed, and now needed the help of those he'd known for only a short time to remember her and memories from a lifetime.

"Winds are at thirty knots," he said. The pencil shook in his unsteady hand. He made a notation. "Marina traffic is light, and should be. Who in blazes would take their boat out with these winds picking up?" The binoculars were trained on the small grocery store on the dock and the building that housed the laundromat and showers for boaters. "Take a look at the flag on the dock. There hasn't been slack in Old Glory for over a week now." He rested the binoculars on his lap. "We've got a storm coming. I hope you're prepared."

"I am." Marianne sat on the edge of the bed.

"If you're not, you'll learn your lesson. You've got no one, but yourself, to look out for you, just remember that." He looked beyond her toward the hall. "Where's Missy?"

This was how it always went; his concern for the youngest, whereas she and Ian were expected to fend for themselves. If he wasn't forgetting her, the man who'd raised them after the accident that had taken the lives of their parents, was being as hard on her as ever. "I'm sure she'll be by later. I saw her this morning."

"Does she have supplies for a power outage?"

"I don't know."

He frowned at her. "Could you make sure she is prepared?"

Ed Dunaway was a complicated man. You never knew if your words and actions were going to gain his respect or disapproval. In her case, generally the latter.

On her last visit, she'd left determined to find a way to not let his bark and bite get to her, knowing deep inside that his personality was what kept her away most of the year. She'd searched the Internet for tips and found an article on dealing with difficult people. The advice was that she couldn't control how others behaved toward her. What she could control how she responded. Today was her first go at her new approach in getting along with her grandpa. The only way to survive a visit with her grandpa would be to take a step back on an emotional level and pretend she was just a volunteer keeping a cranky old man company. Calm and cool. She could do this.

"She is a grownup," Marianne said. "I'm sure she can take care of herself. She also has a boyfriend now." She immediately regretted divulging that much and hoped he hadn't heard. His frown said otherwise.

"Don't for a minute think that no-good nephew of Harold Swan's is doing your sister any good."

"Who told you that her boyfriend was Gerald Cain?"

"I don't remember." He scowled. "There's trouble there. I can see it on her face. Where's that son-of-a-bitch living? Do you know?"

She crossed her fingers behind her back. "No. I don't know. What trouble?"

"That's none of your affair. You can't interfere in her life."

She dug her fingernails into the palms of her hands and counted to ten. "Yet you want me to coddle her and take her supplies."

"It's up to her to stand up for herself. It builds character. You need to stay out of her affairs." He pointedly ignored her and picked up the binoculars once again.

Like a tidal wave, back came the feelings that drove her off this island so many years ago. Who was she kidding? Detaching herself emotionally and remaining objective was going to be impossible with this man.

She was at the door with her coat over her arm when she stopped and glanced back.

Her grandpa leaned at a precarious angle trying to reach the pencil that he'd dropped. She rushed over to keep him from toppling headfirst out of the chair.

"You're supposed to press the button if you need help, Grandpa." She kneeled by his chair and picked up the pencil.

His response was delayed as if he wasn't sure how the pencil came to be back in his hand. After a moment, he placed his hand over hers, and smiled at her in a gentle way that she rarely saw.

"It's good to have you back, Marianne."

Tears welled up in her eyes. She smiled at him. "It's good to be back."

And then the moment was gone. The frown returned as did the important task of keeping track of the world outside his window. Her frustration with him returned. She would regret later the impulse to press his buttons.

"I saw Harold Swan today. Your name came up." She stood.

The binoculars came abruptly down and he barked, "What does that man want with me?"

"I didn't say he wanted anything. I just mentioned that he asked after you, in a round-about way."

"What way?"

Her curiosity over his long-standing feud with the Swan family pushed her on as did her need to follow her instinct that something wasn't right in Missy's life.

"Tell me first, what's wrong with Missy?"

The stubborn Ed Dunaway wasn't one to be easily manipulated. Even as he had his head turned away, she had a feeling that he had his ears tuned to what he might say next on the subject.

"The residents on this island have suspicions about you. That's what he said."

The pencil went slack in his fingers. "Did you believe him?"

"Of course not." She retrieved the photo from her handbag and set the old black and white on top of the journal. "Is that you standing behind Gilly? Were you two once close, long ago?"

He was as frozen as a statue. "Where did you get this?"

"I found it."

A glazed look came over his eyes and Marianne was forgotten.

A young woman stepped into the doorway carrying a tray. "I have your lunch, Mr. Dunaway."

"I'm tired. I want to lie down." He tried to stand.

The attendant quickly set the tray on the dresser and rushed to his side. "Let me help you, Mr. Dunaway."

Another attendant entered the room and her grandpa was helped into bed, leaving his lunch untouched.

Marianne picked up the photo and left with a goodbye at the doorway that wasn't heard as Ed Dunaway closed his eyes to this sudden weariness that had overtaken him.

She stopped at the main office and asked if her grandpa's payment had shown up yet.

It had not.

***

When the rain began to fall in earnest, it thundered on the roof of the Land Rover as she prepared to leave the parking lot of the assisted living center. She turned on the engine to get the wipers going and waited as the defroster did away with the condensation forming on the inside of the windshield.

She checked her phone for messages from her brother. The only message was a text from Missy.

I need Grandpa's briefcase back. Where can I meet you?

She was still angry with her sister for the shove between the shoulder blades. She texted her reply.

I'm not giving it back. You wanted me to take over the finances. I'll do it.

Only after the message was sent did she realize that wasn't the right approach to take if she was going to find out what sort of troubles Missy was having. She'd probably only made things worse and widened the gap between them even more.

Maybe this was going to be the state of their relationship, butting heads, and arguing. It was frustrating. Fiona was right. She'd been absent long enough that she and her sister had become strangers.

She put her vehicle into reverse only to slam on the brakes when a horn sounded behind her.

While the big town car moved at a snail's pace, as the driver attempted to squeeze into a compact parking space, the brief deluge passed.

In her side mirror, she saw a black motorcycle come around the corner. She instinctively scrunched down in her seat, continuing to keep an eye on the rider. He turned on his signal and roared up the steep hill opposite the assisted living center. He pulled over and parked next to the rental office for the cluster of tiny vacation cottages overlooking the marina.

While she waited with fingers crossed that he wouldn't be successful in finding a vacancy, the man who didn't know women's hair colors very well walked in the opposite direction of the rental office. He bypassed the restaurant with big windows that looked out over the harbor and headed straight for a small blue house.

The fact that she'd accused him of following her didn't stop what she did next.

***

Marianne hurried into the newspaper office holding her handbag up to protect her hair from the rain that pummeled the street, leaving her jeans speckled with raindrops and the boot-cut hem soaked. She'd left her vehicle in the parking lot below, hoping that there'd be a longer break in the rain. The unpredictable March weather had other ideas.

On her walk up the hill, she'd come up with an excuse as to why she was here. She didn't have a chance to pull it off. Jack Sanders was nowhere to be seen.

Two wood chairs with cushions sat with their backs to the large window where rainwater streamed down. A coffee table with a tidy arrangement of travel magazines and a glass dish of Tootsie Rolls promised something to do with any waiting time. On the other side of the counter two desks faced each other.

The sole occupant of the office was a young woman who looked up from her computer keyboard. The nameplate on her desk read, '*Rita*'.

"It's days like these that I kick myself for moving to this climate," Rita said as she came to the counter, eying her customer with curiosity. "What can I help you with?" Behind the desks a row of filing cabinets backed up to a wall. In that wall, the curtain covering a doorway still moved.

"I thought I saw someone I know come in here," Marianne said.

"Tall, good-looking guy with dark hair and just an edge of danger about him?"

Marianne smiled. "You should write fiction."

The woman blushed. "Sorry. Bit much?"

"The description fits."

"He just left out the back door with my editor," she said with a grin. "They aren't going far. He wanted to meet Sal. That's my editor's husband. They live just up the stairs to the homes on the hill."

"Yes, I know who Sal is," replied Marianne.

Rita made an apologetic face. "Sorry. I'm still getting familiar with small-town life where everyone knows everyone and everyone's business." She paused. "You're the new owner of Perrigo Mansion, aren't you? One of the Dunaways."

Marianne smiled and held out her hand. "Yes, I'm Marianne. I'm having to get used to the same thing again; how fast news travels in a small community."

Rita smiled. "One minute it's out my lips and the next it ends up as fodder at the coffee shop. Like what's going around right now. Only I didn't start that one." The young woman had spoken innocently enough, yet, her face began to redden. There was suddenly a lot that had to be tidied up at the counter. Brochures straightened in their plastic displays and paper clips and rubber bands swept into a bowl and put under the counter, all with Rita trying to avoid making eye contact. Two people in a single day hinting at town gossip about her family.

"What are they saying about my grandpa?" Marianne said.

Rita looked uncomfortable. "The talk is about you."

"Me?"

"Oh, it's nothing bad," she said. "Just that you must have done really good for yourself to be able to afford Perrigo Mansion."

"I've done okay, as a writer."

She smiled. "You're a writer? As in you have books published?"

"Quite a few, in fact."

"Oh. I don't think anyone in town knows that. I know how to fix that." Rita pulled a colorful flyer out from under the counter. "Sal and Caroline are having their annual party. It's also a fundraiser for a local charity. Sal makes his great chili, of course. The entire town is invited. You could use the opportunity to let everyone know that you're a published writer."

"I'd rather not." Marianne smiled politely.

"Come anyway. You might have fun."

"I'll think about it."

"Great!" Rita's eyes lit up. "In the meantime, I'd be happy to spread the word that you're a writer and that's how you were able to buy the mansion and not with the money your grandfather's pretending he doesn't have." Rita grew even redder this time, wearing a horrified look on her face.

"That's what everyone thinks?" Marianne was stunned. "My grandpa lives off social security. You can spread that around." In the next moment, she was apologizing for taking her frustration out on Rita. "I'm sorry. Any idea how that rumor got started?"

"No."

Marianne thought for a moment. "I'm beginning to think it's just old rivalry."

"Like the one between your grandfather and Mr. Swan?"

"You've heard about that?"

"Yeah. It's quite a story. In fact, that's probably what Sal is telling your friend." She sent a look toward the curtained hallway. "He came in asking for information on Albert and Louise Bullock. My editor told him that her husband was writing a book about what happened long ago when the FBI came looking for Albert Bullock and his sister, and Ed Dunaway, and Harold Swan, all old friends who haven't spoken to each other to this day. Apparently, they each blame the other for something, no one knows exactly what." With barely a pause for breath, Rita added, "You probably knew all that, right?"

"Bits and pieces, I think," Marianne said as her head spun with this new news.

Rita reached out and placed a sympathetic hand on Marianne's. "Their feuding is nothing compared to what we think your sister is going through. I suppose that's why you're really back on the island."

"Come again?"

Chapter 8

The town historian was a large man who filled up the executive-style chair that he sat in. He was bald with a round face and intelligent eyes behind a pair of frameless eyeglasses that looked like they might slide off the end of his shiny nose at any moment.

The low-ceilinged basement office smelled of the damp, mustiness, and many cigars. It wasn't nearly as colorful as the outside of the house that was painted purple with lime green trim and an orange roof.

Jack looked at the upholstered chair by the door and then his rain-soaked jeans.

His host said, "A little rain never hurt anything. Have a seat."

It felt good to ease into the worn chair and gingerly stretched out his leg. The cold day wasn't helping his aching knee.

The surface of the desk between him and the historian was littered with newspapers, thick files, open reference books, and legal-size notepads filled with writing. Over the top of all this, Sal watched him with interest.

"Noticed you were limping some. Sports injury?" Sal asked.

"No." Jack wasn't inclined to say much about his injury, since he couldn't elaborate on the how and where and his blown-to-hell knee wasn't a medal as much as a reminder that his army career might be over. Not if he had a say in it.

On the wall behind Sal, there were several framed photos of a young, decorated marine as well as an older black and white photo of a sailor standing on a dock in front of a gray battleship.

"I was injured in active duty," Jack said, feeling that he was on common ground with the historian. He nodded toward the photos. "Family?"

"My father," Sal said, as he focused on lighting a cigar, "and my son," were the softer words that followed. Only then did Jack notice on a shelf a wood and glass case holding the American flag folded and preserved.

"I'm sorry," Jack said.

Sal nodded his appreciation. "I served for a spell," he said. "Broke my ankle so badly, that was that." He gave a slight grimace. "Tried college. It wasn't for me. Dropped out of trade school, too. Then I met Caroline," Sal referred to his wife with a wink and a smile. "She's been the twinkle in my eye for forty years now." He paused, then sighed heavily. "As far as ever finding a respectable career, well that didn't happen. I ended up here in my basement trying to make ends meet with freelance writing and odd jobs here and there." He leaned back in his chair, taking a long pull on his cigar as smoke filled the space between his bald head and the low ceiling stained with water and draped with cobwebs. "Figured this book I'm writing is my last chance to make something of myself."

Cold sweat trickled along Jack's spine. Sal's timeline from his medical discharge to where he'd ended up in a basement with a mousetrap in the corner was a far more terrifying story than the time when Jack waited it out under a bombed-out house in Afghanistan while the terrorists he hunted searched the rubble for survivors to torture.

Jack unzipped his jacket and ran a finger under the neck of his T-shirt, wishing the door had been left open.

"You're looking for information on the slippery Albert Bullock," Sal said. "Why don't you tell me first, what exactly it is you hope to gain from our conversation? What is your interest in the Bullock family?"

"I recently inherited the old Heron Inn and I understand that Albert Bullock was the former owner. That is, before my grandfather owned it."

Sal looked perplexed for a moment. "I don't recall that property ever changing hands. Who left you the property?"

Jack hesitated. "My grandfather, Albert Smith."

Sal stared at him for several seconds then smiled. "I've always wondered if perhaps they'd changed their name." He looked over the rim of his eyeglasses. "Never expected to have his grandson sitting in my office. My condolences. When did he pass?"

"*My* grandfather passed away last month. Let's not confuse the two Alberts."

Sal made a note on a legal pad. He set down his pen and gave Jack a sharp look over his eyeglasses as if debating whether to argue the point or not. Finally, he leaned back in his chair.

"It was 1945. The war was ending." He spent a few moments fussing with his cigar.

"If this is a history lesson on WWII," Jack began.

"Sit tight, son. You're about to learn a whole lot more." The historian pushed his glasses up onto his bald head and pinched the bridge of his nose before blinking sharply. "What I have learned is that Gilly was back east at a women's college about the same time that Albert was shipped stateside to spend some time in an army hospital. Not long after that, two of Albert's childhood friends were back stateside as well. I'll get to their names shortly. I know they were all together over in the Boston area because they ended up in one of those many photographs in the newspaper of our nation celebrating the end of the war." Sal puffed on his cigar. "I doubt that group of friends have been together since. Something happened to tear them apart, except Albert and his bride, who was Gilly's roommate. The rest came back separately, quiet as can be. Next thing everyone knows is that the FBI is here on the island looking for Albert, his sister, and the rest of the group. That's about the same time Gilly became very ill with polio and the family doctor ordered a quarantine area around Perrigo Mansion. Oh, and of course, your grandfather and his new bride disappeared off the island like a pair of ghosts."

"The Bullocks left the island. *My* grandparents raised a family in Oregon," Jack said.

"Son, you're a stubborn one. You show up saying you inherited the Heron Inn from your grandfather, Albert Smith. I know, for a fact, that the inn hasn't changed owners in the last forty years when Albert Bullock inherited it from his parents. Why don't we quit pretending that you're not seeing what's as clear as day? The Bullocks and Smiths are one, and the same. Unless by chance you've already confirmed that your grandfather has school records and such elsewhere?"

Jack got to his feet. "Thank you for your time."

He shut the door on the nasty cigar, taking a gratifying breath of fresh air.

It wasn't enough.

He lifted his face to the rain that pock-marked the dark earth in the narrow strip of garden and didn't take another step, even as the rain dripped down the back of his neck.

From the moment he'd met Marianne, he knew that he'd have to make his business short on the island and try to get back on his way without any complications or diversions.

It wasn't working out that way.

He didn't know which developing complication was giving him more frustration. The strawberry blonde or that his grandfather might not have been who he said he was.

The good news, if there was any, was that he still might be able to avoid one of those complications.

Jack had chased enough clues to know when they were all lining up as straight as an arrow. It would only take a few additional pieces of the puzzle to conclude that his grandparents had managed to keep a big secret all these years. The question was, why?

Sal didn't look in the least surprised to see him step back through the door.

"Do you have any photos of Albert Bullock?" Jack asked.

Sal dug through one of the thick, manila file folders on his desk. He pulled out a much-handled newspaper clipping. The newspaper photographer had captured the five young adults laughing and clapping each other on the backs as they stood on a street packed with others celebrating the end of the war. The air was littered with confetti. Unfortunately, it blocked getting a good look at the tall, young man with the dark hair. All that could be seen was his big smile.

"That's the best I've got at present," Sal said.

"Why were they of interest to the FBI?" Jack asked.

"They had a description of Albert from a witness who was at the same party where valuable jewels were stolen. The FBI tracked down every guest for questioning."

"Were the jewels ever recovered?"

"Not to my knowledge." Sal sat forward. "As I shared with you, the FBI attempted to pursue the Bullocks for questioning, but the trail went cold. Rumors abounded, though. Most of this island's residents believed back then that the Bullocks left with the stolen jewels, that is, if they were indeed the thieves. In my novel, that's the case. However, of late, events occurring are changing how I'd planned to wrap up my story." The town historian started checking off new developments on his fingers. "A Dunaway bought Perrigo Mansion a few weeks ago. According to our mail carrier, someone recently left a threatening note on the gate with mention of her having 'traitor in her blood', a note that has yet to be reported to the sheriff, according to the dispatcher. Makes me wonder why Ed Dunaway's granddaughter is trying to keep this hush-hush. What does she know? And who on the island is riled up enough to not like that she's living in the mansion?" Sal looked thoughtful. "There is another rumor that never really gained momentum, and that is, that one of Albert's friends sold the jewels and made some nice cash. However, that doesn't hold water either because those involved who remained on the island never seemed to have had a sound financial existence. It seems more plausible that the jewels left with Albert and Louise or are in hiding." His pen scratched across the note pad. "Still need to verify that the note Ed's granddaughter received truly exists, although Eleanor is a fairly reliable source."

"Why would anyone care that she's living in the mansion?" Jack said.

Sal's eyebrows rose above his eyeglasses. "Keep up, son. Only three things could have possibly happened to those jewels. I've told you two. Either they left with Albert and Louise or they were sold or," Sal paused for effect, "someone hid them very carefully and I suspect that location would be somewhere in the mansion."

"Is this granddaughter by chance Marianne Dunaway?"

"You know Marianne?"

"We met on the ferry yesterday."

"Ah." Sal nodded. "So, you haven't met her grandfather, Ed, yet. He's quite a character. Set in his ways and somewhat gruff, but you got to admire the man. He started a family late in life to begin with, then just when he was about to retire, his daughter and her husband were killed in a car accident. Ed and his wife ended up raising their grandkids." He paused. "Does Marianne know of your relation to the Bullocks?"

"*I* just learned of my relation to the Bullocks. Unconfirmed relation," he added, quickly.

"I don't know what Ms. Dunaway's intentions are, but I'd sure hate to see the young woman come to any harm. Let's hope that whoever doesn't like the fact that she now owns the mansion doesn't have the balls to take their threat a step further."

Sal stubbed out his cigar in the ashtray. "Those friends of Albert's that I mentioned are Harold Swan and Ed Dunaway. They used to run in a tight group; Albert and his sister Gilly, and Harold and Ed. They're not friends any longer, that's for sure. The way I see it, the truth seems to want to spill out of wherever it's hiding. It just needs a good shake of the tree." Sal chuckled. "Now here you are. Word gets out that you're on the island and that's certainly going to stir the pot."

***

Jack returned to his motorcycle by way of the street. The walk down provided a panoramic view of the harbor with the marina and the towering hillside opposite as well as evergreen-covered islands farther out. Jack craned his neck to see if he could see his inn. It was too well hidden in the trees.

When he'd parked his motorcycle, he'd noticed a '*vacancy*' sign in the window of the rental office that had the same cedar-shingled roof with green-painted door and trim as the cottages.

Cars were parallel parked along the steep street and tourists were unloading gear in front of their rented cottages while keeping an eye on their kids. Two boys played in the middle of the street throwing a football around. He was almost abreast of the Banner office when a misfired football came flying in his direction. Jack caught it in time to keep the football from hitting a windshield.

"Go out for it," he said to the two young athletes. He waited until they were almost to the bottom of the street then lofted the ball easy enough for one of them to catch. He then nearly plowed into the woman who'd stepped out between the parked cars, not watching where she was going.

He'd grabbed her by the shoulders to keep from knocking her down. It was Strawberry hair, Gigi, whose real name was Marianne. Either way, she smelled good, this close.

"Sorry," she sounded flustered. "I didn't see you." It was the barest movement, her head turning enough to look over his shoulder up the hill toward the house with the orange roof.

Jack felt that it was his due to have some fun with her. "Remind me of your name again?" he began, then snapped his fingers as if it had come to him. "It's Gigi, right?"

"Ah, yeah." She self-consciously tucked her hair behind her ears.

"Have a nice day, Gigi." He crossed the street to his motorcycle.

After a moment, she followed. "Thank you for what you did back at the tavern. I'm sorry I was rude to you."

"Happy to have helped." He wished she would take off her sunglasses, because he couldn't remember if her eyes were green or blue.

"I'm also sorry for nearly running you off the road."

Her genuine sincerity made it easy to put the incident in the past. "All is forgiven," he said.

The wind played with her hair. "Have you found accommodations yet?" she asked.

At that moment, a woman came out of the cottage office and flipped over the sign to the '*no vacancy*' side.

Jack had carried his half helmet with him and he set it on his head, leaving the straps to dangle for now.

"You live nearby?" Although he already knew the answer, he waited to see if his luck would change and she'd offer up a room in her big mansion, now that she was warming up to him. Blue eyes? Green eyes? He couldn't remember any longer the second reason she was on his shit list.

Her reply was as cautious as on the ferry. "I don't live too far. You might have better luck over on San Juan island."

"You keep telling me." He had a feeling that if he pulled down those dark sunglasses, he would see that she was quite pleased that he might have to move on to another island for a good night's sleep.

"In case we don't run into each other again, enjoy your stay, wherever that may be." She gave a small wave and was about to leave when a car came driving up the hill directly towards a big rain puddle.

Jack pulled Strawberry out of the way just as the car's tires splashed through the puddle sending a spray of water in their direction. He didn't stop there. He didn't know what he was thinking, backing her a few steps up against the wall of the cottage office.

Glossy, pink lips below big dark sunglasses smiled softly at him. "Thank you," she said. "That's twice today you've helped me out."

"My pleasure, Gigi," he replied. He was liking the sound of that name, far too much. Maybe that was a good thing. If he kept calling her by her phony name, it might be easier to think of her as a fantasy woman instead of a real woman who might be hard to forget, once he got off this rock.

It was a fight to keep his hands where they were, resting lightly at her hips, and not stray toward the shape outlined beneath the snug-fitting coat that she wore. A pulse beat at the side of her slender neck. A voice in his head told him to step back and quit fantasizing over what she'd look like with her hair all mussed up in the morning after a night of lovemaking.

She broke the moment. "This is crazy." Then she was gone, moving swiftly down the hill without a look back, leaving only her scent behind.

The spray of water had covered his bike. He wiped off the seat with a rag from the saddle bag as he continued to watch her cross the street to a parking lot in front of a long, low building with many windows.

This was no fantasy. This was getting complicated. A smart man would be on the next ferry, if for no other reason than to save his motorcycle from this dangerous woman.

He wouldn't think of the photo again for several hours.

Chapter 9

Something didn't look right. It took Marianne a few seconds to realize that the broken glass on the ground next to her Land Rover wasn't there when she'd parked outside the grocery store.

She put the box of emergency supplies in the back of her vehicle before inspecting the broken rear-passenger window that had left glass on the seat.

A woman pushing a shopping cart stopped. "That's a shame." She shook her head. "We never used to have things like that happen on Orcas."

Although the vehicle still smelled of pipe tobacco, her grandpa's briefcase was gone.

An employee of the grocery store came out and helped sweep up the glass from the pavement and even went as far as to sweep out her back seat. A sheriff's deputy arrived shortly and took her statement. Her next stop was the hardware store one block over for heavy-duty plastic and a role of duct tape.

Conveniently, the bank was two doors down between a candy shop and a bookstore. The manager,

Carla, helped her at the windowed counter where a vase of yellow tulips had an arrangement of plastic orca whales circling its base.

Marianne introduced herself and showed the manager her identification as she explained that her grandpa's checkbook had just been stolen.

"You're one of the grandchildren on Mr. Dunaway's account," Carla confirmed as she quickly typed at the keyboard and pulled up Ed Dunaway's account information. "That's such a shame about the theft."

"It was basically his home office; checkbook, tax documents, bills."

Carla shook her head in dismay followed by a look of sympathy.

"I'm sorry to tell you this, but that's not the only problem with your grandfather's financial affairs. I've tried to contact your sister regarding this matter. She hasn't returned my calls."

The door opened and cold wind moved the paper whale mobiles hanging from the ceiling. Marianne glanced over her shoulder to see if she recognized the person waiting in line. That didn't necessarily mean that Marianne wasn't recognized and anything overheard wouldn't make it to the coffee shop in the next hour.

"What matter?" Marianne asked, barely above a whisper.

Carla leaned forward and spoke in a lowered voice, "We haven't seen a deposit in over a month. Your sister usually brings in his social security check about the tenth. Just not this month. It wouldn't be a problem, as there's generally a healthy balance, but there's been a lot of activity on his account, unusual expenses."

"How low is his balance?"

Carla wrote a figure on a piece of paper and pushed it across the counter to Marianne.

"It's in the negative?" her voice shot up. "Have any checks come back?"

"Not yet."

Marianne pulled out her wallet. "How can we fix this?"

***

It was noisy driving with the wind rattling the plastic covering the broken window. She turned the heat on full and suffered through what was left of the lingering pipe smell. She felt like she'd been in her car all morning and was anxious to get home and relax.

At her sister's, the driveway was empty. Keeping one eye on the rearview mirror for a black Suburban approaching, she quickly wrote out a note for Missy, asking her to call as soon as possible regarding their grandpa's finances. She set the box of emergency supplies in the driest spot next to the back door with the note tucked down between two cans of beef stew.

Her last stop before home was to return to the assisted living center where she used her credit card to cover the unpaid bill and asked that they not let her grandfather know that she'd done so. Her grandpa was a proud man and had refused Marianne's offers in the past to help with his expenses.

Later that evening, the storm front descended on the island. Clouds moved in and blocked out moonlight and starlight. Rain fell in earnest, blowing in through the window over the sink that wouldn't shut all the way. She wedged two dish towels into the open gap of the window frame then pulled the curtains across.

The duct tape came into use again.

She tore off several pieces to hold the curtain in place. It wasn't so much to keep the rain out as she didn't want to see the open window that only reminded her of Gerald's remark about her living alone.

She tried to think of other things instead of how many days she had to go in this big and shadowy mansion. An image of a dangerously-handsome pirate biker came to mind along with his gallant actions at the tavern and again saving her from a spray of mud puddle water.

Due to the unnerving events of the day, she couldn't help the suspicion and wariness that overtook romantic thoughts she might otherwise have indulged in. Why was Jack so interested in speaking to the town historian about the Bullock family? And why did he have a photo of her grandpa and Gilly, a photo that had upset an old man?

She went through the first floor, her steps muffled by the thick oriental area rugs and runners, closing the heavy, pale blue, velvet drapes and turning on a lamp in each room.

She'd forgotten about the red, glass bird she'd left on her desk. This time, she purposely carried it through to the formal dining room to the mahogany table where packing paper and boxes sat at one end. She carefully wrapped it in paper and added it to the box with the rest of the set.

Standing beneath the large, crystal chandelier, she debated if she was up to finishing her project tonight, that of packing up the assortment of antiques and collectibles she'd assembled. Most were destined for a shop to see if she could sell them. One of the antiques she was hoping to repair and keep. The blue and white Japanese ginger jar would make a nice addition to her collection at her home in Seattle. But someone had glued the lid on. She was hoping that she could remove the glue without damaging the antique.

Leave the dining room, she stepped on a hard object in the thick fringe of the blue and gold oriental rug. The red glass handle from a vase glinted up at her. Puzzled as to how it came to be there, she picked it up and her eyes fell on the vase itself that had rolled beneath the sideboard with the dust bunnies. It was the largest piece in the collection. One that she was certain she'd wrapped in paper and packed in the box. Now it was broken and under the sideboard.

Goosebumps prickled along her skin.

Perrigo felt far too big and too quiet.

She hurried back to the kitchen. In passing the large tapestry in the hall that covered the door to the basement, she felt a draft move across the back of her hand. She didn't stop to investigate.

No longer was the swinging kitchen door with a porthole a favorite architectural feature of the old mansion. Now it only meant that a face could suddenly pop up and scare her.

With her heart pounding, she dragged the leather armchair across to block the door. Then she felt ridiculous. She was overreacting.

Or was she?

With shaky hands, she called her brother, only to end up getting his voicemail.

It was difficult to enjoy her dinner of cold chicken and a baked potato as she sat on a stool at the kitchen island, keeping one eye on the swinging door and hearing the wind whistle through the open window. She looked around the kitchen for anything to use as a weapon: the fireplace poker, the straw broom, a heavy flashlight, and maybe forks because the thought of pulling out a big knife and having it turned on her was too much for her imagination.

She assembled her weaponry on the kitchen island. The arsenal looked cold and unfriendly.

She reached for her closest friend at present, a bottle of wine, and while she was at it, added the wine opener to her pile of weapons.

She was happily halfway through her second glass of the smooth-tasting Malbec, and using a chemical she'd found under the sink to try to remove the cement-like glue that held the ginger jar lid in place, when the phone on the wall rang. The shrill and unfamiliar sound startled her so much that she knocked over the bottle of wine.

She didn't have a land line at her condominium and couldn't remember the last time she'd answered a phone wired into a wall. She wiped up the spilled wine as the retro-looking, princess-style phone shrilled again. The stained dish towel went in the sink and she crossed the room to the phone.

"Hello?" she answered.

"Do you hear that music?" Gilly said.

"How did you get this number?"

"It's still my phone number, Numbskull. Guess you haven't changed everything that was once mine."

Not yet. She would disconnect the line tomorrow. "I don't hear any music," Marianne said.

"Pull that long hair of yours out of your ears. There's music coming from the old inn. Nobody should be over there," Gilly said. "If it's that teenager again, I'm going to call the sheriff and make sure he locks him up, this time."

"You don't need to call the sheriff," Marianne said, thinking back to what Tom Harris had shared with her about Royce.

The handset had a long, coiled line and she stretched it across to the kitchen island where she set the phone down.

The covered veranda protected her from the rain as she stood listening for any music coming from the old inn on the hillside.

The high winds easily beat out the sound of the tide, covering up any disturbance from up on the hill, that and the steady drip, drip coming from the downspout.

She zipped up the down vest and pulled up the hood to brave the elements. Ducking her head into the wind and rain, she walked across the back lawn to the water's edge. Away from the dripping downspout, she picked up the faint beat of music.

"It's not as loud as usual," she said to Gilly, once back inside, her face and hands cold from those brief moments out in the storm. The last thing she was going to do tonight was deal with the music. She was too tired and beat from a crazy enough day as it was. "I'm sure he'll turn it off shortly."

"It's only going to get louder," Gilly replied. "Now go over there and take care of it, or I will, with my shotgun."

"Fine," she said with a heavy sigh. "First, I have a question for you."

"What?" snapped her neighbor.

"Have you been in my house?"

There was a long stretch of silence until Gilly said, "City people are way too paranoid." A dial tone buzzed in her ear.

Marianne counted to ten. It didn't help. Then her eyes fell on the kitchen shears in her assembled arsenal. It was easy to wiggle the phone from its mount on the wall and expose a phone line. The shears were on the dull side so it wasn't a neat cut, but she was saved from Gilly bothering her again, in this manner.

With the leftover chicken from her dinner, she made several sandwiches and put these in a shopping bag along with two apples. Tom Harris had yet to find out what had brought Royce to Orcas Island. What he did know, was that the young man was far from home and without enough money to return. Tom, having had a rough start to his own adult years, gave the seventeen-year old odd jobs and hot meals. But the proud teenager had refused any additional charity, including a spare bed that Tom had offered. It was on Tom's word that beneath the awkward and defiant attitude was the heart of a good kid that had Marianne deciding it was time to make peace with the down-on-his-luck teenager.

She slipped her black ski parka over the pink down vest and sheltered the grocery sack inside her coat as she hurried to her vehicle.

The wipers worked madly to clear away the rain, leaves, and pine needles whipped up by the wind. There was little traffic as she drove over the bridge, seeing on her left the warm lights from her kitchen window and hoping that the power stayed on long enough for those lights to be a welcome beacon on her return.

Once she accessed the hill, the night grew darker with the way the tall trees threw shadows across the road. She had to slow so as not to miss the hidden driveway to the inn. Her headlights caught the heart-shape on the cedar tree, the sun-bleached clamshells acting like reflectors.

She parked at the foot of the front steps and was all ready to be a good neighbor. One foot out of the vehicle, and the gusting winds that violently shook the bushes, like an invisible hand, sent her jumping right back in to quickly lock the doors.

It was so tempting to head back home and wait until daylight. The thought that a parent somewhere probably worried about this homeless kid had her shaking off her ninny moment.

She reached for the flashlight in the glove box only to close her hand around a gun she'd forgotten about. A lot of good the Lady Derringer was, without bullets or the nerve to use it.

She shoved the gun into the pocket of her ski jacket, with the intent of burying it in the backyard and seeing how her friend dealt with that. From the back of the vehicle, she took the wool blanket she kept there. Dinner and a warm blanket for Royce and maybe she would be less like the Harold Swans of this world.

On her last visit to the old inn, the front door had swung open with one touch. Tonight, something on the opposite side held it firmly in place. With the flashlight beam guiding her, she made her way around the veranda, stepping carefully along its gleaming wet surface, slippery with green algae.

She followed the music to the bay side, noticing not the familiar base thump of Royce's boom box, but music she liked. That Royce had taste in music from the 70's might give them some common ground, although the song about never leaving an old hotel in California gave her the strangest feeling that she was visiting the place the lyrics described.

Cobwebs brushed against her face. Dry twigs and leaves broke beneath her rubber boots. Just as she approached the rear corner, the music stopped.

A half-beat later her flashlight batteries died leaving her in total blackness.

"Crap," she said, then ran right into a blockade that came crashing down.

If that didn't cause her heart to leap out of her chest, the masculine voice just behind her did.

"I suggest you stop right there."

Chapter 10

She slowly turned around, not quite believing that here he was, again. A friend had once told her to be careful with what she wished for. Hadn't she just been fantasizing about this man?

"A bit late for a neighborly call, isn't it?" Jack said as he snapped on his flashlight.

"You really shouldn't sneak up on people." With her heart continuing to beat wildly, Marianne put a hand up to shield the glare as he ran the flashlight beam over the length of her.

"Keep your hands out to the side," Jack instructed.

Hands skimmed over her waist and hips, patting all her pockets. Hardly the same man who had looked as if he might kiss her earlier today. Hardly the way she'd wanted his hands all over her.

"Hey!" she protested when she saw that he held the Lady Derringer.

He checked the chamber. "Your weapon's not much good without ammo, is it?" He slid the handgun into the pocket of his jacket. "Bet I know why it's empty."

"That was completely unnecessary," Marianne said, and tried to sound like she meant it. Never had she imagined that a weapons search might turn her on.

She could have sworn she'd glimpsed a smile on his face before he disappeared into the darkness of the inn. She hesitated in following.

Moonlight appeared in a break between the fast-moving clouds and cast a beam of silver across the harbor water below. Ship cables clanged making her feel like she wasn't too far from the safety of her own home.

A light came on in the center of the room. Jack stood there, his hand on a small battery-powered lantern that sat in the middle of an old kitchen table.

If she was learning anything about this Jack Sanders, in the short time that she'd known him, it was that he was determined, whatever his purpose on Orcas Island. Men she knew would have left the island by now if a soft bed and a hot shower were not guaranteed. Yet, from the looks of it, Jack was making the best of the situation.

He shoved a gun into the back of his jeans. His was much larger than hers.

"Were you pointing a gun at *me*?" she said, the thought leaving her feeling very unnerved.

"In my line of work, it's not always a good thing when someone comes sneaking along the porch at night." He sat down on one of the three chairs around the table that held his dinner of a wrapped sandwich and bottled water.

"What kind of work is that?" she asked.

He looked at her long and steady over the top of the lantern. "The kind of work I can't talk about."

Her heart skipped a beat. It never occurred to her that he might be criminally dangerous, more so than a pirate. She only thought that she had sexy dangerous to be concerned about.

"Is it illegal work?" she said. "If it is, don't tell me. I don't want to know." She made to retreat.

He held his sandwich poised for a bite. "I work for the United States Government."

She was intrigued. "Are you a spy?"

"No."

Jack had made himself at home. A duffel bag sat on a plastic tarp on the floor as well as a sleeping bag with the price tag still attached. Behind him, the motorcycle was parked half in shadows and looking like a stabled beast, the light from the lantern reflecting off its chrome and single headlight.

She felt bad with her intended purpose here. Even with only the lantern light, she could tell that Jack's jeans were still wet from the deluge earlier. She shivered in the cold wind that came in through the French doors. She could only imagine that the damp and cold were not helping his knee, which she'd noticed he continued to favor.

"You're going to really believe that you're jinxed when it comes to finding a place to stay on this island," she began, "because I have to inform you that you're trespassing. If you keep the music turned down, you can probably get away with staying here tonight. After that, my neighbor is threatening to call the sheriff."

He glanced to what she carried: grocery sack and rolled up blanket. "Are you here to warn my roommate away, as well, or just here to make his stay more comfortable?"

At her look, he added, "The owner of the sleeping bag behind the registration desk has yet to make an appearance."

"His name is Royce and he's just a teenager."

"He's a kid? What's he doing sleeping here?" Jack asked.

Marianne found herself drawn by his concern and took a seat on the chair opposite Jack. As she sat down, one of the legs of the old chair splintered and threatened to give out.

Jack patted the seat of the chair next to him. "You'll have better luck with this one," he said.

She carefully eased into the chair, keeping a grip on the table just in case the frail antique wasn't as solid as Jack assured her.

"I don't know his full story yet," she said, not sure of the feeling she was having sitting close to Jack in the intimacy of the lantern light while everything around them remained dark as the storm brewed outside. It felt like they were having their own private picnic. She worked to keep her mind on her purpose here. "Somehow Royce ended up stuck on this island and has taken shelter here." She set the chicken sandwiches and blanket on the table. "If he even returns tonight, would you see that he gets these? I sort of upset him today, as you probably witnessed."

Jack finished his sandwich and drank from his water bottle. "I don't mind if he stays here."

"That's nice of you, however, it's not your call. You're trespassing," she reminded him.

"It is my call. I happen to own this establishment." A drip began in earnest in a far, darkened corner and the sound of little feet scratched their way up inside a wall. "Not that that's a good thing," Jack said dryly.

Had she heard him correctly? "That's impossible. This property is still in the Bullock name and I don't recall it going on the auction block, yet."

He pushed a large manila envelope across the table. "There's your proof."

Sure enough, his name was on the title. She closed the envelope, trying to recall some of the Bullock family history and, also, realizing that she'd been gone so long that she shouldn't assume the inn still belonged to Gilly's older brother. What she did know, and only from island gossip, was that after the death of their parents, Gilly had inherited the mansion, and her brother the old inn. A brother who hadn't been seen back on the island for decades.

"Did you buy this place from Albert Bullock?" she asked.

The man good at changing subjects did it again. "May I have my photo back?" Jack said.

Instincts told her to stall. At least until she knew a little more about what he wanted with the people in the photo. "I can bring it over in the morning," she said.

"Or I can come get it."

She could almost hear Fiona saying with a wink, "*What are you waiting for, girl? Invite the man over.*"

"Goodnight." She was off the chair and to the French doors before her friend's love advice could be any more of an influence.

"Hold up."

She turned around. Backlit by the lantern, his shadow was thrown up to loom over her from the ceiling. Then the real flesh and blood man stopped directly in front of her, where she'd backed up against the frame of the door.

Nervousness loosened her tongue.

"My real name is Marianne. I live across the harbor in the big yellow house."

"I know," he said. "I got all that from the bartender earlier."

She felt her face warm with pleasure. "You were asking about me?"

"The bartender had a lot to say when I told him I was the new owner of this inn," Jack replied.

"Oh." Now she was embarrassed. What he knew about her was just the locals talking and not due to his wanting to know. Then it occurred to her that he'd continued to call her Gigi even though he'd known her real name.

She supposed that was fair enough, tit-for-tat for her little white lie.

The wind pulled long tendrils of her hair through the door opening to snag on the weathered wood. She attempted to free her hair.

When he reached for her, she held her breath. All he did was put her handgun into one of the pockets of her ski coat and the box of ammunition in the other.

"Thank you," she said, caught off guard that it had ended up being that easy to get the gun and ammo back.

He zipped her pockets closed. "You're welcome."

Despite the inn's negative score on possible romantic get-a-ways, the moment held some intimacy with his closeness. Her head was spinning. Dear God, she was growing more attracted to this man simply by his action in zipping up her coat pockets in a way that felt almost protective, like he was looking out for her. Fiona would think that was sweet. Marianne would have to agree and it was all dangerously interfering with her ability to proceed with caution.

"Do you like wine?" It just blurted out of her.

He was quiet for too long, this man who was so close that she only needed to lean into him, slide her arms in under his jacket and feel the warmth of him. She'd sensed that he'd wanted to kiss her the last time they'd stood like this. Now, in the shadows, she couldn't read his expression. Sometimes a girl had to go with her instincts and hers were telling her that his silence was as good as a 'no'.

"Never mind," she said. "My friend thinks she knows what's best for me and she doesn't. It was a bad idea."

When he reached for his back pocket, she braced herself thinking that he wasn't taking the 'take backs' so well. She'd never been so relieved to see a flashlight come out of its hiding place rather than a big gun.

He clicked on the flashlight. "I'll walk you to your car.

The rain had let up, leaving big puddles in the driveway. As much as her stereotyping of Jack was proving to be way off base, she was still relieved that she'd taken back the date request since it was obvious, at this point, that he wouldn't have accepted. Maybe he had a girlfriend back home. Maybe Marianne just wasn't his type. At least she wouldn't have to worry about being out-experienced in the bedroom with this pirate, because that was never going to happen.

As they walked around to the driver's side, his flashlight moved over her rain-beaded vehicle and reflected off the silver duct tape.

"What happened?"

"Someone broke into my car today."

He opened the driver's door and shone the flashlight around inside. "Did they take anything?" He went to the back and opened the rear door as well and continued his inspection by moving the beam of light around inside.

"My grandpa's briefcase."

She thought it was a bit much when he bent down and looked under her vehicle. He waited while she climbed behind the wheel and told her to start the engine.

He kept his hand on the door. As it turned out, he liked closure. "I should make it clear that I'm not here to start anything over a bottle of wine."

The turn down burned.

"That's more than clear," she said. "In case you missed it back there, I'd already retracted the offer of wine because it would be a very bad idea. You have no idea how bad."

The look on his face reminded her of her first impression of Jack; a bad pirate you wouldn't want to mess with. "Good thing we never got that far," he said.

Exiting gracefully wasn't her call either. Back tires spun in the slippery driveway and mud flew all over the man standing in the glow of her taillights. There was only one thing to do at that point and that was to put distance between herself and trouble.

***

She didn't sleep well. Wind and rain pelted the bedroom window through the night. Guilt that she was warm and dry almost had her returning to the inn to offer Jack and Royce a decent place to sleep.

Almost.

Jack under the same roof would be dangerous.

Besides, she was still angry that his last words had only made her want that date even more.

The storm had died down, leaving Deer Harbor without power.

The bedroom was cold as she dressed that next morning. When she opened her lingerie drawer and debated whether to wear the cotton panties or the all lace, and realized why it would matter, she slammed the drawer shut in frustration.

She opened the curtains and natural light fell across the dresser where the ginger jar now sat. She'd brought the antique upstairs last night to try using nail polish remover on the stubborn cement and to stay busy and keep her mind off Jack. She'd been unsuccessful in each endeavor.

The kitchen was colder than the rest of the house with its bare floors and windows facing the water. It took her only a few minutes to get a fire going in the wood burning stove.

Dealing with a power outage was second nature to her. All the Dunaway kids had learned from their grandpa what he felt were the basic skills everyone should know when the power went out; how to build a fire for warmth and cooking, along with how to make what he called 'camping coffee', and that just about anything could be heated up in a cast iron skillet.

She thought about her grandfather as she measured out coffee grounds for the stainless-steel coffee pot. Despite how cantankerous and difficult he could be, and how it felt, at times, that his love had to be earned, she had to admit that she'd learned a lot from him. Maybe that was how he showed his love, by teaching his grandkids how to survive. Ed Dunaway had been raised in another era, he'd lived through the Great Depression, served his country in peacetime, and then called to duty again during the war. He did double duty as a parent, as well, when at the age of sixty-two, he'd taken his orphaned grandkids into his home. Maybe she was the one being too hard on him and not the other way around. Feeling a little lighter on the relationship between her and her grandpa, she noticed something out of the corner of her eye.

There was a pair of muddy footprints next to the pantry door.

Her blood froze.

That print wasn't there last night as she sat at the kitchen island collecting arsenal and drinking wine. The fact that someone could have been in the house while she slept sent a jolt of fear racing through her veins. What she did know, was that the muddy print wasn't hers. She'd left her muddy boots on the veranda upon her return to the house last night.

A knock on the back door sent the spoonful of coffee grounds spilling across the counter. The man she'd tossed and turned over hadn't slept well either, not by the looks of him through the window in the door. Two happenings in a matter of minutes making her heart take dips and dives; this morning was getting off to a great start. Jack's appearance at least got her mind off mysterious footprints.

She quickly looked down to make sure she had put on a pair of jeans. Most mornings she walked around in her alma-mater T-shirt, panties, and something warm on her bare feet. Due to the chilly conditions today, she had more on her bottom before noon. She wore skinny jeans tucked into sheepskin suede boots and a pink, cable-knit sweater.

There wasn't much she could do about the fact that she was makeup-less and her hair was pulled up into a sloppy ponytail.

Jack had cold-reddened cheeks and nose, and purple shadows under his eyes. He'd added another layer under the motorcycle jacket. The collar of a denim jacket was pulled up to his ears. Across the front of his jacket was a splattering of drying mud.

"Did I do that?" she said upon opening the back door.

During his short time on the island thus far, she'd done nothing but bump into this man, land on him, and now make his miserably, cold night even worse. From the look on his face, he was thinking the same thing.

He reached his arm out to the side and pulled Royce into view. The green-eyed teenager looked worse than Jack. The ends of his soft brown hair curled up like duck tails and he had a cut above one eye. Dried blood was mixed in with white plaster.

"A section of the ceiling fell in last night. Do you have a first aid kit?" Jack asked.

"It's nothing," Royce mumbled, looking uncomfortable from the attention and unsure of his welcome.

"Come in." She held the door open. "I don't have power but I can make a hot breakfast."

Both man and teenager went immediately to warm their hands and backsides in front of the wood burning stove. They each carried the smell of the damp inn on their rumpled clothing. Jack wore another day's growth along his jawline. Royce's freckled baby face, with just a start of peach fuzz along his upper lip, had the crease of whatever he'd laid his cheek against through the night.

She brought the first aid kit from the powder room along with a wetted wash rag. Jack set to cleaning up Royce's cut while she returned to the coffee makings. Before either might notice that she was braless beneath her sweater, she slipped on her pink, down vest from the coat hooks.

To help the young teen feel more at ease in her kitchen, she put the bandaged Royce in charge of monitoring the coffee pot as it perked on the wood burning stove.

"Ever make camping coffee before?" she asked.

"No, ma'am."

She felt Jack's eyes on her as she taught Royce what her grandpa had taught her. "When the water starts to boil, you'll see water bubble up in the glass cap. Watch the color. Soon as it's dark brown, it's ready. There are hot mitts behind you." She indicated the brick wall adjacent to the wood burning stove.

When their eyes met briefly behind Royce's back, it was evident that the tension that resulted from their standoff last night had yet to diffuse. The last thing she wanted to hear was a more detailed explanation of why he'd refused the offer of sharing a bottle of wine with her. And maybe he didn't want to give one because he now appeared more interested in the dated kitchen.

She imagined he was having the same reaction as she when she'd stepped inside the kitchen as the new owner. The cabinetry was dark and grimy looking. The gold-colored appliances had rust stains circling just about every screw that held them together. And it was hit and miss which light switch in the kitchen still worked.

"How's the patching up going?" he asked.

"I've done what's absolutely necessary. The rest I don't care about."

"Why?"

If he was trying to break the frosty air between them, it was going to take more than neighborly chit-chat about her outdated home.

"Because I don't plan to be here this time next year." She pulled a carton of eggs and a package of bacon from the refrigerator.

Jack offered to cook their breakfast. He went as far as to take the food right from her hands and then opened an obvious cupboard near the stove and pull out two cast-iron frying pans.

Both man and teenager stood side-by-side at the wood burning stove, as if they did this on a regular basis: Royce carefully monitoring the glass top on the coffee pot and Jack turning bacon in one cast iron skillet and heating up another skillet for the eggs.

She'd feed them and find an excuse to run errands and they'd be on their way before Fiona's advice started to work on her again.

While they both had their backs to her, she quickly wiped up the muddy print with paper towels, its presence only an unsettling reminder that she'd need to deal with this intruder, sooner, or later.

Her eyes found their way back to Jack's broad shoulders and easy, confident stance. She had a fleeting thought that, if he was under the same roof, only a fool might take the risk of breaking in.

"You just bought this place." Jack turned, catching her staring at him. "Why so determined to be gone after only a few short weeks?"

She put her back to him and began to set the breakfast table. "How do you know how long I've owned Perrigo?"

"Word around town." Jack cracked open an egg on the rim of the skillet.

"I knew, too," piped-in Royce, who had said very little since stepping through the door.

She pulled silverware out of the drawer. "I forgot how information moves around this island. Who needs the Internet?"

Royce looked even more uncomfortable than before.

"How did you find out?" she asked him. "You didn't show up until a week ago."

"Just heard it from someone, that's all."

Jack nudged him back to paying attention to the perking coffee. "Not too black," he said.

Bacon sizzled in the larger skillet. With his back to her, his jacket did too good of a job covering any sign that he might have his large gun tucked down the back of his jeans. Her eyes traveled over to where he'd set his saddle bags on the floor by the back door, next to Royce's backpack.

"What do you know about your neighbor?" Jack said.

Until she knew why Jack had that photo in the first place, she wouldn't give anyone up to a man she'd only known for less than forty-eight hours. She would defend the home front, first, and foremost.

"Which neighbor?" she asked innocently.

A shotgun blast ended their quiet morning.

Chapter 11

A black cloud of crows circled overhead. Their noise was deafening, so much that she had difficulty hearing what Jack was saying. His hand gesture made it clear that she and Royce were to stay behind the brick pillars that supported the wrought iron gate.

As Jack went forward to investigate, keeping his handgun discreetly behind him, Royce picked up a hefty branch from the wind debris.

"He may need my help," he said, and followed Jack.

A grouping of lilac trees and tall rhododendrons just outside her gate blocked the view of her neighbor's front porch. She could hear Jack's deep voice talking calmly until a door slammed. Her two breakfast guests came into view, walking back around the bushes.

"What happened?" Marianne said.

"She saw someone at your gate and fired off a shot," Jack said. "She gave us a brief description: about your height, skinny, had a hood over their head, and according to your neighbor wore sissy, white, tennis shoes."

"Yeah," Royce added, "and the guy took off through the orchard."

Jack was staring at a point above her head.

"That wasn't there earlier," he said.

Marianne turned slowly around, knowing what she'd see. Why else this morning's trespasser?

What she wasn't expecting, was how this note had been delivered.

The large wingspan of a dead crow stood out like a slash of black across the iron bars. Silky, black feathers ruffled in the wind and the crow's head hung at an unnatural angle from where it was tied to the gate.

"Oh, no!" Marianne exclaimed.

The note was tied to the poor crow's feet.

Together Royce and Jack gently removed the crow from the gate.

"Everyone inside." Jack ushered them quickly back around to the kitchen door.

The flock of crows flew to the top of the willow tree, their cries fainter as they grew farther away.

"They're mourning their friend." Royce looked upset. He cradled the dead crow in both hands. "I think we should bury him and at least give him a name."

"We'll give him a name," Jack said. "We just can't bury him, yet. The bird is evidence."

Once inside, Marianne found an old towel and handed it to Royce who wrapped the dead bird in a protective manner and then placed the bundle on the dryer in the laundry room off the kitchen.

Jack looked up from reading the latest note. "Where is the other note?" he said.

"How did you know about the other note?" The island's communication system came swiftly to mind. "Never mind," she added. Still, she hesitated in letting someone she hardly knew get close to her personal problems. "Let me see that," she said of the note he still held.

"It's disturbing," he said.

"Look," she said, "I'm not the prissy, mall girl that you think I am. Besides, it can't be any worse than the other one."

He handed over the note.

Time to give up what isn't yours. If you don't want harm to come to those you love, you'll do exactly as I instruct. I'll leave further instructions tomorrow.

Fear sent her heart into a dive.

"I need to make a phone call," she said.

She left Jack and Royce in the kitchen, hoping that neither saw how shaky she was as she pushed through the swinging door. She waited until she'd reached the library before making her phone call. The receptionist at the assisted living center answered on the first ring.

Marianne asked to speak to the manager and was promptly transferred.

"This is Lynn," answered a warm voice.

Marianne identified herself. "How's my grandpa? Has anyone been in to see him that he doesn't know?"

"Yes. In fact, I was just about to contact you. He had a visitor a few minutes ago. An attendant heard raised voices in your grandfather's room. It appeared that this woman was threatening him. We've contacted the sheriff."

"Did anyone recognize this woman?"

"No one, so far. I'm still asking around. She was quite rude when she was asked to leave."

"Please don't let anyone into his room unless it's your staff or a member of my family."

Jack was studying the notes and drinking coffee when she returned to the kitchen. Royce, although still looking sad about the crow, did his best to dig into the plate of burnt bacon and overcooked eggs that Jack had set before him.

She pulled on her ski jacket, finding it difficult to manage the zipper with her shaking hands.

"Where are you going?" Jack leaned against the kitchen counter.

"I need to check on my sister. Then I'm going to call my brother. He's FBI. He'll know what to do. You're both welcome to stay here and keep warm."

"You don't need the FBI." Royce lifted his head from his meal. "Jack can help. He's Army Special Ops."

She would expect that most would want to avoid getting involved with anyone who had dead birds and threatening notes at her gate. Jack just looked steadily at her as if he waited for her to make the decision.

"I can't drag you into this," she said. "You're only here for a few days and I don't want to make your visit to Orcas any more miserable than I've made it already."

"I've managed to stop a few bad people in my life. What's one more?"

"No." She shook her head, adamant. "It's too much to ask. Why would you want to help, anyway? You hardly know me."

"True." He took his coffee mug to the sink and rinsed it out. When he turned around, he wore a look like he'd been hatching a plan. "How about I help you in exchange for a couple of rooms for me and Royce for a few days?"

Royce stopped with a forkful of eggs halfway to his mouth as he waited to see what she might say. She looked away from the hopeful expectation in his eyes only to see the steady look in Jack's eyes.

They needed her, that was for certain, even if it was only for decent accommodations and hot meals. And two more people under her roof might make the shadows feel smaller. She'd certainly feel safer with Jack around. Which could bring up a problem.

How much could he help without getting too close? She still didn't know why he had a photo with her grandpa in it. What she did know was that he'd rescued her twice already; minor incidences, yet, he hadn't hesitated. Right now, he was the only sure thing she might be able to trust. And from the looks of the two of them, hot showers and warm beds with clean sheets tonight would be heaven sent.

The trick would be keeping this all business.

"Okay," she said.

"This is going to be so dope!" Royce punched the air.

***

"Easy on the corners," Jack said from the passenger seat, although he would be driving equally fast if he were in her shoes.

Marianne slowed, only long enough to get safely through the corner. Then the speedometer shot back up.

"One thing to consider," Jack began, "is that the notes are only intended to shake you up so that you're more willing to do as they ask. Did you try calling your sister first, to see if she was okay?"

"She doesn't answer my calls and her voicemail box is full."

Jack already knew the answer to the question he was about to ask, but if she were to learn how much he knew about her family, already, it would mean having to explain why. It was easier, for now, to let her tell him. "Do you have any other family on the island?"

She sent him a quick look, like she had something else to say, before she returned to focusing on her driving.

"Got your seatbelt on back there?" he said to Royce in the back seat.

They came around a corner to see a half-dozen chickens up ahead, slowly pecking their way across the road.

The woman he'd entrusted his life to decreased her speed while blindly feeling around in the console until she held up a silver tube of lipstick. Using one knee to steer, she flipped down the visor mirror with one hand while holding the lipstick in the other. She popped the cap off with her thumb.

"Come on, work for me, work for me," she said as she ran the pink lipstick across her bottom lip, never taking her eyes from the road.

Suddenly a barking dog raced into the road sending the chickens scurrying with their short wings flapping until the road was clear. She capped the lipstick and let fly with the silver tube. Both of her hands were once again on the steering wheel as her foot slammed the accelerator to the floor.

Royce was thrown back against his seat and the lipstick ended up in Jack's lap.

Other than he was impressed with her effortless maneuvers in keeping the car under control while putting on lipstick, he said nothing as the white-knuckled driver accelerated out of another curve.

The next time his cell phone had a signal, he began to dial 9-1-1.

"Are you calling the sheriff?" Marianne asked.

His thumb hovered over the call button. "I think it's a good idea."

"If you call the sheriff," Royce said, his voice taking on an angry tone, "he's going to think this was me. I'm in the wrong place at the wrong time, again, and I'll get blamed, again."

"I'll vouch for you," Jack said over his shoulder.

Royce sat forward. "You will?"

"In case you've forgotten, you were learning to make camping coffee about the time the note was left." Jack checked his cell phone; still no signal. "Wrong place, wrong time?" he said to Royce.

"It's nothing," their rear passenger mumbled.

"I think we should keep the sheriff out of this, for now," Marianne said.

"You were ready to call the FBI a moment ago," Jack said.

Her hair moved back and forth across her shoulders as she shook her head. "Not officially, I wasn't. I just wanted to see how my brother could help. I have two problems here. One is these notes and the other is that someone's been in my home. I don't know how to stop one without drawing attention to the other. Which brings me back to Gilly. I think she's been in my house taking stuff. I'm not too upset if she is, because I told her to take what she wanted. I just didn't expect her to do so when I wasn't there." She sent him a quick look. "At least I think it's her breaking in. All I have to go on is that things have gone missing and there have been muddy footprints."

Jack waited while she passed the slower vehicle ahead. "When did this start happening?"

"Almost as soon as I moved in," she said.

He held onto the door handle as they swept through another curve. "When did the first note arrive?"

"The first week. Do you think the notes and the missing items are connected?"

"Very coincidental, and you could be right that the missing items may only be your neighbor doing some midnight requisitioning." Jack recalled what Sal had told him about Gilly losing the mansion.

Worry creased her brow. "I just don't understand the motive behind the notes. What do I have that this person wants?"

It was her bewildered and frustrated tone that had Jack doubting Sal's assumption of why this Dunaway might have purchased Perrigo Mansion. There was a blip of a signal on his phone and then it was gone, again, as they entered another dead zone.

"That's her house up ahead." She slowed their approach.

Between the houses on his right, he could see a line of sun-bleached driftwood and gray, choppy water just beyond.

"Pull over here," Jack instructed.

She brought the vehicle to a braking halt on the shoulder, tires locking up in the gravel.

"Without drawing too much attention," he added a bit late.

Two driveways away, a blue Buick sat parked in the driveway alongside a post-war home with white paint and blue trim. It wasn't the only vehicle in the driveway.

"I've seen that Suburban before," he said.

"That's Gerald. The creep from the tavern. He was also on the ferry with us Friday night."

"Gerald Cain lives with your sister?" Royce said in a tone of disgust and alarm.

"Unfortunately."

"Let's keep going," Jack said. "Pull up in front of the house."

"Wait!" The rear door opened and Royce jumped out. "I've got to get to work."

As they pulled forward, Jack watched as Royce jogged back the way they had come, his backpack bouncing between his thin shoulders.

The residential street was quiet. They eased to a gentle stop in front of the mail box. However, their quiet approach was for naught. Someone watched from between the opening in the window coverings. Then the face was gone.

"That's him." She put her hand to the door.

Jack stopped her. "We don't go in without a plan."

A lot of good his advice did. She was out of the vehicle.

He ignored the sharp twinge of pain in his knee and checked Marianne's determined stride in the driveway. He pulled her out of sight of the front window, using the side of the house as cover.

"Stay behind me," he said.

There was no argument from her. Instead, she grabbed ahold of the back of his jacket.

"Go to the back door," she said. "I'm guessing Gerald moved furniture around to make room for his big television and the piano now blocks the front door."

Missy's boyfriend waited in a nonchalant fashion on the back porch as he smoked a cigarette. The wind off the shore blew the smoke straight past his ear. He wore a white, cable-knit sweater over a pair of jeans. Both looked brand new. His feet were sockless in a pair of navy topsiders. Gold flashed at his neck and on his pinky finger.

Gerald's relaxed posture belied the cold look in his eyes as they approached the back step.

"You two hitched up pretty quick for just being strangers yesterday."

"Can you let Missy know I'm here?" Marianne said. "I need to speak with her."

"You're here to see your sister and not me? My feelings are hurt." Gerald flicked his cigarette into the rain-soaked lawn. "She isn't here."

"Her car's in the driveway."

"Like I said, she's not here."

"When will she be back?" Jack said.

Gerald delayed replying as he lit another cigarette, cupping the white stick of nicotine in his hands to protect it from the wind. "I can't be certain. It's my best guess that she caught the morning ferry to Anacortes. She and a girlfriend were talking about going shopping in Burlington and staying over."

"Which girlfriend?" Marianne asked.

"The one from the tavern."

"I don't believe him," she whispered in Jack's ear.

"Can we have a look inside?" Jack asked.

The cigarette landed at Jack's feet. "You think I'm lying?"

"You said you can't be certain where she is. Maybe she's still in bed," Jack said.

"I know she's not because I was just in that warm, sheet-rumpled bed." Gerald's smile sent chills down Marianne's spine.

"What time are you expecting her tomorrow?" Jack asked.

"Jesus, you're annoying me. I don't know!"

"As soon as she walks in the door, will you tell her to call her sister?" Jack turned Marianne back toward the street.

"Not so fast," Gerald said. "You want to tell me what this little sticky note is all about?"

He held the note she'd left on the canned food.

"It's a personal matter," she said.

"Missy and I share everything. I'd be happy to pass the message along to her."

"It's none of your business," Marianne said.

An angry, red stain left his neck blotchy. "If you're going to be like that, then maybe I won't remember to give her any of your messages." He crumbled up the note and tossed it into the yard. "Now get off my property."

Chapter 12

"Why do I have this feeling that Gerald was expecting us?" Marianne said.

They'd travelled a few miles in silence, heading back toward Eastsound. She was thankful that Jack had been with her in confronting Gerald. Missy's boyfriend's behavior was creepier than usual today. "I have to admit that I almost want him to be behind these notes just to have a reason for Missy to throw him out."

"He's bad news, that's for certain," Jack said from the passenger seat where he carefully eased his leg out in front of him in the confined space.

"Do you think Missy is safe?" she asked.

"Is going shopping with a friend something she might do?"

"I don't know," Marianne said. She kept one eye on the road while she tried to send her brother a text message.

Jack plucked the cellphone from her hand. "I've had enough close calls with you behind the wheel."

She was too startled to be angry. "I was trying to send my brother a message."

"Tell me what you want to say," he said.

"I want him to call me. It's urgent."

"Done," Jack said, deftly texting with his thumbs.

The cellphone went into the drink holder in the console. More than once he'd massaged his knee since they'd left Perrigo. With the announcement from Royce that Jack was Special Ops, she'd started to speculate that his injury had occurred while on active duty.

"How did you come to own the Heron Inn?" she asked, just to make conversation as they followed behind a slow truck pulling a boat and trailer.

Jack watched the passing scenery. "I inherited the property from my grandfather."

It took her a few seconds for that meaning to sink in. She looked at him so quickly that the vehicle swerved. "The Bullocks owned that property."

"Yeah," he said dryly. "I've been told."

The Bullock name was another family her grandpa had warned her to stay away from. "You're a Bullock," she stated, battling with the shock. "Is that why you have a photo of the five when they were friends? And why were you asking Sal questions about the family if you're one of them?"

"Correction," Jack said. "You have the photo that I'd like back very much, as it's one of the rare photos my mom has of my grandfather. I'd like to add that it's unconfirmed that I'm related to the Bullocks."

He turned in his seat to face her. "How do you know I was asking questions about the Bullocks?"

She was over her surprise in this new news and could only think of protecting her grandpa. "Don't try to sidetrack this discussion. Are you a Bullock or not?"

"Like I said," Jack sat forward, "it's unconfirmed."

"You just said that you inherited the property."

"I'm hoping that there was a card game in there somewhere and that my grandfather, Albert Smith, won it from this Albert Bullock." There was more than a little sarcasm in his tone.

That didn't change the obvious.

She hit the brakes. "They had the same first names?"

"Yes," Jack said. "That's not the only strange thing I've discovered."

"What else?" she said.

"Let's find a place to have coffee. I'd prefer to tell you when you're not operating a moving vehicle."

***

Tom Harris looked up as they approached the bar together and took seats directly in front of him. He stared at them for a moment before grabbing two white mugs.

He set the pair of mugs down side by side and said, "Are you two together?"

Jack and Marianne just looked at each other, not answering.

Tom moved the mugs farther apart. "You're not together?"

Jack draped his jacket over the empty stool next to him then reached for the mugs and moved them closer together, just not touching. "We'll take two coffees and two menus."

"Good enough," Tom said. He filled the mugs with coffee and set menus before them. "I'll be back in a sec' to take your order."

"Tom," Marianne reached out to stop the bar owner from leaving. "Where's Julia?"

"She had to take a few unexpected days off to go help a friend."

"She didn't go shopping with Missy?"

"Nope," Tom said. "How is your sister? We haven't seen much of her since she quite."

"Missy doesn't work her any longer?"

Tom shook his head. "She started missing a lot of work and then one day called to say she had to quit. I've got an order to check on. Be right back." He hurried into the kitchen.

Marianne put her hands around the warmth of the coffee mug. "I've never known my sister to not have a job. She told me once that she loves to work because she gets to be around people. She's a people person, at least she was. You wouldn't know it by how she treats me these days." She checked again for a message from Missy.

Jack sat so close that his knee brushed against hers.

"Maybe she hasn't checked her messages yet," he said.

"Or she's ignoring me."

"Does she do that a lot?"

143

"Seems to be the current trend and I made it worse yesterday."

"Have anything to do with the boyfriend hitting on you?"

"She doesn't know about that. He hits on every woman, just to set that straight." She looked around to make sure they didn't have any eavesdroppers. "How dare he tell us to get off *his* property. That is my grandpa's property. I want him out of there."

"He's playing king on a throne that he knows isn't rightly his. It's just a matter of time before he's found out and he knows it." Jack opened the menu. "What are you having?"

"I'm not hungry."

Tom came back to take their orders.

"We'll have two of the salmon and scrambled eggs with the island hash browns," Jack said.

Marianne tried to change the order only to be told by Jack that she needed to eat something.

"I expected to see Royce in here, unless he's still hoofing it into town," Jack said. "Did you notice how fast he took off as soon as he heard the name Gerald Cain?"

"Royce used to work over at the Swan Pawn Shop," Marianne said. "Gerald's uncle told me that he fired Royce last week."

Jack slowly set down his coffee mug. "Whose Gerald's uncle?"

"Harold Swan, owner of the pawn shop."

In the mirror over the bar, their reflection showed them sitting as close as the couple at the far end of the bar who were holding hands while sipping their coffee.

"You said there was something else you discovered," Marianne said. "What was it?"

Jack set down his coffee mug. "It has to do with Albert Bullock and several of his friends."

The tavern door opened behind them.

"Where've you been, son?" the bartender said. "Get stuck in the mud somewhere?"

Royce was red-faced from the cold and there was mud on the knees of his jeans and on the toes of his hiking boots.

"Sorry I'm late," he said, out of breath. He caught sight of Jack and Marianne and smiled sheepishly. "Guess I should have stuck with you guys."

"I expect you had your reasons for getting to town on your own." Jack swung around on the bar stool to talk to the teen, but Royce had already pushed through the swinging doors to the kitchen "There he goes, disappearing again."

Tom refilled their coffee mugs and moved off to attend to other customers.

"My grandfather passed away last month," Jack said.

"I'm sorry." Then the realization hit her. "I wonder if Gilly knows. I mean, if your grandfather was indeed Albert Bullock."

Jack rubbed his hand along the back of his neck. "I wouldn't want to upset her, unnecessarily. What I need is confirmation."

"Of course. But what if he was? That doesn't really change anything, other than you have an aunt you didn't know about."

He gave her a half smile. "If he was my grandfather, then our grandfathers used to be friends."

"I know."

"Any idea why that friendship ended?"

There was something about how he'd asked that question that led her to suspect he knew something.

"I don't know," she said.

His jacket on the stool beside him drew his attention. Jack pulled his cellphone from the inner pocket. He unlocked the phone with a password and read a text message. Then he stood. "Excuse me. I need to make a phone call."

He stepped outside.

Marianne stared at her reflection in the mirror across the bar. "*Don't enjoy his company too much*," she said softly to herself. "*He's not going to be around for long.*" If only she could think of reasons not to like Jack, this might be easier.

Royce was on the family side of the tavern dining area clearing tables. She walked over to the railing that separated the two sections and signaled to Royce. He came over holding the tub of dirty dishes.

"Did you and Jack talk much last night?" she said.

"Some," he said warily, glancing over her shoulder to the empty bar stools where they had sat. "Where'd Jack go?"

"He's outside making a phone call."

"Why don't you ask him what we talked about?"

"I'm asking you." She added a smile.

Royce looked torn between taking sides. "He asked me where I was from and why I wasn't in school."

"Is that all?"

"No." Royce shifted the tub to his other hip. "I tried to get him to tell me how he got shot. All he said was that it happened in Afghanistan and he couldn't talk about it." He looked proud to know this much about Jack. "He said he'll be going back soon."

Hearing it said left her with a hollow feeling inside. A part of her was relieved that Jack hadn't readily accepted her invitation to share a bottle of wine. That didn't mean that she wouldn't always wonder what it would've been like to get to know him better. Even for just one night.

She put the brakes on that bit of wondering and got back to finding ways not to like Jack Sanders.

"What else did you talk about? Did he say anything about why he's here?" she said.

Royce shrugged as if it were unimportant. "We mostly talked sports, guy stuff. He's a cool Dude. I've got to get back to work."

"Wait." She put a hand out to stop him.

Her instincts told her that Jack was a good man. And Fiona would accuse her of sabotaging a good feeling, a move that was completely out of character for Marianne. Desperate times, however, sometimes required the down and the dirty. She looked toward the door to make sure Jack wasn't on his way back inside.

She wasn't sure what she wanted Royce to unintentionally reveal that would lower Jack to the levels of the Gerald Cains of this world, making it much easier to stop liking Jack Sanders.

"If you had plans to check out a piece of property," she said to Royce, "wouldn't you call ahead and make reservations? Jack didn't. Makes me wonder if he just didn't want anyone to know he was ever here."

Royce suddenly became very defensive. "Maybe his plans just didn't work out! Like mine!"

"What plan was that?" Jack said as he walked up to them, making them both jump.

She hoped that she didn't look as guilty as Royce. She turned a smile on Jack. "Business call?"

"Something like that." His attention was on Royce. "Why don't you like Gerald Cain?"

"What's with the twenty questions?" Royce glowered like a rebellious teen being grilled by his parents.

"What were you asking him?" Jack turned to Marianne.

"Just little things; where he's from, things like that."

Blue eyes scrutinized her for a few lengthy minutes. "Just little things?" Jack said.

Watching the teenager's eyes dart back and forth between her and Jack was all the body language anyone needed to see. Royce had something to say. It was just hard to know what to expect from him next.

"She wants to know why you're *really* on the island."

"Royce." Tom Harris pointed to a table that needed clearing.

"We'll take the check," Marianne said to Tom as she walked swiftly back to their seats.

Jack followed at a measured pace. "I'll tell you anything you want to know. You just have to ask."

She slipped on her ski jacket before turning around to face him. Jack looked like a steady rock.

Her nosing around hadn't even riled him to reveal a bad side. Steady rocks were good things. What she needed was to see bad things from him.

She pushed harder. "If you didn't know you were related to the Bullocks until you'd arrived here, how is it you had a photo of Albert and Gilly and their friends?"

Other than his eyes narrowed a bit at her accusing tone, his reply came without hesitation, "My grandfather's estate attorney gave it to me along with the information on the property. I expect it was to help me identify the property."

"Or to show you who your grandfather really was, a man who up and left this island one night, and obviously had a reason to change his name. Why do you think that was, Jack? Did he get himself into trouble?"

From his momentary quietness, she knew she had struck a nerve.

"I believe the trouble happened before he left. I take it that you don't know about the FBI coming to the island looking for Albert and his friends." He paused. "Including your grandfather."

Marianne was too stunned to speak at first. "What did the FBI want?"

"You really don't know?"

She felt her face redden, not from guilt, but because he'd said it like she was the one hiding something.

"No. I don't know," she replied. "I have a feeling that you're about to enlighten me."

Jack moved her out of earshot of the other customers. "I'm sorry. I should not have broken it to you that way. However, your town historian has done enough research to conclude that Albert Bullock and company may have all been involved in a crime, or at least were considered suspects, at one time."

She couldn't believe what she was hearing. Someone was seriously mistaken.

"Ed Dunaway is one of the most honest men I've ever known! If anyone was in trouble, it had to be your grandfather, if I went by how crazy his sister is." She slung her handbag over her shoulder. "Now I know what you're after. You're trying to clear your grandfather's name and place the blame on mine." Finally, she had a reason to not like Jack.

"You think so, do you?" He walked back to pay for their breakfast, signing the charge slip with a slash of the pen against paper.

She took a step back as he rejoined her on the square of floor space in the bar that was beginning to feel like their fighting ring. It was the same spot where she'd corrected him on hair color the day before.

"From what I'm discovering," Jack said as he slipped his arms into his jacket, "it's not just my grandfather who can keep a good secret. Maybe you should ask yours why he was a suspect in a crime." Although his words were curt and to the point, there was no anger in his direct gaze. Or if it had been there, it was no longer. "Look, I don't want to blow the chance of Royce having a dry place to sleep tonight. Can we table this until we've both calmed down? Temporary truce?"

His decency, in looking out for another and being more the adult, when she just wanted to stomp her foot, wasn't helping at all.

"Truce," she said, "for however long it will last. And just so you know, your new friend, Sal, doesn't have his facts straight, I assure you."

"Maybe we can discuss that further tonight." His eyes held hers. "Just an amicable conversation and we'll see where it leads."

Just like that, he was ready to put their differences aside? The forgive and forget personality along with his charm? That wasn't helping Marianne with her dilemma. What had she just done? She'd had an opportunity to keep him from sleeping under her roof and instead they were going to pick up this conversation later tonight at her place.

Good neighbor gesture, or not, she'd invited temptation to sleep in her home.

Her pulse strummed. "I don't know where you think a conversation will take this. You do know that we can't seem to get along for even five minutes."

"We'd better work on that."

She grew warm beneath her sweater, and her hair was falling out of its ponytail and across her eyes, making her feel frumpy and uncomfortable. Yet, he continued to look at her with interest. Time to set down some rules.

"If we talk at all," she said "we keep it to our grandfathers and anything you can do to help me with the notes, which I see as your service in exchange for room and board. Agreed?"

Daylight shot across the tavern floor as the door opened behind them.

"Jack Sanders?" purred the slender and attractive blonde woman who sauntered over to Jack, looking like he was her next meal. "So glad you called. I had a feeling this was my lucky day."

Chapter 13

Just like that, her bodyguard slash bad-guy hunter had something of a higher priority to attend to. Despite the obvious, that she might not have to worry about an intimate encounter with Jack due to the sexy distraction that had just pulled him from the tavern, she felt dumped for the second time by this man.

Jack had asked her to wait and have another cup of coffee while he walked over to the realtor's office.

"This is going to take longer than a cup of coffee, hon'," the realtor said as Jack held the tavern door open for her to proceed him out to the sidewalk. Jack had smiled in return.

Did he really think that she was going to patiently wait while he engaged with the pretty realtor who, by her island reputation, Marianne knew would be offering Jack more than just her professional expertise?

The pirate biker had a full social calendar already: a blonde realtor looking determined to monopolize his time today, and tentative plans for a so-called discussion about their grandfathers later tonight.

Not if she could help it.

And especially since he hadn't agreed to agree to her boundary lines. Once, again, he'd just looked at her without telling her what she wanted to hear.

Tom stopped her on the way out the door. "Jack asked me to keep an eye on you."

"Tell Jack I can take care of myself."

She stepped out into a gust of strong wind that sliced right through her clothing and whipped her hair across her eyes. They'd left Perrigo in such a hurry this morning that she only had the down vest over the cable knit sweater and it wasn't enough for this rainy, damp day. But by the time she'd made it back to her car, she was no longer feeling the cold as her temper was simmering.

***

The dispatcher at the sheriff's office looked up sharply when Marianne screeched into the parking space in front of the large glass window.

It wasn't until she walked into the office smelling of burnt coffee and popcorn that she remembered that Jack had the notes in his jacket pocket.

"What can I help you with?" The tall man wearing a brown uniform with a sheriff's badge turned from filling up his coffee mug.

Behind him sat a table pushed up against a wall of maps. A coffee maker, box of donuts, and a popcorn popper occupied the table stained with brown coffee rings.

The sheriff was a man in his mid-forties with brown hair, smile lines around his eyes, and an angular, freckled face to go along with his lean, muscular frame. A wad of chewing gum was stuck to the side of his Starbuck's mug with a Seattle skyline design.

The dispatcher, a former classmate of Marianne's, was on the phone. She sent her a brief nod of recognition before resuming with her call, although her eyes followed Marianne as she walked up to the sheriff.

Marianne introduced herself.

"Sheriff Bradshaw," he said. Her hand was grasped in a crushing handshake. "I hear you had a little trouble yesterday. Wish I had some good news on the whereabouts of what was taken. We'll keep our eyes and ears open."

She flexed her fingers to make sure they were still working. "Thank you. That's not why I'm here."

He sipped at his coffee. "You recently purchased Perrigo Mansion," he stated.

"That's correct."

The dispatcher was all-ears. That was all she was going to get as the sheriff first offered coffee to Marianne, who declined, then showed her into his office.

"You have a sister on the island, don't you?" he said as soon as he'd closed the door.

"Missy. My grandfather is Ed Dunaway."

"Ah, yes, Ed. How's he adjusting to the assisted living center? Hasn't he been there a couple of years now?"

"Yes. Some days he likes it and some days he just wants to go back home."

Sheriff Bradshaw nodded his understanding as he sat in the oak, swivel chair behind his large desk. At his back, a window, with horizontal blinds, opened to a view of the town park and rudimentary amphitheater.

"When I'd heard that you had moved back to the island, I wondered how long before I saw you in here. Are you here about Missy?"

"That's one of my reasons. How did you know?"

He sat back in his chair and made a temple of his fingers. The chair creaked as he rocked back and forth.

Finally, he sat forward. "I don't have any hard evidence, yet. Only concerned friends of your sisters having sat in that very chair telling me that they suspect your sister is being abused by her boyfriend."

Marianne was stunned and speechless, at first. That didn't last long. She'd jumped to her feet so fast that her handbag fell off her lap. "That son-of-a-bitch! I'll kill him!"

"Hold on there, Ms. Dunaway. I can understand your anger, but let's dial that vigilante button back down to zero."

"How did I not know this?" she exclaimed as she took her seat again. "Why didn't she come to me?" Even as she asked this, she knew why. Missy had lost faith in her as a trusted confidant. She had difficulty swallowing past the lump in her throat. "Why hasn't she thrown him out?"

"Leaving an abusive relationship is never easy," the sheriff said. "Getting the abuser to leave is even harder. And I need to remind you that there is no proof, yet, and won't be until your sister files charges." He paused.

"What?" Marianne was shaking all over, fearing more bad news was about to come from the sheriff. When she spoke, her voice didn't sound like her own. "What else do you know?"

"Your sister did approach me on the street last month. She looked like she wanted to say something, but she didn't and then suddenly rushed away."

"I saw her yesterday," Marianne said. "She looked like she was hurt. She said she'd fallen."

Sheriff Bradshaw pushed his coffee mug to the side, plucking off the wad of gum to put back in his mouth. Then he placed his forearms on the desk. "The reports I've received are all about the same, which leaves me to believe that if Gerald is indeed physically abusing her, he does it in areas that can be covered up with clothing. It's my hope that she walks through that door one day soon and files a report. Until that happens, I can't do anything, other than to painfully observe from a distance, just like everyone else on this island who cares about your sister."

Marianne's eyes burned with tears. "I think he did something to her, recently." She sat on the edge of her seat. She had her hands on her knees to keep them from shaking.

The sheriff pushed a box of tissue across to her. "What makes you think that?"

"Someone has been leaving threatening notes on my gate. The one this morning threatened to do harm to someone I love. That's why I drove over to check on Missy. Gerald said that she'd gone shopping on the mainland with Julia Harris. That's a lie. If she's shopping with a friend, it isn't Julia because they don't know each other that well. At least I think they don't. I've been sort of absent for a few years. Okay, more than a few years. Even if they do know each other, Tom said that his daughter is out of town helping a friend. Then Jack said that maybe the notes have something to do with what he'd learned from Sal. I still think that something has happened to Missy. And I don't want Royce to get into trouble or Gilly."

"Okay, slow down." The sheriff donned a pair of reading glasses and began jotting down notes. Then he set down his pen. Intelligent and patient green eyes looked at her over the top of his eyeglasses. "Let's take this one bit of information at a time, here. Who is Jack?"

***

Sheriff Bradshaw had one deputy to spare and asked him to follow Gerald around and keep him posted on his activities. He'd then phoned the ticket booth at the ferry dock in Orcas Village to speak with the employee there who knew Missy, requesting she keep an eye out for her return.

While in his office, Marianne received a text message from Fiona, who wanted her to check in, and, also saw that she'd missed a call from her brother.

But as the sheriff had said, out of the side of his mouth, "Just give me a reason to get Gerald Cain out of my Jurisdiction," he was now moving like a man on a mission. He wanted to look around her property and see the notes.

"I understand your concern for your sister," he'd said, "but before we raise the alarm, let's give her the chance to show herself. There's a chance that she may not have told Gerald the truth of her whereabouts today."

Marianne didn't agree, but put off saying so. It was her hope that once the sheriff read the notes, he'd think otherwise. In her hurry to get back to Perrigo, she put off replying to either message and led the way to Deer Harbor.

On the stretch of road with the marina in the distance, a blue BMW sped past only to have its red brake lights flash on as soon as they saw the sheriff's vehicle. The sheriff kept on, following Marianne onto her private lane.

Jack sat on his motorcycle, waiting just inside the gate to Perrigo. His mouth was set in a straight line as she pulled past him to park in front of the garage, the sheriff right behind her.

"Who might you be?" Sheriff Bradshaw didn't mince words as he stepped from his vehicle.

"Jack Sanders."

The two men shook hands. Even though Jack out-muscled the sheriff's slighter frame, Jack did as she had done, and tested that there was still life in his fingers by flexing them at his side.

"You okay?" he asked. It was hard to tell if Jack was angry with her or just concerned.

She averted her red-rimmed eyes, certain that the end of her nose was just as telling. "I'm fine."

The sheriff wore a black, fleece-lined winter hat with the ear flaps flipped up. His green jacket with 'sheriff' written across the back was zipped up to his chin. Jack seemed impervious to the chilling wind that ruffled his hair. Both his Kevlar outer jacket and the denim coat beneath were open. She felt a flash of jealousy that the promiscuous blonde might have opened his jacket to run her hands over the black T-shirt material stretched tight across his chest.

"Your girlfriend didn't stick around," Marianne said.

"My realtor, you mean."

"Is that what she's selling now?"

Rain began to fall, a light pattering of drops on the ground and the tops of their heads.

"Whatever is going on between you two, let's put it to one side and talk about these notes and how we can help Missy," said Sheriff Bradshaw.

"There's nothing going on between us," Marianne flatly stated, shoving her hands into the pockets of her down vest to keep them warm in the cold air.

"I second that," Jack said, locking eyes with her and looking like a man not about to give an inch.

"Can we get inside before this opens up?" the sheriff said.

Marianne was already moving in that direction.

The air in the kitchen was chilly and they all kept their outer wear on. The musky scent of rain swept in through the window as the deluge began outside. While Jack added wood to the still-glowing coals in the wood burning stove, Marianne put a pot of coffee together then turned to find Jack ready to take it from her to set on the wood stove as if they'd done this, many times, before.

It was a strange feeling of domesticity that she wasn't used to and one that frustrated her because she'd found that she liked it.

The sheriff looked around the kitchen. The light fixture that dangled from the ceiling caught his eye. The princess-style phone sitting on the kitchen island with the line cut raised an eyebrow.

"Can't say I've ever been in this place before," he said. "How's the upkeep?"

Her eyes went to the window over the kitchen sink. "If I made a list of all the repairs needed, it would probably convince me to move out tomorrow. But I can't leave."

She and Jack were both standing by the wood burning stove, warming their hands. She tried not to feel badly that he still smelled of a damp inn. Then she caught a whiff of perfume.

"Why can't you leave?" The sheriff pulled out a chair at the kitchen table. He flipped open his notebook. "Is it because of your sister?"

"Yes. It's my sister." She wasn't about to tell them about the dare. It all seemed ridiculous now. Especially the fact that she'd impulsively bought a relic that had only brought her trouble.

That trouble now had a sheriff at her table along with a man who, unknowingly, had brought her a different sort of trouble. She had to get a rein on her emotions when it came to Jack. One minute she was acting defensive, not liking what he'd implied about her grandpa, and the next she was behaving like a jealous girlfriend.

They still had to get through a night under the same roof.

Chapter 14

"What order did these arrive in?" The sheriff had the notes spread out before him.

Marianne set the mugs on the oak pedestal table and then reached between the two men to place the notes in order.

"Who do you think is behind this?" Sheriff Bradshaw asked.

She and Jack exchanged looks.

"At first, I thought it was Gilly," Marianne said. "Then I realized that the notes were tied up fairly high. I had to reach for them. Gilly has to be less than five feet tall."

Jack dragged another chair around to rest his leg on. This didn't go unnoticed by the sheriff who said nothing.

"I spoke with Sal yesterday on another matter," Jack said. "He knew about the first note."

"How did Sal know?" the sheriff asked what Marianne was thinking.

"Your mail carrier."

"Ah, yes," the sheriff said, "our ever-helpful eyes and ears of the island. I'll check with her to see if she recalls seeing anything or anyone looking out of place."

"We have a description," Jack said. "Gillian saw someone leave this morning's note. She fired off a shot."

The sheriff winced. "She's going to hurt someone, someday." He pulled his notepad out of his jacket pocket. "How is it again that you're involved in all this?" The sheriff looked at Jack over the top of his reading glasses.

"Jack owns the old Heron Inn." Marianne was tired, worried about Missy, and now beginning to grow hungry. Information she thought would help move this along faster spilled out of her mouth as she continued, "He's Special Ops and has offered to help find whoever wrote these notes. I think I trust him, although, I can't tell you why. I know, sounds crazy." She got up and went to the cupboard above the stove where she kept the bourbon.

Jack looked as if he thought she'd said too much or maybe not enough.

The sheriff had a fleeting smile at the corner of his mouth. "I've heard crazier."

While Jack gave the description of the suspect that Gilly had given him, Marianne retrieved the perking coffee from the top of the wood stove and filled three mugs with the hot beverage. Then she added a shot of bourbon to her mug and set the bottle in the middle of the table.

The fire in the wood stove glowed hot through the glass door, slowly taking some of the chill out of the room.

"Why do you call her Gillian?" the sheriff asked while writing. "To my knowledge, Gilly is the only name she uses."

"He's a Bullock." Marianne mimicked Jack in putting her boots up on the one remaining chair as she sipped from her hot drink. "He said her full name is Gillian Bullock."

"I never said that. The only way you would know that is from the back of the photo you took from my bag."

The sheriff stopped writing and looked over the top of his eyeglasses. "Do you have this photo?"

She swung her boots to the floor and walked across the room to retrieve her handbag.

The sheriff stuck his wad of chewing gum to the side of his coffee mug as she handed him the photo.

He briefly looked at the photograph before flipping it over. The names were penciled on the back in a diagonal pattern following the order of those in the photo, starting with the first row.

The sheriff read them off, "Gillian, Albert, Louise, back row, E.D. and H.S."

"Those are my grandpa's initials and Harold Swan's," Marianne said.

"Why did you take this from Jack?" the sheriff asked, pushing the photo to the center of the table with the notes.

"I mistakenly took it. I was trying to get my bullets back."

"You carry?"

"No."

"What are the bullets for?"

"A friend lent me her Lady Derringer believing I needed protection."

"Ever thought about getting a dog?" the sheriff said. "That might be a better idea if you're not comfortable with a gun."

"Who said I wasn't comfortable with a gun?"

"Where is it now?"

She had to think for a moment. Jack pointed to the black ski jacket hanging from the coat hook.

She brought both the box of bullets and the gun to the table, holding the grip of the Lady Derringer like it was the tail of a mouse.

"I'd be curious as to the last time that was fired. It's quite the," the sheriff searched for words, "antique."

Seeing that the diminutive gun would once again get little respect, Marianne felt the need to defend its presence. "My friend meant well in lending me this weapon."

"That's not a weapon," Jack said. "That's a stage prop."

"Just because your gun is bigger," she began.

"Okay, you two, let's stay on track here." Sheriff Bradshaw got up and refilled his coffee mug. He stood with his back to the wood stove. "Other than Gilly, who I think we are close to ruling out, who else do you suspect left these notes?"

"It wasn't until the second note that I suspected Gerald," Marianne said. "Only because I believe he lied when I asked him where my sister was this morning."

"He's got my vote simply because he's an ass," Jack said. "Although, he doesn't fit the description of who Gilly saw. My guess is that he has someone doing his dirty work."

"Well, well, Mr. Cain enters the picture once again," the sheriff said. "Unfortunately, being the end of a horse isn't enough. We need motive."

"He's been pestering me to have a look at the antiques in my home. He won't let up." She understood now why she so badly wanted this to be Gilly breaking in. The thought of the intruder being Gerald was far more disturbing and upsetting. "Someone has been in my home as there are items missing," she continued. "I've unfairly suspected Gilly. The more I think about it, maybe it is Gerald."

"Why didn't you report a break-in?" the sheriff said.

"Because if it is Gilly, she's only taking what she may feel is rightfully hers, and I really don't have a problem with that. Other than I wish she'd arrange it with me first."

Jack had been sitting quietly, his coffee untouched. "There's something you need to know that may be tied to these notes," he said to Sheriff Bradshaw.

"What is that?"

"According to your town historian, the FBI followed jewel thieves to this island back in 1945. They were looking to talk to the five in that photo. They started with the Bullocks. Then Albert and Louise disappeared and the trail went cold. Sal believes that Marianne moving into the mansion has triggered old resentment over whatever happened long ago. Someone doesn't like that she lives here. There's an assumption that her family may know where the jewels are hidden."

"That's ridiculous!" Marianne exclaimed.

The sheriff took his seat again and sat back with his arms folded as he contemplated what Jack had told him.

"I've heard some of that story over the years. Never really thought there was any truth to it." The sheriff took a sip of his coffee before continuing, "Seems to me that there's a catalyst, something that has triggered renewed interest in the stolen jewels, if they really are on the island. Can you think of anything that may have brought this to the surface after all these years?"

Jack spoke first, "I'm here because my grandfather, Albert Smith, passed away and I inherited the Heron Inn."

"Albert Smith? I thought you said you were a Bullock."

"From what I've recently discovered, it appears that my grandfather may have changed his name."

"You don't sound one hundred percent convinced of that."

"I wouldn't mind seeing some proof."

The sheriff looked at Marianne. "How about you?"

"I bought this place at auction. I moved in two weeks ago."

"That's it?"

"Pretty much. Except," it came to mind the conversation she'd had on the ferry with Gerald and the subsequent denial from Gilly, "Gerald told me that he sold a pair of jeweled opera glasses for Gilly and wanted me to ask her if there was more to the set. I've tried to ask Gilly, and she became very upset with me. She told me to stay out of her business and that I shouldn't believe anything Gerald says."

"What about you?" the sheriff said.

"What about me?"

"It's not clear to me why you're back on the island. I asked you earlier if you had moved back because of your sister. Yet, you didn't know about the alleged abuse."

"What abuse?" Jack said.

"I've moved back temporarily."

"You bought this place temporarily?" the sheriff said.

"What abuse?" Jack said a little louder, then directly to Marianne. "Is that sleaze-ball hitting your sister?"

The thought of it made her stomach clench. "Yes! I think so," she said, feeling both angry and helpless again. "She told me that she fell. The sheriff says he's heard enough from others to suspect that Gerald is hitting her."

"Allegedly," the sheriff said just before they were interrupted. His radio crackled.

A female voice spoke from the radio clipped to his shoulder, "Sheriff, this is Tilly."

He pressed the side button on the radio. "Go ahead, Tilly."

"Jan from the ferry dock called in. She had the first shift today. She didn't recall seeing Missy get on any of the ferry runs this morning. She said that she'd know if she did because she and Missy always chat when Missy's waiting for a ferry. She hasn't seen her leave the island in a long time."

"Thank you, Tilly."

"There's more, sheriff. My sister is here with me, and when she went to work this morning, she's pretty sure that she saw Missy talking with Sal's wife in the alley behind the yarn shop."

The sheriff thanked Tilly and signed off.

"Well," he said to Marianne, "it's looking like Gerald was telling the truth, although he wasn't accurate on where your sister was this morning. Again, she may not have wanted him to know. But at least it sounds like she's okay."

"For now," Marianne said, his words bringing only temporary comfort.

She understood that the sheriff had to remain objective until enough occurred to initiate the involvement of law enforcement. She wasn't the sheriff.

Sheriff Bradshaw plucked his chewing gum off the coffee mug and popped it back into his mouth. He chewed thoughtfully for a moment.

"Let me think on these notes," he said. "I'll ask around town to see if that description you gave me fits anyone. Might stop and have a chat with Gilly to see if there's anything else that she remembers. As for your sister, and I'm sure I don't need to tell you this, but it wouldn't hurt to connect with her today and see for yourself if she's okay. And let me know when you do. I'd sleep better." He gathered up the notes. "In the meantime, I don't see why you need a gun when you've got Jack."

***

"Why didn't you wait for me at the tavern?" Jack said.

The sheriff had let himself out. Jack and Marianne were still sitting at the oak table.

She carried their empty coffee mugs to the sink and returned the bourbon to its place. Only then did she turn to face him from the safety of where she leaned against the kitchen sink.

"You looked like you were going to be awhile," she said.

"I told you that I'd be right back."

"From what I can remember of Just Babs, she can be pretty convincing." She began to rinse out coffee mugs at the sink. "I didn't expect to see you back here."

"Why wouldn't I be? We have an arrangement."

She looked at him. "An arrangement? Is that what you're calling it? You're helping me find out who wrote the notes, and I'm letting you and Royce be my guests for a few days. That's not an arrangement. An arrangement is what my heroines might get themselves involved in." She stopped when Jack began to look amused. "Never mind." She went back to washing the coffee mugs.

The aroma of brewed coffee hung in the air and the fire crackled in the wood burning stove. Just then, a sound rumbled up from the basement.

"What's that noise?" Jack asked.

Marianne smiled. "The furnace. The power's back on."

Jack reached over and flipped on a light switch. The light fixture overhead flickered on, however weakly, and the conversation returned to what Jack found more interesting.

"What kind of arrangements do your heroines get themselves involved in?"

"That's not up for discussion." Her face heated up. "Besides, we should be figuring out who wrote these notes and how we're going to help my sister." She rinsed off the last mug and set it in the dish drain, turning toward Jack as she wiped her hands on the dishtowel. "What if you can't find this person in a few days? You said you were a short-timer."

For the first time since moving into the mansion, it didn't feel empty. Jack made the mansion feel more like a home. Maybe it was the way that he seemed to care more about the people around him than his own comforts. He cared where Royce, the homeless teen, slept. And he was protective of her, even if it was merely from a harmless spray of water from a mud puddle. That had a way of getting to a woman's heart, at least hers.

"I need to be in Virginia by the end of this week," Jack said from where he looked relaxed at her kitchen table. "Hey, it's a small island. Someone's bound to have seen something or knows something. It will just take some asking around and keeping my eyes open."

"Are you returning to active duty?" Marianne asked.

"That's my intention."

She glanced to the leg that he favored. "I was under the impression that you were still recovering from your bullet wound."

"I'm further along than it looks." He lowered his leg to the floor, making a slight grimace that he tried to cover. "It's this damp air that's giving me trouble. This doesn't impede my ability to complete my missions."

"Hunting bad guys?" she asked.

"At present, hunting your bad guy."

"Where should we start looking?" she said.

There was a hesitation before he spoke, "There's no 'we'," he said.

He got to his feet and walked over to inspect the window over the sink. "I prefer to work alone."

"I intend to help. This isn't just about who is delivering the threats. I want to get her away from Gerald."

"I understand your concern for your sister. You just need to realize that this could get ugly before it's over." He leaned against the counter only a few feet from her and folded his arms across his chest. Strong arms that could hold a woman and make her feel safe.

"You won't talk me out of this." She planted her hands on her hips. "Besides, I have an idea of where and how you might glean information from the locals."

"What's your idea?"

"There's a party tonight."

Chapter 15

From the floor above, the old water pipes stopped their creaky protest when Jack turned off the shower in the guest bathroom.

He'd been in there long enough to deplete the hot water in the tank.

She couldn't blame him, considering where he'd spent the night and that some of the mud he wore came from her back tires.

The bathroom closer to her room had its own water tank and she should be up there now getting ready for the party. The thought of showering on just the other side of the wall from Jack sent a flurry of butterflies dancing in her stomach.

She knew it was nerves that had her fluffing the pillows on the sofa and picking up the magazines from the place in front of the fire where she liked to sit with hot cocoa in the evenings. Then she realized that she was tidying up, not just because she had a houseguest, but to impress Jack, and for what reason. He'd made it clear that he wasn't here to start anything and she'd made it clear that a date with him was a bad idea.

They'd both drawn a big boundary line between each other. How much clearer could that be?

Was he lying like she was?

She knocked a magazine off the coffee table, threw a pillow back on the floor and messed up the knit afghan that she'd folded neatly on the back of the sofa. And because he was a curious man and didn't miss details, she closed her laptop and stuffed manuscript pages into drawers. She didn't need Jack picking out the name Gigi Divine in the notes and manuscript on her desk and learning the secret desires that repeatedly got her heroine into trouble.

The bathroom door opened on the floor above and footsteps moved down the hall to the guest bedroom where the door closed.

Warm, shower steam, and the masculine fragrance from the expensive soap she'd bought for the guest bath wafted down the stairs. She closed her eyes and breathed it in. When she'd bought that soap, it was intended for her brother to use should he stay over. Now all she could think about was Jack using that soap all over his naked body.

A step on the landing above sent her seeking clearer thoughts in a room where the cold draft from the window, dated cupboards, and yellowed, broken light fixtures would have flat-lined anyone's romantic thoughts about a man who likely wouldn't and couldn't return them.

The ugly kitchen wasn't doing what she'd hoped it would do. The scented soap had followed her.

She spun around with her hand over her heart. "I'm going to tie a bell on you."

Jack smiled and made no apologies for his silent entrance through the swinging door. "Hadn't you better get upstairs to get ready for our date?"

That caught her by surprise. "This is a mission. Not a date. We should not get those two confused."

"If you say so." He sent her the subtlest of winks as he walked over to the kitchen sink to fill a drinking glass with water.

Her pulse hammered away at the base of her throat as she checked out how nicely Jack had cleaned up, and good. Showered, shaved, and wearing a change of clothing, he'd draw more than a few admiring looks from the female guests tonight with those broad shoulders beneath a thin black sweater that fit him like a second skin. His jeans hung low on narrow hips and he'd cleaned the mud from his black boots.

"I mean it," she said.

"I'm sure you do." He had his back to her so she couldn't be sure if he was teasing or not.

She couldn't stop the impulse to look him over again from head to foot. And what was it with her and anything that smelled good on this man? Last night it had been simply the fresh air clinging to his jacket and blending nicely with his subtle cologne. Now it was the innocent soap she'd bought that was turning out to be highly dangerous.

"At least you smell a lot better," she said.

He slowly turned around as he drank from the water glass, watching her until the glass was empty and he'd set it down on the counter. The shower had made more than just an improvement on the cleanliness factor.

Or maybe she was seeing the improved mood of a man who didn't have to sleep on the hard floor in a decaying inn with rats running around in the dark. Instead, he would be sleeping on a soft mattress between clean, cotton sheets with a thick down comforter to ward away the chill at night.

Last evening, when he'd basically passed on her invitation to share a bottle of wine, he'd looked cold, wet, and disagreeable to the core. This was a complete turnaround.

The man that she didn't need any encouragement from wore a lazy smile.

"Talk like that could get you into trouble on our mission," he said.

***

The purple and orange house at the top of the hill had every light ablaze. Sal and Caroline Johnson's three-story home with dormer windows was as narrow as the lot it sat on. The shingled house had evergreen clematis vines climbing to the upper windows. Candles in mason jars lined the walk and even the white picket fence wore a festive string of tiny, white lights.

Marianne found a parking spot on the shoulder of the steep street and turned off her headlights.

Jack came around to open the driver's side door.

Down below, the lights from the marina reflected off the quiet water. With the storm system having moved on, the night was peaceful and a silvery slice of the moon smiled down on Deer Harbor. A light wind played with the hem of her silky, black dress that swayed around her ankles.

"You look nice," Jack said, warmly, making her more aware of how the dress fit to her curves.

She'd swept her hair up to hold in place with a jeweled clip. A few rebelliously, curling tendrils had already escaped to tease against the side of her neck.

"What's the plan?" Marianne asked, wrapping the silky shawl closer.

"We mingle and keep our eyes and ears open." With a hand lightly at her back, he escorted her across the road to the house where loud music played.

It was on their way through the open gate to the lit path, that Jack laced his fingers through hers.

She stopped. "What are you doing?"

"We need to act like a couple. Couples hold hands."

They stepped up to the porch where the beat of music could be felt through the wood planks. One didn't need to hear the lyrics clearly to get the feel of the song.

"Sounds like a Woodstock reunion going on," Jack said.

"How would you know that?" she teased.

"My mom still has all her albums from that music era. She could beat the pants off anyone when it comes to Woodstock trivia." His eyes smiled warmly as he talked about his mother. "Did you know that the Beatles were invited to Woodstock, but not everyone in the group wanted to do it, so it didn't happen."

"No, I didn't know that."

She liked the feel of his warm, strong hand around hers, but the intimacy had sent her pulse pounding and put her nerves on edge. The fine line between whether this was truly just a mission or dangerously close to becoming a date was getting thinner by the minute. More so because he kept glancing to her lips.

"Why is it a good idea to act like a couple?" she said.

"Because whoever is behind these notes is angry that a Dunaway has moved into Perrigo Mansion. Imagine what they'll think when they see a Bullock and a Dunaway together. They may think we've teamed up."

"Then what might they do?"

"Reveal themselves. That's the plan." He gave her hand a squeeze. "Are you ready for this?"

She gave him a nod and he rang the doorbell. "One more thing," he said.

"What's that?"

"Be prepared in case we need to do some real convincing."

"What kind of convincing?"

"Use your imagination, Dunaway. You're the romance writer." A smile worked at the corner of his mouth.

Try as she might, she couldn't resist this man. So much that she instinctively leaned against his shoulder.

His hand found the curve of her hip. Dark eyes locked with hers before he lowered his gaze to her mouth. It was enough to make her glad she'd chosen to wear the lace panties and thigh-high stockings.

Very slowly his hand went astray, moving down the silky material of her dress toward the curve of her bottom.

Suddenly the front door swung open.

A smiling woman beamed at them. "Jack Sanders, so good to see you again. Welcome! Come in. Come in."

Their hostess wore her dark hair twisted up into a French knot. In the light from the many tiny lights that decorated the front door, the faintest of gray hairs shone like silver threads woven through her hair. Her tall frame was draped in a flowing, chiffon pantsuit of lemon yellow. Daisy earrings of the same color swung from her ears and a heavy hand of dark eyeliner enhanced large, brown eyes.

Caroline pulled them into the foyer and shut the door. She cocked her head to one side as she looked at Marianne. "Marianne, right? One of Ed's grandkids."

Marianne held out her hand. "Nice to see you, again."

"A handshake is way too formal for us." She gave Marianne a big hug.

On impulse, Marianne asked. "Did you see my sister this morning?"

Their hostess looked caught off guard. "Was she coming to the knitting circle?" she said. "We have new people joining all the time."

Marianne felt the weight of worry return. "Someone thought they saw you two together. They must have been mistaken."

A comforting hand patted her arm. "Come find me in the kitchen, later." Then she cupped her hands to her mouth and announced over the music and buzz of conversations, "Everyone! This is Jack and Marianne!"

People turned holding drinks and appetizer plates, smiled, nodded, said hello, and went back to their party. Some eyes remained curiously in their direction.

A baby grand piano draped with a purple shawl was set up as a bar.

"Sal's the man to see for your drink of choice," Caroline said. "There's chili in the kitchen. Bathroom's down the hall to your left. Make yourself at home."

From what Marianne could see, from where she stood, the narrow house was crammed full, of both people, and furniture. If a guest didn't occupy one of the floral-print sofas or armchairs, a stack of books or a casually tossed coat or sweater did.

Floor to ceiling bookshelves looked ready to collapse beneath the weight of books and record albums. Trailing vines of tropical plants were draped across the tops of bookshelves and over the curtain rods, so many vines that it was hard to tell which plant they belonged to.

The house smelled of cigars and wet dog. The house also burst with light, warmth, and the joyful sounds of a gathering.

An old black lab, with gray at the muzzle and his tail swinging lazily back and forth, worked the room, lifting his nose to sniff at plates that were set on the edge of side tables. He'd stop long enough to allow a guest to pet his big head before his nose guided him to the next unattended plate.

Jack took her by the hand as they wove their way to the piano. A large man wearing a blue and yellow Hawaiian-style shirt over linen pants saw them coming and waved them over.

"Son, good to see you again. What'll you have," Sal said as he heartily shook Jack's hand all while his eyes were curiously on Marianne.

"Hello, Sal," she said.

"Haven't seen you in years, young lady. You're looking splendid."

Jack took a cold beer and Marianne accepted a glass of chilled chardonnay just as a tail smacked her on the back of the legs. The smell of wet dog disappeared under the piano after receiving a pat on its rear from Sal.

"Can't say I was expecting to see you two together," Sal said.

Jack smiled. "Stirring the pot."

Sal pushed his eyeglasses back up to the bridge of his nose and practically licked his lips in anticipation. "This should be interesting. Let me know what develops, if you wouldn't mind?"

Music came from the dining room and they followed the sound. A turntable was almost hidden under the fronds of a giant fern. A stack of record albums teetered on a dining room chair, the top one was worn around the edges and a band from the 60's graced the cover. The speakers had a dual job as they also served as a plant stand for the large ferns.

The dining table held an array of desserts, from chocolate cakes to pies to plates of cookies. In the center of the table was a large, clear plastic tub filling up with money. A sign on the tub asked for donations to a women's shelter.

A figure in a gray, pullover sweatshirt with the hood pulled up turned toward them. Royce, looking freshly showered and wearing clean jeans, smiled at them through a mouthful of chocolate chip cookies.

"Hi," he said. He noticed that Jack held her hand. His grin widened and they saw more of the chocolate mashed up cookie in his mouth. "Are you two on a date?"

"No," Marianne began to say, then Jack gently squeezed her hand. "Sort of."

"It's a hot date." Jack winked and took a long pull from his beer. "Spread the word."

Yellow chiffon swept in through the open French doors that connected the dining room to the kitchen. Bell sleeves billowed as Caroline set a tray of brownies on the table, smiling at the sight of Royce.

"Put down those cookies and go eat your dinner, young man."

The teenager complied, smiling.

"He's hungry all the time," Caroline said.

"Has he been eating here?" Jack asked.

"Oh, I just dragged him home with me today. Tom Harris told me some of Royce's story. I'm concerned because I suspect he's under age. The sheriff is checking to make sure there are no worried parents looking for him. Royce, however, is adamant that his dad doesn't care where he is. Sal and I would like to help the young man, but Royce just keeps telling us that he's fine. He said he's been staying at a friend's house and that the plumbing isn't working. I had him shower here and found him some clean clothes."

"He's been staying at the Heron Inn," Marianne informed her. "Jack is the new owner."

"Royce has been sleeping in that dump?" Caroline looked shocked.

"That's about to change," Jack said. "I've made arrangements so that we both have clean beds to sleep in for the next few days."

"What about after that?" Caroline asked. "If he ends up staying on Orcas, he's going to need a safe place to call home."

"I couldn't agree more," Jack said.

"And return to high school as I suspect he's dropped out."

"I gathered that, too."

"And tonight, for example, my granddaughter has invited him to movie night down at the teen center. What the boy needs to know is that someone cares what time he comes home tonight. Don't you agree?"

"Absolutely."

Caroline studied Jack with her head to one side. "He'd be lucky to have someone like you in his life."

Jack appeared to be at a loss for words.

Marianne felt a change of subject might help. "Jack's a Bullock," she announced.

Silence dropped like a heavy theater curtain, cutting off all talk in the dining room. Even the record player had gone silent.

Following the silence came some odd vibes.

"Overkill," Jack said, near her ear. "I wanted to stir the pot, not get shot."

Chapter 16

Their hostess abandoned them after the Bullock announcement and busied herself changing out the record album on the turntable.

"I feel like I'm about to get a knife in the back," Jack said.

Was Marianne just paranoid, again, or did it feel like eyes drilled into them? The back of her neck tingled uncomfortably. She squeezed Jack's hand. He squeezed back.

"I think we need another drink," Marianne said.

They were cut off from escaping the uncomfortable atmosphere they'd created.

Rita from the newspaper practically jumped in front of them. "I see that you've found your friend," she said, nudging her in the ribs, and giving Jack a smile. "Did you wait for him outside the Banner?"

Marianne felt her face heat up.

"Answer the question," Jack said. "The curiosity is killing me."

She was saved as Rita continued to attempt to be helpful. "I heard that you had your grandfather's checkbook stolen yesterday, along with some of his mail. That's too bad. That happened to my grandma's friend. They got her social security check and even cashed it." The dessert table drew her attention.

"Where exactly did this happen?" Jack asked Marianne.

"In the parking lot at the grocery store. I didn't think that his social security check might have been in the briefcase. The one from last month didn't get deposited by Missy and he was short on funds in his bank account."

"You might want to call the social security office and see if that check has cleared," Jack said.

"That's a good idea," she said.

A group of people trying to get from one room to another bumped into them as they passed. Jack's hand settled at her waist.

Royce suddenly ejected himself out of the crowded kitchen, carrying a bowl of chili and with his pockets bulging.

It only took Marianne a moment to figure out why the teen was in such a hurry to leave the kitchen. She caught a glimpse of the bent frame of the pawn shop owner standing next to the refrigerator.

There was very little space around the table as guests crowded in to fill their plates. To whisper in Jack's ear meant turning toward him. It seemed so natural to let her hand rest on the belt at his hip. It was a feeling she could get used to, if she wasn't careful. She reminded herself that this was only a mission.

"Gerald's uncle is at two o'clock in the kitchen," she said.

"The old guy?"

"That's him."

"You go on in and start introducing yourself around," Jack said. "Don't be shy about letting people know that you love living in the mansion. Be creative. See what reaction you get out of Harold. I need to let Royce know that he's got a bed to sleep in tonight and figure out how he's getting home."

Home. That word had come so naturally from Jack. She wondered if he realized that he'd sounded like a parent. She watched as he caught up with Royce at the far end of the dining room where a sofa, armchair, and older model television made for a cozy place tucked into the bay window.

A group of teenagers were sitting elbow to elbow on the sofa with the window at their backs where the twinkling lights of the marina could be seen in the distance. They were having fun throwing M&Ms into the air and trying to catch them in their open mouths. Royce was right in the middle of it.

In the blue and white kitchen, guests helped themselves to the chili and corn bread. A breakfast bar separated the kitchen from the eating area.

Harold stood next to the refrigerator dipping a plastic spoon into the bowl of chili he held while listening to the couple beside him talk as they sipped at their cocktails.

The owner of the pawn shop had yet to see her in the crowded kitchen.

An arched doorway next to the refrigerator led to the front room where Sal tended bar. The dog suddenly came trotting through the doorway at a fast clip. Much like Royce's behavior, the dog was on the move to avoid someone and pushed between the legs of guests to exit out through the French doors into the formal dining room.

From what little she could see through the doorway into the front room, someone new had joined the party. She caught a glimpse of the tails of a navy-blue sports jacket mingling near Sal's bright Hawaiian-shirted backside. The sports coat looked new and was worn over a pair of khaki slacks. The owner wore leather slip-on shoes with no socks. A tanned hand belonging to the navy blazer flashed a gold ring as it rested on Sal's shoulder.

She held her breath waiting to see if that hand belonged to Gerald. The volume of conversation and music was so loud that Marianne couldn't hear what the man was saying to Sal. Before she could catch a glimpse to see if it was Gerald, her view was cut off by a growing crowd entering the kitchen in search of food.

She introduced herself to the couple scooping chili into their bowls. "Hi. I'm Ed Dunaway's granddaughter."

"Oh, yes. You're the one who bought Perrigo Mansion at auction."

"I did and everything in it. I'm finding treasures galore," Marianne said, keeping watch for Harold Swan's reaction. So far, her tactic wasn't working. She raised her voice. "The Bullock family had some valuable jewels in their collection of antiques. I'm hoping to get them appraised. In the meantime, I should probably find a safer place to keep them. It's like having the crown jewels in my kitchen. Makes me nervous."

The couple's polite smile revealed how little they were interested in her boasting. They simply wished her luck and added that she might not love the place so much when a cold winter set in and she grew tired of the power outages.

She turned to find Harold Swan staring at her over the breakfast bar. Then he abruptly left the kitchen.

She stood on tiptoe to look for Jack over the heads and shoulders lining up for the chili. There was no dark-haired, broad-shouldered, pretend-to-be-my-date man to be seen.

Caroline appeared at her elbow holding a large bowl of salad to place on the table.

"I need to talk to you about your sister," she whispered in her ear. "Go out through the mudroom and wait for me at the bottom of the stairs."

***

A few stars appeared against the dark sky above, their silvery light brief witness to her descent down the wet stairs at the back of the house. Clouds moved across the moon and she had to grab ahold of the railing and feel her way down the farther she moved away from the porch light.

The air smelled of mud and salt water. Inky darkness saturated the small, backyard where her heels sank into the soft ground. The light from the house shot over her head to the top of the blackberry vines at the edge of the lawn.

She thought she was alone for a moment until a figure moved at the far end of the backyard. Yellow pant legs beneath a dark, hooded coat, and Caroline's white hand as she beckoned, were all that she could see before her newly-made friend disappeared into the shadows.

She nearly bumped into her hostess as she came around the corner. The shadows were denser on the side of the house, and the ground firmer on the gravel path.

Caroline took her hand and pulled her up the path and out of any light from the windows above.

"Is Missy okay? Do you know where she is?" Marianne asked.

Half of Caroline's face was in shadow. "I can tell you this much. A group of us are working to help your sister get away from her boyfriend. That's why I met with her this morning. Sorry I had to be deceitful. If this doesn't work, the wall will go up higher around her and it will be even more difficult for her to get away. And we don't know what the consequences will be. He's unpredictable."

"Why hasn't she gone to the sheriff?"

"Gerald has threatened to hurt your grandfather if she does. That's why we must do this carefully and cleverly. We have to outsmart him."

"I want to help."

Caroline gently covered her hands. "I know that you are concerned, but your moving into Perrigo Mansion seems to have changed his behavior for the worse. He's watching her more closely than ever. Whatever happens in the next few days, that is, if we're successful, you can't go to the sheriff. You need to trust that our plan will work."

"Can you tell me what the plan is?" Marianne said.

"I can't tell you too much other than we just need an opportunity when he's not watching her."

A voice shouted the hostess's name from the back of the house. "Caroline, where are you? We can't get your coffee maker to work."

Caroline grabbed Marianne's hand and pulled her deeper into the shadows from the house next door.

"Gerald is an intelligent man in a very scary way," Caroline said as she kept her voice lowered. "He's a smooth one. That charm of his wins over more women than I'd like to say. I speak from experience. I was married to someone like him, once. You know that they're lying, but they manage to convince you that you're the crazy one and not them. You need help getting away from men like him." She pulled a cellphone from her coat pocket. "Give me your phone number. I'll call you when I have news. In the meantime, don't discuss this with anyone. I know this is a lot to ask. You need to trust us."

The sole of a shoe scraped on gravel. Caroline put a finger to her lips and listened toward the front of the house where street lights gleamed off the many parked cars. She silently urged Marianne back the way they had come then stopped her beneath the window of the dining room.

"That was probably just a guest leaving," Caroline said. "Let's not take chances. We shouldn't be seen talking to each other. I think that most of the Swan clan is here tonight. I sent invitations out to as many as I could, hoping that tonight would be the chance Missy needs. The one I really wanted to come tonight isn't here, yet, or if he is, I haven't seen him. But the bait is set, right smack in the middle of the dessert table."

Marianne had an idea. "I have a friend who may be able help."

Caroline shook her head. "We are already set up to move at a moment's notice. I don't dare tweak the plan," her voice trailed off as something caught her eye in the window above their heads.

It was the profile of her sister, Missy, talking to several of the teenagers as she sipped from a wine goblet.

Relief swept over Marianne. Her sister was okay, so far.

"Do you think Gerald is here with her?" Marianne whispered.

Caroline looked over her shoulder toward the front of the house. "We should always assume that he is."

"If only you could get her away from him now. There are so many people here tonight he might not realize she's missing for the few minutes that you'll need."

"Oh, he would notice, I assure you. At best, we would have only seconds to act," Caroline said, as she bit her lip in thought. "We just need to find a way to distract Gerald. Now let's get back inside before we're missed. You go first."

Marianne hurried toward the stairs then came to an abrupt stop when the door above opened. Having been in the shadows, the porch light blinded her for a few seconds when she looked up. When she saw a head of blonde hair above navy-blue shoulders and a flash of gold, she instinctively wanted to run. She even began to back up under the stairs to hide. Then realized that this was how she could help Missy.

Caroline had seen Gerald at the same time and beckoned for her to join her in the shadows against the house. Marianne stayed put and signaled to her to make the call to set the rescue in motion.

The leader of the knitting circle shook her head madly to dissuade Marianne's intentions.

Marianne stepped out of her hiding place and called up to Gerald who was lighting a cigarette.

"Hi."

His eyes slid her way, his body language guarded and suspicious. "What are you doing out here?"

"Needed the fresh air. Look, I think that's Venus showing itself tonight."

As Gerald looked up at the sky, she caught a glimpse of yellow chiffon slipping into the shadows at the far end of the backyard.

Marianne hoped that she could stand to engage this man for however long was necessary. The fact that she instinctively flinched when Gerald put his weight on the stairs to descend, told her otherwise.

Chapter 17

Jack searched every room of the house and could not find Marianne. He was regretting thinking it was okay to let her out of his sight while he talked to Royce.

Through the packed room, he caught sight of a bent frame belonging to thinning, gray hair. Harold Swan quietly collected his coat from the many coats draped over the stair railing.

"Goodnight, there, Harold. Glad you could join us," Sal called over to his departing guest, who either didn't hear him, or ignored him, as he pulled on a trench coat.

A petite, dark-haired woman bumped Jack's shoulder as she moved past with a wine goblet in her hand. She murmured an apology and kept going. A black raincoat covered her thin frame and she wore a pair of jeans stuffed down into rubber boots. The receptionist from the Banner greeted her and Jack knew then why the young woman looked familiar; she resembled Marianne with the shape of her eyes and high cheekbones.

Rita fanned herself with a napkin. "There're so many people here, we need to open a window. Missy, aren't you warm in that coat?"

The younger woman pulled the coat collar up around her neck. "I'm fine," she said, darting a look over her shoulder as if checking to see if someone stood behind her.

The record player began to skip and the dog growled from under the dining room table. Jack felt his bad-guy vibe go off right before Gerald came down the hall from the bathroom. In the foyer, uncle and nephew conferred in low tones next to the open door, letting in a cold draft that fluttered napkins and dresses. Several of the guests looked with annoyance toward the two. Then another guest stepped through the front door.

Just Babs looked out of place in a short, leopard-print coat. Fishnet stockings filled the gap between coat hem and the top of her boots. After speaking briefly with Gerald and Harold, she walked towards the dining room. Jack wasn't in the mood to talk real estate with the hungry tigress. One of the houseplants worked as a shield to mask his presence as she moved past.

Harold went out the door. His nephew sauntered over to the bar and flashed a phony smile at the host.

"I'll take another beer, old man," Gerald said as he slapped their host on the back, his eyes searching the room.

Gerald had yet to see Jack and soon disappeared amongst the guests. One had only to follow the smell of cheap cologne and the trail led around to the kitchen.

It was clear that Jack wasn't the only one attempting to avoid Just Babs. Missy saw the realtor coming and pivoted on her heels. Keeping his eyes off Gerald for a few seconds too long, proved to be a mistake. He was no longer in the line for food.

"If you're looking for your date," Rita said at his elbow. "I saw her go out that same door Gerald just left by, only about fifteen minutes ago."

On Jack's prior visit to Sal's office, he remembered that one side of the house was fenced off from the neighbor's and the other had a path that ran from front to back.

He went out the front door and nearly slammed into Harold Swan standing on the steps smoking a cigarette. As much as he'd like the opportunity to see what he could get out of Harold, he had a bad feeling that needed attending to.

"Excuse me," he said to the man who was either blind to the fact that he was in his way or didn't care.

"I hear you're related to the Bullocks," Harold said as he dropped his cigarette to the path where the end burned a bright orange in the night.

"I've heard things about you as well." Jack didn't wait to see what reaction this brought from the older man. He left the smell of cigarette and musty old shop and lengthened his stride across the narrow front lawn.

The shadows were long as he moved down the gravel path. In passing the door to Sal's office, he detected movement behind a door not closed all the way. Since he didn't smell cheap cologne, he kept going, his concern for Marianne increasing as he came around to an empty backyard.

Voices came from the far side of the house.

"I wondered when you were going to come to your senses and quit avoiding me. You know we got chemistry, darlin'." Gerald had someone cornered where the fence was attached to the house.

Clouds moved across the night sky, and there was very little moonlight overhead. At first it looked like Marianne wasn't opposed to Gerald's closeness. Until the sleaze-ball put a hand to her waist and she nearly fell back against the house.

"Now you got me confused, Sweetcakes," Gerald said in annoyance, "you're back to acting like you're too good for me."

"That's because she is," Jack said. "Step away from her."

"Jack, don't," Marianne warned.

A glowing ember flicked by Jack's ear. "Get lost, Gimp." Gerald was dumb enough to show Jack his back again.

Jack only needed a fistful of collar and he had Gerald off the ground and flying toward the blackberry vines.

Gerald remained stunned for a few moments before struggling to his feet trying to keep his balance on the muddy grass and get his fists up at the same time. Wet grass and twigs clung to his pants and jacket. Mud stained his backside. Stringy hair covered eyes gleaming with hate and spittle showed white at the corner of his mouth. "I'll kill you," he said, breathing hard.

"You may have just made things worse," Marianne said as Jack took her hand to get her as far from Gerald as possible.

"I've only just started," Jack said. "Let's get out of here."

***

From her vehicle, they watched as Gerald escorted Missy across the street to the black Suburban.

She looked at Jack to see if he was seeing what she was seeing. Her sister was laughing and Gerald wasn't pulling her to his vehicle like the monster she was beginning to believe he was. He had a hand lightly at her sister's waist. From the front porch, Caroline and two other women watched the couple as well.

"I don't get it," Marianne said. "She's acting like she likes him."

"Maybe that's exactly what it is, an act."

"I'm following them home." She put the keys in the ignition.

"Not a good idea. We've pushed Gerald far enough tonight. For your sister's safety, we're going to have to back down, for now."

It was difficult to watch and do nothing as the taillights of Gerald's vehicle grew more distant. Once they were out of sight, she started up the engine. It was an uncomfortable drive the short distance to Perrigo Mansion. Their earlier comradery had been replaced with the tension resulting from her tangling with the dangerous Gerald.

Even when a deer shot across the road and through the beams of her headlights, and she stood on the brakes, Jack remained silent. Although the look he'd sent her after he'd been thrown forward against the seat belt said plenty.

"Stop here," he said.

She pulled over to the shoulder just before her private lane. Jack got out of the vehicle.

"I thought you were staying with me? I mean, in one of my guestrooms." She was glad for the darkened interior of the vehicle, to cover her embarrassment on how that had sounded.

Wind ruffled his hair as he ducked his head back inside. "I'm taking a walk. Call me if you have any trouble." He nodded toward a folded piece of paper in her consol.

He set off on foot to his inn. As she proceeded on toward home, she could see his silhouette as he accessed the footbridge over the water.

It was a struggle not to feel like this was a date that had ended badly. What it was, was a failed mission with a man whom she was beginning to like far too much. And now he preferred to distance himself rather than see where the evening might lead.

That was probably for the best.

Just in case she needed him for another reason, she copied into her cellphone the number he'd left.

***

Maxwell answered after a few rings, "Hey, buddy."

"Is this a bad time?" Jack stood on the back veranda of the inn where he could see the lights in Marianne's home across the water.

"I don't have the answer you're looking for."

"That's not why I'm calling."

His friend of twenty years didn't miss much. "You're not sounding like yourself."

Considering what Marianne had been through tonight, Jack felt a twinge of guilt for not seeing her home properly and making sure all her doors were locked. Was it too much to rely on his suspicions that Gerald was behind the notes? Was it false security knowing that the one man he felt was responsible for disrupting the peace and security of the island was too busy keeping an eye on what he felt was his personal property?

Jack sat down on the step. "I'm not feeling like myself, to tell you the truth. A lot has happened since I arrived here."

"You mean to check out the property?"

"Something like that."

A small animal scurried away from the foundation near where Jack sat and hurried into the patch of ferns. Jack picked up a fir cone and tossed it into the still moving vegetation.

"Keep on going," he said to one of his roommates from the previous night.

"Who are you talking to?" Maxwell said.

"Just chasing away rats."

"Seriously?"

"Yes, unfortunately. And it's not the only rat I need to chase away," Jack said, rubbing his hand across his brow. "Problem is he's just going to keep coming back as soon as I'm gone."

"We're not talking about a rat with four legs, are we?" Maxwell said.

"No."

"And this is bothering you because," there was a pause, "there's a woman involved, isn't there?"

Before Jack could deny it, his friend continued, "Holy smokes, I never thought I'd see the day when a woman had you thinking otherwise."

"Just hold on there," Jack attempted to stop the assumptions.

"What's her name?"

"Marianne."

There was dead silence on the line. "You gave me a name, this time. I need to sit down."

"Knock it off, smartass. I need some help here."

"You need some help regarding a woman?" Maxwell said, as if not believing what he was hearing. Then his tone changed. "Yeah, maybe you do because this is unfamiliar territory for you. Caring enough about her that you're either acting stupid or scared shitless that you're going to muck it up."

"Max, I'm going to hang up."

"Okay. Okay. What can I do to help?"

Jack got to his feet, not liking this feeling of indecision. As dangerous as it was hunting the bad guys of this world, it was familiar territory, his expertise. His expertise with a woman was more in the physical way. He sure didn't always know what to do, otherwise.

Jack closed his eyes and thought about what he would do if he was hunting a bad guy and found himself in a new situation. He would rely on instinct to make his way and survive.

"Never mind," he said. "I think I just found the answer myself."

"You sound awfully sure of yourself for someone in unfamiliar territory," Maxwell said. "You're not backing away from this, are you?"

"I gotta go."

"Hold on, Jack. If you really like this woman, you're going to regret getting on that plane. I did. But I was smart enough to turn around and go back and I've never regretted my decision. Not for one minute."

"I'll take that into consideration."

"Sure you will, just like my professional advice. If I was there right now, I'd smack you on the side of the head."

Jack had walked back to the middle of the veranda where he had the best view of the mansion. A pair of headlights had just turned down her private lane.

"I'll call you later." Jack ended the call abruptly.

The car idled at the far end of the lane. Moonlight gleamed off the chrome trim across the top of the windshield. It was impossible to tell the make and model from this distance in the dark.

Securing his inn was pointless. The wind blew the French doors wide open, again. He cursed himself for making the walk up to his inn, leaving his motorcycle at the mansion. Prior to his gunshot wound, he could run a mile in nine minutes.

The hobbling run back down the hill to the footbridge gave him plenty of time to think. Not about what he'd do if the driver had ill intentions, that would all come instinctively. He was thinking about how much his life had changed since he'd arrived on Orcas Island.

In the short time that he'd allotted for taking care of business on the island, to unload material things, he'd gone and acquired something he hadn't expected to: feelings of responsibility for a teenager and a feisty, strawberry blonde. Didn't mean they needed him.

These feelings in no way tied him to this place.

Chances were good that someone would look out for Royce.

Chances were even greater that another man would enter her life. The problem was, that didn't sit well with him.

And that brought him to realize that he was beginning to care. A dangerous emotion that could change things, if he let it.

Chapter 18

She opened the back door when she saw Jack standing by his motorcycle where he'd parked it earlier that day.

He turned from unstrapping his helmet from the back of the bike.

Her heart plummeted.

Would he really do this to her? Promise to help her and then take off like this, unexpectedly, and for what reason?

She stopped a few feet from where he stood in the halo of light from the garage floodlight.

"I'm sorry I messed up the mission," she said, thinking that might be the reason he was leaving sooner than planned.

"You should go inside," he said, looking toward the gate. "You're cold."

Jack was breathing hard.

"Did you run back here?" she asked.

He had something hiding under the helmet that rested on the seat. Light glinted off metal. And Jack looked deadly serious.

"What's wrong?" she said, turning to look toward the gate.

"Were you expecting any visitors tonight?"

"No." She made to walk toward the gate to see better down the lane. Jack stopped her with a hand to her arm.

She caught a glimpse of headlights at the far end of the lane as a car turned around, its engine not running so smoothly. Red taillights flashed before the car drove off.

"Whoever that was, sat there for a good fifteen minutes," Jack said.

A scary thought occurred to her. Perhaps she'd baited the hook too well.

"Maybe I shouldn't have said as much as I did at the party."

"What did you say?"

"I made it sound like I had the crown jewels in my kitchen, easy for the taking."

He remained a little too quiet for her comfort.

"You said get creative," she added in her defense.

A glimpse of a smile hovered at the corner of his mouth, then it was gone. "You take me literally, don't you?"

A reminder of how little they knew one another. "Yes. Since I don't know you very well and I can't read your mind."

Light glinted once again off the gun as he expertly relocated the weapon to the back of his jeans.

He held his helmet like he was deciding whether to put it on, or not.

"Are you expecting more trouble tonight?" she asked. She hoped the answer was no. She'd had enough excitement for one day.

The look he gave her didn't give her the answer she wanted. Then again, maybe they weren't talking about the same kind of trouble. Her heart skipped a beat.

There had to be a way to get past the security vault to what he was feeling inside. She'd felt it a few times now, in how he'd looked at her, and the control she knew he'd used to keep from kissing her. He'd rescued her tonight from Gerald like a man looking out for his woman. Now where had that man gone? It felt like they were back to square-one as strangers and she was beginning to wonder if she'd imagined everything else.

The night air was chilling her skin. She wrapped her arms tighter about her middle. Jack kept looking toward the gate. It was hard to tell if that was the look of a man keeping watch or one mapping out his escape route.

It had been a long time since she'd felt her way in getting to know a man. She didn't know what to do next. She had only instinct to rely on; one blind step after another into unknown territory. The saying that you never know until you try prodded her on. She wanted him physically and emotionally, yet she wasn't sure she was ready for what came next because, quite honestly, she'd never felt this way before and didn't know what to expect next.

Even worse, she wasn't sure her heart would recover if it turned out that Jack wasn't even remotely thinking along the same lines.

There was nothing certain or promised in taking another step toward him. Chances were he'd just get on that motorcycle and go. If not tonight, then tomorrow. She had nothing to lose and all that she might get out of this would be a moment in time, a forever sweet memory. If she could get his attention on her.

She didn't know what he found so much more interesting than her as he searched the roofline above her head and seemed to be counting off her windows, even going as far as to sweep the backyard with his eyes from tree line to shoreline. One again this felt like the end of a date gone bad with the guy hoping that you don't ask, '*when can I see you again?*'

"You're leaving, aren't you?" she said.

That got his attention. About the same time her emotions got the best of her.

"I thought we had a deal," she said. "You help me find out who's leaving the notes in exchange for a room and a hot meal?"

"Was that our deal?"

"It was your idea," she said to the man she was going to need a chisel and hammer to get through to, if her pride would allow.

Whatever he was thinking, she seriously doubted he'd be sharing with her. The cold brought her around sharply. He was a realist. She was a romantic. What chance would they have even if he did stay?

Maybe that's why he was leaving. He'd figured that out already.

She should have just stayed in her car on the ferry and never shared a booth with him and a bad cup of coffee. She should just be thankful that she didn't get any more involved. Still didn't mean he'd be easy to forget.

Sometimes the only life preserver a girl had was her pride.

"Fine. Leave. Don't let me keep you." She spun on her heels and marched angrily away.

"You didn't do too badly on your first mission," he called after her.

She slammed the door shut as hard as she could.

Furious that, despite it all, she still liked his charm, his curious nature, the way that he would glance to her legs when he thought she wasn't looking, and the way that he sat relaxed in a chair while looking interested in what she was saying.

The swinging door received the brunt of her anger. She gave it a hard push just as the back door opened and shut again.

"I never said I was leaving." Jack hung his helmet on the coat hook. His gun went into his saddle bags that were still by the door.

Caught off guard, she was halfway between still being angry and feeling immense relief wash over her.

"What were you doing out there, then?" she said.

In all fairness, she really didn't even give him time to form a decent response.

"This better be good," she said before he could even reply. "And just for the record, you and I are totally different from each other. Even if you did stay, it would never work."

It was hard to tell if that was a gleam of amusement or something more primitive that flickered in his eyes.

"What has that got to do with room and board for a night or two?"

Never had silence felt so awkward as embarrassed heat flooded her face.

"I have no idea where that came from," she could finally speak. "Flashback to an old boyfriend is my best guess."

The seconds ticked painfully by as she waited to see if he would stay or run, after her slip-up.

"A bit lame, but not a bad recovery." He took a step toward her. "You saw me about to put on my helmet because I was considering following that car."

"Why didn't you?"

"Because there's a chance they may have wanted me to, thereby leaving you here alone."

Just the thought of what someone had planned if they'd successfully pulled Jack away had her imagination going into overtime. She shivered even though the kitchen was warm.

"Did you lock the door?" she said.

To her relief, he did just that. When he turned back to her, she could tell he had more to say. How much worse could it be than hearing his thoughts of how bad people thought? She braced for impact.

"To be honest with you, before I saw those headlights, the thought did cross my mind to get on my motorcycle and not look back."

That rubbed her the wrong way. "You still can," she said. And she began to harden her heart in preparation of that happening.

"I can't leave just yet," he said, "because I did say I'd help you and I'm good on my word."

He came closer.

She didn't know what it was he was expecting; to have that nice amicable talk about their grandfathers?

She wasn't feeling amicable.

Her emotions had had a rough night so far. Pretending to be Jack's hot date had left her feeling like she wanted that all the time. Then her attempt to try to help Missy had failed. Now Jack admitting to wanting to leave.

She took a step back. "I release you from any obligation you may feel in having to help me. You're off the hook. If you leave in the middle of the night, I won't be surprised. After all, you are a Bullock."

His eyes narrowed dangerously. The clock on the wall behind her ticked like a bomb counting down. Yet the man didn't blow. His words were controlled and his tone neutral as if he were negotiating with a bad guy.

"If I didn't want a soft, clean bed to sleep in so badly," he said, "I'd tell you what I think of that nasty comment of yours."

She slapped her chest. "Hit me with it. I can take it and maybe you'll still have that bed to sleep in. If not, I know where there's a moldy, old inn with vacancies."

The clock tick-ticked toward detonation.

Jack's hand hung idly by his side. Very subtly he flexed his fingers like a gun slinger poised to draw. Which made her realize that she probably shouldn't be trying to anger a man with a gun bigger than hers.

"I'm thinking I should just shut up and kiss you," Jack said.

She didn't see that coming.

Nor how smoothly he closed the distance between them, catching her up against him with a hand to her lower back and the other delving deep into the thickness of her hair.

"What if I don't want you to kiss me?" Her heart thundered against her ribcage.

The cold air from his clothes penetrated her own, chilling her skin momentarily until his body heat began to warm her where his denim clad thighs pressed against hers and where their torsos met.

"Considering how much abuse my motorcycle and I have taken from you in the past few days, I don't much care what you want." His mouth hovered over hers before gently taking her bottom lip between his and caressing it with the tip of his tongue. His hand slid down to cup her bottom. He nuzzled her neck. "On second thought, I'll let you decide. Here, or somewhere more comfortable."

A sweet pulse began beneath the lacy black panties she was thankful she'd worn.

His timing was perfect, in that regard.

Not so much with her heart. She'd yet to close the steel door around that vulnerable organ and it was at the mercy of what the rest of her body wanted to do.

"Anywhere," she whispered and wound her arms around his neck.

They made it through the swinging doors before Jack pinned her against the wall between two oil paintings.

He hiked up her dress and hooked her legs around his hips. There was no denying where this was going when his hand slid down the back of her panties. She moaned against his mouth. His tongue swept seductively across her tongue, a slow, deliberate message of what he wanted and intended to have.

She cupped him between the legs.

In his attempt to brace her against the wall and pull her dress straps off her shoulders at the same time, he knocked one of the painting off its hook. His move to avoid the other painting centered her over the light switch that pressed into her back.

"That way." She pointed.

They bumped into the foyer table and things went crashing to the floor.

"Wait!" she gasped, pulling her mouth from his. "I'm not on the pill."

"I've got that covered." His kisses were heating up, growing in their intensity.

It was quickly apparent that the foyer table just wasn't big enough. Jack's eyes fell on the sofa in the library and they were on the move, again.

She thought that his setting her down on the back of the sofa was temporary while he whipped her dress over her head before his sweater followed.

He took one look at her thigh-high black stockings. "Those stay on," he said. "This doesn't." And her black, lacey bra flew over his shoulder.

He pulled out his wallet and let his jeans drop to the floor. She barely caught a glimpse of a gold foil packet in his hand before he put his other hand flat to her bare breasts to give her a gentle push. She fell back onto the sofa cushions seeing only a flash of what commando style revealed.

Experienced fingers slid beneath the crotch of her panties. She gasped and arched up, her hair cascading off the cushions and onto the floor as feather-light touches stroked her, leaving her wanting him not to be so gentle.

So exquisite was the sensation that she bit down on the corner of the accent pillow to keep from screaming.

"You like that." Jack touched her again.

She couldn't take the torture. The pillow went flying, knocking the stack of books and magazines off the end table. "Just—"

Jack pulled her upright, taking a fistful of her hair. "Just what?" His mouth was against hers.

"Bend me over the sofa."

"No."

"Please," she begged, running her hands through his hair and nibbling on his earlobe.

"Maybe round two."

He yanked off her panties and her heart raced, unsure of what he had planned. Her breasts were flattened against him. They were both breathing hard, their skin hot and damp with perspiration.

She caught his bottom lip between her teeth. He growled low. Holding her bottom tight, he made a slow and deliberate entry and then he stopped all movement. The instinct to move on him was too much. She grasped his shoulders and tried to ride him. He held her in place.

Marianne put her nose against his and locked eyes with her pirate. "I want you," she said.

"You'll get it," he said. "When I decide."

A thrill went down her spine. She had ideas of her own. She smiled into his eyes then suddenly pushed off and arched back onto the sofa cushions again, unlocking her legs from his hips, she presented Jack with a view of where they were joined hoping to excite him further and push him over the edge, wanting to see all that the dark look under half-hooded eyes had in store for her.

Yet he remained in control, splaying his hand seductively slow across the flat of her tummy and up to cup each breast.

Then his hand trailed down and he began to massage the area where she'd spent plenty of time taking care of herself. She did something that Gigi Divine would do. She put her hand over his and began to guide him, showing him just how she liked being touched there.

"Like that. I like that," she said.

"That's sexy," Jack said huskily. Then he lost control.

It happened so fast.

She was pulled up tight against him once again only to have Jack roll them both over the sofa and onto the floor. He ended up on top. She had no complaints as strong hands imprisoned her slender ankles and placed them over his shoulders. It was more than Gigi Divine had ever experienced.

***

She'd fallen asleep with her head resting on his shoulder and the soft afghan covering them.

Jack gently shook her awake. "We're not alone," he whispered in her ear.

He gathered up their clothes and they dressed quickly by the light of the candles she'd lit and the low-burning flames in the fireplace. The wind was gusting, again, and the tree outside the window scraped against the glass.

"What if that car came back?" she said.

"We would have heard it," he said. "The owner of that car needs a new fan belt." Jack turned on the lamp. "Were you expecting anyone?" he said.

She shook her head a second before she remembered that Jack wouldn't be the only guest under her roof tonight.

"It's probably Royce!" She hurriedly snatched her bra from off the lamp shade and looked around for a place to hide the lacy lingerie.

"Not unless their movie ended early. By the way he was looking at Caroline's granddaughter, I doubt he'd cut the night short. Stay here by the fire," he said.

Just as she was thinking that the last time they'd separated things went badly, as in her run-in with Gerald, Jack came back into the library, striding across the room to where she was removing a flashlight from the desk drawer.

"On second thought," he said, "I'm not letting you out of my sight this time." He saw the hefty silver flashlight she gripped. "You plan to hit someone over the head with that?"

"Yes. Especially if it's you-know-who."

"It's not him," Jack said. "I would have smelled him by now." In the foyer, he pulled her close. "Did you hear that?" he said against her hair.

There was no sound at first, then she heard a faint whirring sound and that of an object brushing against another.

It came from upstairs. They proceeded to investigate, moving quietly up the blue paisley runner that carpeted the grand staircase.

At the landing on the second floor, the whirring and brushing sound pulled them to the left of the stairs, the opposite direction of her bedroom. The noise began to grow fainter as if it was now going away from them toward the main floor.

She thought at first that Jack was suddenly interested in the seascape oil paintings and heavy tapestries on the walls along the hallway, until he started rapping on the wallpapered spaces between the gilded frames and looking behind the tapestries. He did this along a five-foot section of one wall before turning to do the same on the opposite. When he moved aside a tapestry, a narrow door was revealed.

"A secret room?" she said.

"If my guess is correct, it's an elevator."

The wood door opened stiffly. In the poor light thrown out by the dated wall sconces, they could see that a cage door kept anyone from stepping into the dark cavity. It creaked open and they both peered in to cautiously look down. Jack shone the flashlight beam on the dusty top of a small elevator that had come to rest several floors down.

"Looks like it goes all the way to the basement." He reached out and closed his hand around one of the cables. "Feels warm."

The knowledge that the elevator wasn't moving on its own hit her. She gripped his arm with both hands. "Where's your big gun?"

Jack shut both the cage door and the wood door. The tapestry swung back into place. "In your kitchen," he said.

Alarmed that they were unprotected with an intruder a few floors down, she said, "What's it doing down there? We need it up here."

"I figured you wouldn't appreciate me walking around armed," he replied. "Where's your gun?"

"In the flour bin. Why are you so calm? We have an intruder."

"I've dealt with worse. Now here's what you're going to do." He ushered her down the hall to her bedroom. "Stay in here. You'll be safe. This next part is where I work alone." He closed the door soundly.

It took her about two seconds to decide that that wasn't okay with her. This was her house, her intruder.

The hallway was empty. He'd disappeared like a ghost.

If she'd learned one thing from growing up on the island during winter storms, it was to keep a flashlight in every room of the house. Taking a lighter-weight flashlight from her nightstand drawer, and wishing it was the heavier one that Jack had with him, she followed the brave pirate.

Jack was nowhere on the second floor. She descended to the first floor as quietly as she could. Something looked different in the hallway to the kitchen. One of the tapestries had been pushed aside, held open by a narrow wood door like the one on the landing above. This elevator door wasn't like the cage style on the floor above. The accordion style fabric door was open.

She moved forward on tip-toe to peek inside the elevator when the power went out.

A strong arm hooked around her waist and a hand clamped over her mouth and she was pulled into the darkness of the elevator.

The power flickered back on.

"Thank God it's you!" she exclaimed. "Must you scare me like that?"

Jack loosened his hold on her. "Figured it was you."

Before he could eject her out of the elevator and continue his investigation without her, she closed the elevator door and pressed the down button.

"That may not have been such a good idea," he said as the elevator began to descend. "What if the power goes out again? It could be a long night stuck in here together." His breath gently moved the hair at her temples.

The rest of her began to heat up with every inch of her pressed up against him in the tight confines.

"You might need my help. What's the plan?" she said as the elevator came to a stop.

A small, flat light fixture sat flush with the ceiling a few inches above Jack's head. The yellowish glow illuminated the old elevator with its fake paneling and brass handrails.

"For starters," Jack said, "I've already been to the basement. Whoever was in here left out the storm door leaving a trail of muddy footprints."

"We're not chasing anybody?" she said.

"You're a few minutes late. He or she is long gone."

The thought of someone in the house moving about while they were minding their own business, of sorts, sent a shiver up her spine.

She grabbed Jack's arm. "Do you think they saw us?"

"I'm not so much concerned about that as to who it was and what they were looking for." He made a lopsided grin. "Although, we might have heard them sooner if you didn't scream so much."

She punched him on the shoulder. "I wasn't screaming."

"Oh, yes you were. Good thing you live at the end of a long private road or you'd have neighbors complaining."

"I suppose you want full credit for that?" she said, feeling her cheeks heating up.

His grin widened and he winked at her. "Damn straight." He reached behind her and pressed the button. The elevator gave a jerk but nothing happened. Jack pressed the button again. The elevator began to ascend.

"For a minute there, I was afraid we were stuck." She rubbed her arms, feeling nervous and unsettled knowing that someone had been in her home. "I think we should call the sheriff and report an intruder." Her rear-end bumped into the controls. The elevator stopped. "Oops," she said.

"Quit moving around," he teased.

His warm body pressed closer to hers as he reached around to the control panel. Before he could correct their situation, the light overhead flickered out.

"Figures," Jack said.

She could hear him pressing buttons to no avail.

She sighed. "Why did I buy this place? I've got intruders, windows that won't close, and these power outages."

Jack's body heat had increased and his hand now rested on her hip. "We could make the most of this." His thighs pressed against hers and she felt the brass railing against her lower back.

She put a hand flat to his hard chest. "How can you want to make-out at a time like this? I'm scared, Jack. Someone has figured out how to get into my home and go about doing whatever they please. What if you weren't here?"

He pulled her close and wrapped her in a hug. "It's okay. I don't believe this person meant any harm. I think they were looking for something because they weren't interested in bothering us." He kissed the top of her head. "I'm thinking it was your sweet neighbor."

"Gilly?"

"She knows this place better than you, obviously. You didn't know about the elevator." He smoothed a hand over her hair. "We'll let the sheriff know in the morning and I'll stay close to you tonight. You'll be okay."

His reassurance eased her fears, so did the way that he played with a long, strand of her hair where it rested on her shoulder.

She knew what he was trying to do, get her mind off her worries for a spell. He was doing a good job. Even more so when he had no trouble finding her mouth in the dark.

Unlike earlier, when their kiss had ignited an out of control wildfire, this kiss was slow and sweet, a deep kiss in the pitch black of the elevator as she wrapped her arms around his torso and felt the tension leave her body.

Suddenly the overhead light flickered on. A moment later the elevator began to climb.

"Did your ass do that?" Jack asked.

"No. Your hand must have since it's back there on my butt."

"It wasn't me." Jack pushed her behind him as the elevator came to a stop and the accordion door slowly slid open.

Chapter 19

It was a mystery as to where Jack had kept his gun in the crowded confines of the elevator. It was now pointed at the dark-haired man wearing a black-hooded sweatshirt and a 49ers hat stained with car oil.

Since she wasn't expecting her brother, it took her a moment to recognize the handsome and broad-shouldered man with a day's growth of beard and a gold hoop glinting off his earlobe.

"Ian, what are you doing here?" Marianne said from where she stood on tip-toe looking over Jack's shoulder.

Jack lowered his weapon.

"You sent me a message," Ian said. He'd held up his arms at the sight of Jack's gun. Now he lowered them with a non-too-friendly look toward Jack and the gun he slid into the back of his jeans.

Royce stuck his head around the kitchen door. "We've been looking all over for you guys."

"Since when did you get your ear pierced?" she said to her brother.

"It's part of my cover," he said. "Who are you?" he demanded of Jack.

"Nice to meet you, too," Jack said. The two men of equal height and body weight circled each other in the hall until Marianne stepped between them and made the introductions.

"Jack is my guest in exchange for helping me."

"What exactly is he helping you with?" growled Ian. "And what is going on here? Did you have a break-in? Is this what was so urgent?"

Gold-framed, oil paintings of landscapes leaned cockeyed against the wall. The foyer table they'd bumped into was pushed away from the wall and the mail that had sat in a shallow wood bowl was scattered across the marble floor with the overturned bowl in the middle of the mess.

Jack only smiled.

"We did have a break-in," Marianne said quickly. "That's what we were investigating."

"Dude! Seriously!" Royce looked awed. "Did you shoot him?" he asked Jack.

"Sorry to disappoint you." Jack patted the teenager on the shoulder.

Ian's eyes narrowed in suspicion. "I need a drink."

They followed him into the kitchen where he began opening kitchen cupboards.

"Tell me you have something besides wine."

She retrieved the bourbon from the cupboard and set out glass tumblers.

"I needed you here because Missy's in trouble," she said.

Her brother slowly set down his glass. "What kind of trouble?" he said, directing the question to her and rudely ignoring Jack.

"Jack," Marianne began, "you can summarize it better. Will you please tell Ian about the notes and why we suspect Gerald?"

Jack spoke directly to Marianne, ignoring Ian. "He can go see the sheriff tomorrow and let him bring him up to speed. Although, I'll have this problem solved before he's even out of bed in the morning."

Royce pulled air in between his teeth and waited with excitement in his eyes to see how Ian would respond to Jack's challenge. The teenager hoisted himself up on the kitchen island where he had a good view and was safely out of the way.

Ian's hand rested on the table next to his glass. His hand didn't move but for his index finger that slowly tapped on the table. Something he did when things weren't going as he'd like and, as Marianne remembered from their young adult years, the finger tapping proceeded either Ian getting up and walking out or kicking over a chair or two.

"We think that Gerald may be hitting Missy," Marianne said quickly.

The finger tapping stopped as Ian went very still. "I'll kill the son-of-a-bitch."

That one statement seemed to pull Jack and Ian onto the same team, however momentarily.

Jack leaned forward to rest his forearms on the table where he sat across from her brother. "He likely is also the one leaving threatening notes on Marianne's gate and we think it has something to do with stolen jewels."

Ian was on his feet, pulling a set of car keys out of his pocket. "I'll take care of this."

"You can't go charging over there. You'll only interfere in the rescue plan," Marianne said.

"What rescue plan?" Jack asked.

"Why are you even involved?" Ian was back to being rude.

"Ian, didn't you hear Jack?" Marianne said. "This may have something to do with stolen jewels."

"Jack is Army Special Ops," Royce interjected excitedly. "He's on medical leave because someone shot his knee all to hell."

"What did I say about 'need-to-know' basis?" Jack sent Royce a look. To Ian he said, "I've experience hunting bad guys."

Ian didn't look convinced of Jack's credentials. Once again, he pointedly ignored Jack when he asked Marianne, "Have you called the authorities about any of this?"

Jack rolled his eyes.

"Sheriff Bradshaw was here today," Marianne began. "He has the notes and he is aware of the alleged abuse. His hands are tied until Missy comes forward and presses charges. That is why a group of women who meet regularly at the knitting shop have a plan to help Missy get away from Gerald." Her next words were more for Jack to explain her actions at the party. "We thought we had an opportunity for Missy to get away tonight when Gerald went out the back door for a cigarette. I was trying to keep him occupied and then you showed up."

Jack didn't dwell on the incident. He provided Ian with additional information. "There's a possibility that Gerald and his uncle, Harold Swan, feel strongly that the stolen jewels are rightly theirs. Whatever is driving Gerald to desperate acts, it's escalating."

"What jewels?"

"That's what we've been trying to tell you!" Marianne threw up her hands.

The next half hour involved bringing Ian up to speed on the notes and that Jack was the new owner of the old Heron Inn and had Bullock in his blood. And that five friends from long ago allegedly stole valuable jewels and that one of them was Ed Dunaway.

"Where's the proof that Grandpa was involved?" Ian asked. FBI agent and man struggled with the possibilities.

"There is no proof," Jack said. The mutual animosity between the men couldn't hold up as their similar professions came together in analyzing the details. "However, Gerald and his uncle may know enough to change that. Something's driving them or someone to leave threatening notes."

Marianne paced the room. "It's killing me that we can't go over there and get Missy."

"Why can't we?" her brother asked.

"Because Caroline told me that Gerald is controlling Missy by telling her that he will hurt Grandpa if she tries to leave him."

"Keeping control of Missy may be part of his plan," Jack said. "He can negotiate with us using her welfare or even use her as a hostage to get off the island with the jewels, once they find them."

"Can I have a shot of the whiskey?" Royce said.

"Not a chance." Jack moved the bottle out of the teen's reach. Then he continued supplying information. "Someone was in the house prior to your arrival tonight." He paused with a frown between his eyes. "How did you get in?" he asked Ian.

"He picked the lock," Royce said with a grin. "The power was out when Mrs. Johnson dropped me off. I came around the back corner just as your porch light went on and I saw him. Then he showed me his badge and told me who he was. I told him I was renting a room here and he believed me."

"You're not?" Ian asked with a dark look.

"He and Jack are both my guests," Marianne said.

"Royce," Jack said, "maybe now's a good time to tell us why you don't like Gerald Cain. Does it have anything to do with why you were fired from the pawn shop?"

Royce nervously plucked at the button on the cuff of his green army jacket. "Promise me I won't get into trouble," he suddenly blurted out.

"Did you commit a crime?" Jack said.

"No! But he wanted me to!"

"Tell us what you know, kid," Ian said.

With an encouraging nod from Jack, Royce did just that.

"He hired me as a furniture mover. Only when I got here to the island, the first house he took me to, the people weren't home and he wanted me to break in. I wouldn't do it. That's why he fired me. He said that if I went to the sheriff, he would tell him that he caught me breaking in. That's a lie. I don't steal. At least not anymore. I stole once back in my hometown, but it was on a dare and only a candy bar. That's why my dad kicked me out. He said I was too much trouble." Royce had spilled his troubles, talking fast like he had to get it off his chest. He said to Marianne, "Are you going to throw me out?"

He looked so dejected that it went right to her heart. Marianne put her arms around the teenager and hugged him. "I'm not throwing you out."

Although he looked embarrassed by the attention, and his face turned red, he didn't resist and the tension went out of his shoulders.

"Jack, are you sure it couldn't have been Gerald in the house tonight looking for the jewels?" Marianne said after ruffling Royce's head and facing the table again. "He's been very persistent in wanting access to my home, telling me that I should let him sell some of these antiques."

"Has he been here before?" Jack asked.

"Not since I've been the owner," she stated firmly. "And I seriously doubt Gilly would ever let him in through the front door. She's said worse things about Harold Swan and his family than our family."

"It makes more sense that it was Gilly in the house tonight. Question is, why?" Jack tossed down the remains of his drink.

"I suspected her at first. When she said that didn't want anything from here, I began to think it had to be someone else leaving the footprints and taking things."

"There's a difference between just taking what you feel is yours and having to accept it as charity," Jack said.

"Bold enough to break in when I'm at home?"

"Spells desperation," he said. "My guess is that she's looking for something and is willing to take a risk to find it. Gerald and his uncle could be pressuring her for the jewels, trying all avenues to get what they want."

Ian glanced to the old photograph. The light from the brass fixture over the table spotlighted the group that long ago had reason to smile at one another. "What do you think we'd get out of them if we put Gilly and Grandpa in the same room together?"

"How is that a good idea? It's fairly clear that they don't like each other," Marianne said.

"They used to," Ian said "Whatever happened might still be haunting them. What they tell us could be what we need to stop Gerald. Even so, I'm not waiting around for a knitting group to put their plan into action."

"They know Gerald better than we do," she said.

"I agree with Ian," Jack said. "After what I've seen tonight, your sister's friends shouldn't try to take this guy on.

Royce threw in his observation, "This Dude is so crazy you don't know what he'll do next."

***

More than once, Jack did a walk-through of the lower level checking doors and windows. He was set on fixing the window over the sink but the eager Royce wanted to show his appreciation in having a warm bed to sleep in. Jack left him with a few tools to work on the window.

It was later, when two of her houseguests had said goodnight, that one remained downstairs and in a pensive mood.

A restless Ian elected to sleep on the sofa. She brought him a thick comforter and a pillow. He stood from adding another log to the fire.

The books and magazines were back on the end table. Ian had also straightened the sofa and put the coffee table back where it belonged on the oriental rug.

"Looks like you had a struggle with an intruder in here, as well," he said.

"We never saw the intruder. I told you that," Marianne said.

It was only when she saw the teasing light in his eyes that she knew he'd figured a few things out. She straightened one of the accents pillows that was still askew.

"How long have you known Jack?"

"We met on the ferry a few days ago."

Her brother's eyebrows lifted.

"Don't worry," she said. "Jack's a good guy."

"I get that impression. My concern is that you haven't known him long and I see the way you look at him."

"I'm not looking at him in any special way." Internally she was hoping that she hadn't given herself away so easily. What had Jack seen on her face?

"Just be careful, sis."

If only he knew how much she'd fought these feelings so far, to no avail. She hadn't wanted to fall for Jack, knowing that he wasn't here for long. Her heart was in a dangerous predicament.

She might write about love and throw in many hurdles and conflicts for the hero and heroine to overcome to be with one another, in reality, doubt, as to whether the other felt the same, was the biggest villain of all.

As for feeling something for a man the moment you fell into his lap and bad coffee in a Styrofoam cup failed to kill that feeling, that would make for a great scene in a romance novel. And in her novels, she could let love happen that quickly because in writing fiction she could create any scenario she wanted. She basically had license to make stuff up. To have it happen to her? Her head was reeling as she fought to remain practical. Ian's words just made her realize how crazy it sounded to fall in love so easily.

"There's nothing go on between us," she said, trying to convince herself of the same as she did damage control. The fact that this good feeling she had about Jack might not even get a chance to get off the ground made her angry. "Just because you got hurt long ago, Ian, doesn't mean you get to go around sabotaging romance, killing it for everyone else before it can even get started."

"I'm not doing that."

"Yes, you are. If you believed in love, you'd be encouraging me. Not shooting it down."

He sat on the ottoman and unlaced his boots. "You're over reacting. All I'm saying is that there's a lot going on right now with Missy and this crazy guy and it seems to me that maybe you're seeing Jack as the hero rather than a real guy. Maybe you're falling in love with that instead of the real man."

"Ian, you're an ass!" She picked up the pillow and threw it as hard as she could at his head.

He caught the pillow in time to keep it from knocking a candle off the fireplace mantle.

"Easy, sis."

He was talking to her back as she stormed out of the room.

Even as she knew that her brother's observation was exactly what she might throw in the path of two lovers in one of her novels, she now knew just how destructive it could be.

***

Jack knocked on her bedroom door after she'd showered and was preparing for bed. At first, she went eagerly to open the door, determined to prove that her brother was wrong. She'd even put on a pink, silky nightgown, the back low enough to reveal that she wore no panties.

Instead of opening the door, she leaned her forehead against the wood. She wanted Jack.

She was also afraid.

Fear that it could never be, doubt that Jack even felt the same, reality that this might be happening too fast, all ganged up. If passion had pumped her blood before, now fear chilled it like ice and the brakes went on.

That didn't stop temptation from putting up a fight.

What would it be like to share her bed with Jack tonight, to lie awake through the sleeping hours and talk with him and make love, again, and again? To have him kiss her like he had in the elevator, a kiss that held feelings, or had she imagined those feelings?

What if her brother was right? What if Jack was only her temporary hero and she was only playing the role of Gigi Divine whose story was set in dangerous times when one lived for the moment because it could all be gone tomorrow?

"I'm tired," she said through the thick wood door. "And maybe this wasn't a good idea to begin with."

There was no immediate reply. She almost opened the door to see if the hallway was empty.

"Sleep well," he said.

She put her hand over the place where his deep voice had vibrated through the door.

"Goodnight," she said softly.

A door closed down the hall.

Marianne remained there for several minutes even though her bare feet grew cold. The lamp threw a warm glow of light onto her bed where thick comforters and many pillows awaited, not two people, but now only one.

She blew out the votive candles she'd lit, climbed into bed, and pulled the blankets over her head. Sleep well? Fat chance. Her heart was too heavy.

Chapter 20

Jack had slept with the window open.

Morning light crept in between the velvet drapes and fell across the corduroy comforter now rumpled with his tossing and turning all night. The white, cotton sheets had smelled freshly laundered when he'd crawled into bed last night. This morning, all he could smell was acrid smoke that made his eyes water.

He sat up fast, kicked free of the covers and strode bare-ass to the set of windows to throw open the drapes.

Black smoke billowed up from the hillside across the water. He recalled the line of site from where he could see Marianne's house as he stood on the back veranda of his inn. He reversed that.

"Shit!"

If there was one thing Jack could do fast, it was to pull on a pair of jeans and T-shirt while grabbing up gun and cellphone at the same time.

Ian snored on the sofa. He opened his eyes the moment Jack stood over him.

"My inn is on fire," Jack said.

He had his cellphone to his ear as he pushed through the swinging door to the kitchen.

The door pushed open right behind him as Ian strode through. He'd slept in his clothes and had pulled on his boots.

Jack sat down to pull on socks and boots with his cellphone tucked between jaw and shoulder. "I don't even know my address," he said.

The FBI agent, who Jack's first impression of was that he would be a pain-in-the-ass to work with, took the cellphone from him as the 9-1-1 dispatcher answered.

Ian gave the dispatcher the details along with the address. He handed the cellphone back. "They're already on the scene. I'll drive."

It was then that the sound of sirens could be heard drawing closer.

They went out the door, grabbing up jackets, the wind catching the door and slamming it shut behind them.

Outside, the smoke was pungent. Both men put their noses and mouths into the crooks of their elbows as the wind current carried black smoke right over their heads.

"Dude," Ian said as he unlocked the jeep, his eyes watering, "this may not be the best time to say this," and he gestured over the top of his jeep to where smoke billowed out of the hillside, "if you hurt my sister, I'll hunt you down and kick your ass." He climbed into the driver's seat.

Jack took the passenger seat, his day not getting any better with Marianne's brother interfering.

"Dude," Jack shot back, "I'd tell you to mind your own business but your sister made it clear last night that this isn't going anywhere."

Ian hesitated in turning the key in the ignition. "I guess I was a bit premature."

"Just drive," Jack said. His lousy night of sleep had left him wanting to bite everyone's head off and now his inn was burning.

Ian had backed into his sister's driveway. Coming directly at them down the private lane was a speeding vehicle with flashing emergency lights. The wheels of the sheriff's vehicle locked up as he came to a stop just a few feet from the gate.

Sheriff Bradshaw jumped out of his vehicle. He wasn't chewing gum this morning. He wore a worried expression as he stood on the running board.

Both Ian and Jack climbed out of the jeep.

"Tell me that Royce is here with you, Jack," the sheriff said.

"I'm here." Royce came jogging toward them from around the back of the mansion, pulling on his army jacket. His hair stood straight up, having gone to bed with wet hair after his shower the night before. He'd dressed but hadn't time to lace up his sneakers.

Marianne came running up behind him, her hair mussed from sleep. She wore jeans tucked into rubber boots and a thick, white turtleneck sweater that fell to just above her knees.

"Jack," the sheriff began.

"I know. My inn is on fire," Jack said. He was impatient to be on their way.

"Fire department is on the scene as we speak," the sheriff said. "On another concern, I've got a mail carrier missing and I'm hoping that's not two on my list to look for this morning. Marianne, have you heard from your sister?"

"Sheriff, I'm sorry we didn't let you know last night. We saw Missy at Sal and Caroline Johnson's party. Unfortunately, she's still with Gerald," Marianne said. "There's more you should know."

Wind blew thick smoke across the driveway, burning their eyes.

"Let's reconvene on that once this fire is under control. Can I give anyone a ride up the hill?"

Marianne and Royce jumped in with the sheriff who reversed into Gilly's driveway. The moment the sheriff's vehicle was out of the way, Ian jettisoned his jeep out through the gate and they shot toward the road. The sheriff was right behind.

A volunteer in firefighting gear flagged traffic on their approach to the inn. Residents and the curious were being turned around. Ian rolled down his window and told the firefighter that Jack was the owner. They were directed to park on the shoulder behind the vehicles already lining the road, volunteer fire department stickers on their bumpers or rear windows.

Up ahead, a fire truck was parked directly across from the inn. Fire hoses ran across the narrow road.

They covered the remaining distance on foot only to be stopped again as they drew abreast of the driveway. Once again, Jack stated that he was the owner. They were then allowed to remain, at a safe distance.

A half-dozen volunteer firefighters were on the scene manning the fire hoses and continuing to access the situation. The noise of chainsaws filled the air. Trees too close to the roofline were being cut down to keep the fire from spreading to the forested hill.

The patch of ferns was no more, having been trampled into the muddy earth. What was flammable and could be pulled away from the inn was now in a heap clear of the driveway. The beautifully etched front door was now only blackened, shattered glass. Flames leaped from the turret windows. Every few minutes, another window popped and shattered from the intense heat.

Mist filled the air from the powerful stream of water arching onto the roof. The wind blew the smoke out over the water and away from where they stood on the road, making it easier to breathe.

As the sheriff joined them, a tall firefighter turned from the blaze and approached. He walked through the river of water that ran from the driveway to turn downhill and carve its way through the soft shoulder, spreading a thin film of muddy water across the road.

Marianne and Royce walked up to Jack just as the chimney crumbled and crashed through the roof. Embers shot high into the sky as fresh tongues of fire licked up and a wave of heat sent everyone taking a step back.

Jack put his arm out to keep both Marianne and Royce from getting any closer. As hot embers floated above their heads, he took both by the arm and walked them over to the line of parked cars, away from any potential danger.

"We could have been in there," Royce said, looking pale.

"But we weren't."

"I'm sorry about your inn, Jack." Marianne put a hand on his arm, concern in her eyes. She had an arm around Royce's thin shoulders.

Additional volunteer firefighters were arriving, taking gear from their vehicles.

Royce brightened a bit when he saw a familiar face in firefighter gear. "There's my boss." He lifted a hand to wave to Tom Harris.

Tom walked out from the driveway wearing protective gear. Rivulets of sweat ran down through the black soot on his face.

The pickup truck next to them had the tailgate lowered. A woman in a yellow raincoat filled paper cups with water from a plastic water jug. She handed one to Tom.

"Sorry about your inn," Tom said. His expression changed when his eyes fell on Ian, who'd sent him a nod of recognition. "Julia didn't tell me you were on the island," Tom called over to Ian.

"I doubt she knows I'm here," Ian replied, his expression guarded.

"Staying long?"

"No."

"Maybe that's for the best," Tom said. He handed his empty cup back to the woman then returned to fighting the fire.

"You two stay here where it's safe," Jack said and rejoined the sheriff and Ian.

He jostled Ian's shoulder. "Sounds to me like Tom doesn't want you near his daughter or he'd have to hunt you down and kick your ass. Or am I a bit premature on that?"

Ian sent him a dark look.

The sheriff introduced the firefighter in charge as Ned.

"Who reported this?" Jack asked. He'd pulled the neck of his shirt up over his nose.

"House up above," said Ned, pointing to a steep driveway across the road. "She saw the smoke and called it in."

"Royce," said Sheriff Bradshaw, coughing into the sleeve of his jacket. "I've got to ask if you left anything in the inn burning. Cigarettes, camp stove, anything to keep warm?"

"He didn't," Jack said, "and neither did I."

The sheriff nodded as if satisfied. "Ned, can you let me know what you find? There've been too many crazy things going on lately. I need to rule out if this is at all connected."

"Will do."

"This was deliberate," Jack's deep voice rumbled dangerously.

"What makes you say that?" Ned said.

"Smells of it."

A dark blue BMW purred to a halt down the hill and parked behind the last vehicle on the side of the road. Just Babs jumped out.

Pinching her nose closed, she jogged up the road, springing off the toes of her white shoes. Once again, she looked out of place, wearing a zebra-print tracksuit with gold bangles jingling at her wrist. On her shoulder was an oversized, glossy, black purse, held in such a way that all could see the designer's initials in metallic gold.

"Hon', I came as fast as I could." Red manicured nails clamped onto his arm. She didn't even glance at the scene. "Look at the good side. Most buyers would have wanted that old thing gone."

"It might have been salvageable," Jack said.

"Poor baby." She pouted her lips and repositioned herself enough to put her back to Marianne. The move of a needy, possessive woman trying to cut him off from any possible competition wasn't lost on him. "Why don't you buy me breakfast and we'll get this listed today," she said.

"And how exactly would you describe the property?" he said. "Rubble with a view?"

Last night he'd been hoping to sit on that back veranda again to watch a sunset while sipping a cold one, then think about selling, or not.

"I'm clever, just you see." She pressed her breasts against his arm. "Why are you so reluctant today? Remember what you said? 'Help me get this tear-down sold so I can get off this rock, the sooner the better'. I'm gonna do that for you, hon'."

"Get off this rock, the sooner the better?" Twin spots of color stood out on Marianne's cheeks and her eyes flashed.

That uncertain look the teenager had worn when they'd come face to face in the inn, was back on Royce's face.

Jack ran his hand along his jaw. "Did I really say that?"

Just Babs threw back her head and let out a high-pitched laugh that had Ian pulling back and moving away.

"That and more, darlin'. Now let's get out of here before my new purse that cost a fortune gets to smelling like a campfire." She pulled on his arm and he went along with her, just to get her away from Marianne and Royce before she could say anything further that could upset them.

They were halfway to the BMW when he put on the brakes. "Give me a second," he said.

Marianne moved swiftly down the road toward him. Not to speak with him, as it soon became apparent. She attempted to evade him by suddenly veering off between two parked cars to get to the passenger side of her brother's jeep.

He cut her off by coming around the rear bumper.

"In all fairness," he began, in the small space of privacy between the jeep and the ditch and a steep slope of ferns, "I said that out of frustration when you took off from the tavern without waiting for me and I was then at the mercy of having to accept a ride with that woman."

"You don't need to explain." She had her hands on her hips in that sexy way of hers that he liked. "Let's be adults about this," she said. "We had our fun, but I'd just as soon not get any more involved with someone who has an airline ticket which I'm guessing is to get you as far away from this rock as possible. Can't say I really blame you. That's probably the one thing we have in common other than our grandparents possibly having their hands stained with a crime."

She climbed into the jeep and slammed the door shut. Then stared straight ahead through the windshield, completely ignoring Jack who stood by the window as rain began to fall down the back of his neck.

Knowing that here and now wasn't the place for this, he walked around the hood of the jeep just as Ian came walking up.

"Royce wants to hang around and watch the firefighters then he'll catch a ride to work with Tom Harris," Ian said. He sent a look to where his passenger sat. "Everything okay?" he asked Jack.

"No. Thanks to her," he said, indicating the overly-perfumed, abrasive huntress he wouldn't have wished on any friend.

The steep slope of the street wasn't kind to his knee as he walked down to the waiting BMW.

Behind him, the red jeep pulled away from the shoulder, did a U-turn, and sped past with Ian sending him a brief wave.

An official vehicle pulled up alongside Jack. The sheriff lowered his window.

"Thought you should know who you're working with." The sheriff kept one eye on the realtor who was climbing into her car. "Just Babs is a niece of Harold Swan. She and her cousin Gerald have had their heads together a lot lately."

He recalled that Just Babs had arrived right on Gerald's heels at the party last night. And that Missy's body language had clearly showed that she didn't care for the realtor's company. Just Bab's clinging behavior was now beginning to have another motive behind it, other than that of a man-hungry huntress.

"Thanks for the warning." Jack was wishing for a shot of whiskey as he reached into his pocket for the bottle of pain relievers.

The sheriff turned on the windshield wipers. "This rain will help put your fire out. Not so great for our search for Eleanor."

"How's that going?" Jack asked. The loss of personal property was nothing compared to the worry the family of the mail carrier had to be going through. It helped Jack put his loss in perspective.

"This is a great community that pulls together to help one of their own. I'm heading over to talk with the family now."

"Let me get rid of this realtor, then I'd like to assist."

"Appreciate it, Jack, however, you may very well find out some things in the next hour that will require your attention. For starters, take a closer look at the shoes she's wearing."

"Why do I care what shoes she's wearing?"

"You'll see soon enough. Let's talk later. Watch your back in the meantime." The sheriff drove off.

The BMW passenger door was open, waiting for him. The car smelled of a choking combination of perfume and cigarette smoke. His eyes went to the shoes on her feet and the wheels in his head began to turn.

***

Behind them, a siren beeped once to get their attention and headlights flashed in their rearview mirror. Ian stopped once over the bridge and the sheriff pulled up alongside the jeep.

Just as they lowered their window to see why the sheriff had pulled them over, he received a call from dispatch. They heard every word and it wasn't good.

With the driver's side window down, and Ian ignoring the rain and cold coming in, Marianne pulled the neck of her sweater up to her ears as she leaned closer to hear the news that brought another level of somberness to the morning.

"They've found Eleanor's car," the dispatcher reported over the radio. "It's at Massacre Bay. Correction. It's *in* Massacre Bay. The passenger door was open and her purse was floating on the floorboards. This could be those pranksters again. Eleanor's a safe driver. There's no way she wouldn't have set the parking brake."

"To be certain, let's get some boats out there searching the bay and get our volunteers to walk the shoreline. Continue to spread the word around the island. Maybe she just didn't tell her family what her plans were."

Sheriff Bradshaw pinched the bridge of his nose after signing off.

"We can help look for Eleanor," Marianne said from the passenger seat.

The sheriff shook his head in puzzlement. "The inn burns and now I've got a car in the water and its driver is missing. Why is something telling me that these may all be lures to get our attention away from the obvious?" He looked to where Perrigo Mansion sat visible through the bare branches of the orchard.

"You're saying we should stick around and keep our eyes open?" Ian said.

"It wouldn't hurt. Jack may learn something in the next hour or so as well."

Several of the volunteer firefighter vehicles were coming down off the hill and passing them, their vehicles wearing a coat of ash now mixing with the rain.

Marianne brought the sheriff up to speed on Jack's priorities. "He's busy selling his property, what's left of it." She worked to keep her emotions under control. "Those are his priorities."

"Don't be so sure of that," the sheriff replied. "My money's on that he's following a lead. Our sweet-talking town realtor was wearing white Keds."

It took Marianne a moment to remember the details that Gilly had given them of the bearer of yesterday's note. Stunned, she quickly filled Ian in on the description.

"If she's working with her cousin, Jack could have walked into a trap," Ian said. "She may have deliberately lured him away."

"That's why I gave him a heads up that she's related to Gerald." The sheriff glanced to his side mirror for cars as he prepared to pull away. "What was the other information you wanted to share with me?"

"Someone was in my house again yesterday, while I was home." Marianne elected to leave out that she wasn't entirely alone at the time of the break-in.

The sheriff's brow furrowed with concern. "I'll check back with you shortly and get more details from you. In the meantime, I'm running priors on Mr. Cain. Wouldn't be surprised if we come up with something."

***

Marianne was having a hard time recalling everything she might have said to Jack in her spat of jealousy. Hot coffee didn't help as she warmed herself in front of the wood burning stove in Perrigo's kitchen. It only revealed what a mess she felt inside as coffee spilled over the rim.

"I don't want to sit here and wait for something to happen. Maybe we should help look for Eleanor." She couldn't keep her even bigger concern inside any longer. "Do you think Jack's okay? What if Just Babs is as crazy as Gerald?"

Ian poured coffee into a mug. He wasn't one to sip at coffee. He drained it and set his empty mug on the table.

"Jack can handle himself." Her brother leaned against the kitchen island, his arms folded across his chest. "I'd tell you not to worry, but I can see that I'd be wasting my time. You really like him, don't you?"

"What difference does that make? You're right. I do need to be careful. And since his plans are to return to the army, what's the point in starting anything?"

"Two people who truly care about one another would find a way to work around that."

She stared at her brother with her mouth open. "What's with the change of heart? Last night you were a total romance killer."

Ian shrugged. "I've seen the way he looks at you."

She should have walked out of the room and ended this conversation. Her mind was made up that she couldn't possibly feel this way about a man after only knowing him for a few days. It wasn't practical.

"How does he look at me?" she said.

Ian refilled his coffee mug and she had to wait until he drained it, again.

"Protectively."

"That doesn't tell me anything. You're protective over me."

"There's a difference," Ian said. "There's protective over your sister and then there's protective over your woman."

Beethoven played a tune in her back pocket.

It repeated three times before Ian said, "You'd better get that."

"Hello?" she said, fumbling with trying to get the cellphone to her ear.

"Marianne, this is Lynn from the assisted living center. That woman was here again. She's gone, but your grandfather is very upset and trying to leave."

"I'll be right there." Marianne ended the call.

"What happened?" Ian said.

"Grandpa had that unwanted visitor again. Now he's trying to leave. I've got to get over there." She pulled on her ski jacket. The movement disturbing the pungent smell of the smoke clinging to her sweater and hair.

The sheriff's words came back to her, that Gerald might be setting them all up to make this easier for him.

"Ian," she said, "if we both leave won't we be doing exactly what Gerald wants us to do?"

"I've been thinking about that," her brother said as he pulled on his jacket. "If he's watching the place and makes his move, I'm guessing that he won't have Missy with him."

"And your plan is?" Marianne asked.

His next move startled her. Ian pulled out his gun and checked the clip. "I'm going over to Missy's.

I'm getting her out of there. Don't try to talk me out of it."

She had to walk fast to keep up with his longer legs as they hurried out to their vehicles.

"Ian, be careful. Gerald assigns one of his relatives to keep an eye on Missy if he's not around."

"I can handle the Swan family," he said.

At her own vehicle, she stopped and spun around. She called out to Ian as he opened the door to his jeep. He waited while she walked up to him.

She put her arms around her big brother and buried her face in his jacket. "I miss you and I wish we weren't all so far apart all the time."

He engulfed her in a big hug and held her close. "Me, too." He kissed the top of her head. "Let me know what's going on with Grandpa, okay?"

"I will and let me know as soon as you have Missy."

As her brother headed toward the north end of the island to their sister's, Marianne crossed her fingers that he would be successful. She drove the short distance to the assisted living center, unsure of what she'd find.

Chapter 21

Ed Dunaway waited in the lobby supported by his walker and one of the aids who remained at his side. The manager broke away from a discussion on the far side of the room and came forward to greet Marianne.

"Thank you for coming so quickly," Lynn said. "One of our staff recognized the woman and I should have, too. It's been years since I've seen her and she looks very different. Her name is Shawnee Swan. She's a twin to Just Babs, one of the realtors on the island." She put her attention to comforting her resident by placing a gentle hand on Ed Dunaway's shoulder. "Can you tell us now what that woman said to upset you?"

"She gave me this." He reached into the pocket of his bathrobe and withdrew a white folded note. It shook in his unsteady hand.

It was the same notepaper used for the previous notes. Marianne took a step away from the concerned expression on the manager's face, wanting to read in privacy what had put such a grave look on her grandpa's face.

If you want to see Missy ever again, cough up the hiding place of the necklace. Have the stuck-up one put the necklace in a shopping bag and leave it at the end of her driveway. You have until 2pm or your youngest grandkid goes for a swim in the channel.

Marianne let out a gasp. She hadn't expected this level of a threat. She moved back to her grandpa's side, trying to think of what she could say that would put some color back in his face.

"This may all just be a bluff." She tried to comfort him. "Ian's on his way over to her house and I'm sure he'll find her there."

"No. He won't." Ed Dunaway shook his head so adamantly that it threw him off balance. He fell against his walker. The aid and the manager were there to assist him.

"Let's get him back to his room," Lynn said.

"Yes. My room." Her grandpa's anxiety increased. His breathing was rapid as he worked hard to turn his walker around. "There's more you need to see."

It was slow progress walking to his room. He tried to walk as fast as he could. The aid placed a hand on the walker to slow him.

"Easy there, Mr. Dunaway, it's been a while since you've ventured this far in one day."

In his room, his journal and the binoculars were on the floor where they'd tumbled from his lap. Marianne picked them up and her grandpa nearly snatched his journal from her hands as he was helped into his chair.

Arthritic hands made painfully slow progress in turning pages until he reached the entries for today. She read a notation of a time and a description of a boat.

"Missy," he said, pointing toward the marina with a shaking hand. His lips continued to move soundlessly.

"I'll get the nurse." Lynn left the room with quick strides.

Marianne held the binoculars to her eyes, searching the marina.

"The boat left," he could finally speak. His hand shook as he pointed to the clock on the wall. "Almost an hour ago."

"Was she with someone?" Marianne's heart hammered against her ribs. The reality of what was happening was sinking in, that her sister was in imminent danger.

"Yes," her grandpa sounded even more distressed. "That no-good boyfriend. He was pulling on her arm." He jabbed a finger toward the note she still held. "They're all in on this."

"Who is?"

"The Swan family. They have Missy and want the jewels in return."

She gently placed her hand on his blue-veined one. "Do you know about these jewels?"

He looked even frailer and older. "Yes."

"Do you know where they are?"

***

Her brother answered on the first ring. "You may have been right about Gerald keeping Missy under guard," he said. "Her car's in the driveway, but she's not here. How about Grandpa? Is he okay?"

"I know where she is," Marianne said in a rush. "Or at least where she was taken. Grandpa saw Gerald down at the marina. He had Missy. The boat left almost an hour ago. That's not all. Gerald had a relative deliver a note to Grandpa this time. He's very upset. I'm really worried about him."

"What did the note say?"

Her voice broke as she told him, struggling to control her fear. "We have until 2pm. Ian, you know she can't swim. They're going to throw her in the channel if we can't find the necklace."

Whatever her brother was thinking, or whatever plan he had formulating in his head, he only had two words, "Find Jack."

It was the same thought prominent in her mind. Find Jack.

Although she and Missy had their brother to turn to, it was Jack's hunting skills they needed right now.

She put her arms around her grandpa's thin shoulders. "I'll come back as soon as I can."

Knowing that he would need to keep occupied to get through this, she made sure his binoculars, journal, and pen were within reach.

"Write down anything else that you see that doesn't look right," she told him.

Lynn returned with a cup of hot tea. The nurse right on her heels. Marianne requested that someone remain with her grandpa until she or a family member could return.

"Marianne," her grandpa's feeble voice stopped her at the doorway. "I shouldn't have told you to stay out of her business. She needs your help."

"I know and that's exactly what I'm going to do."

***

Finding Jack wasn't so easy. When she finally got a signal on her cellphone, he didn't answer. Could she blame him after the freeze-out she gave him?

She had no idea where to find the realtor's office and had begun cruising down each street in Eastsound when she saw a familiar figure on the sidewalk. She slowed and rolled down her window.

"Rita," she called out to the woman in the lime green raincoat, "do you know where the realtor's office is? The one where Just Babs works?"

"Go back one block and take a left."

Marianne waved her thanks and pulled a U-turn in the street. She sped back up the street, the plastic over the rear passenger window snapping in the wind. Her race into town had loosened it and it was now barely attached by a single piece of duct tape.

A blue BMW sat parked in front of an older house converted to business offices. She parked on the opposite side of the street.

Just Bab's eyes widened when Marianne stepped inside. This didn't slow the white Keds nervously tapping under the desk or the way that she flipped a pen back and forth between her manicured fingers.

The man she needed sat in one of the two chairs across the desk from the realtor. It looked odd that the realtor's desk was bare but for the far corner where a grouping of heavy objects had been pushed to the edge.

It soon became clear why Jack guarded the tall glass vase, stapler, and a rhinestone covered cellphone. On the floor behind Jack, a broken paperweight lay against the baseboard.

"I've been looking all over for you," Marianne said.

About the same time that she recognized the musty, stale smell in the air, she noticed the worn briefcase that sat near his boots. "That's my grandpa's!" she exclaimed. "Where did you find it?"

Just Babs did the telling. "I told you, I didn't steal it!" The realtor did a poor job of sounding insulted. "One of my clients brought that smelly thing to me." She waved her hand in front of her nose. "They found it in the alley. I was going to take it to the sheriff. I swear I was."

"Like I'm going to believe you?" Marianne exclaimed angrily. "Your entire family is messed up!" She turned to Jack. "I think Gerald has kidnapped Missy. Grandpa saw them at the marina. Missy would never willingly go out on a boat. She's terrified of water." Her emotions were getting the better of her. She turned angrily on Just Babs. "Your sister has been threatening my grandpa. Where is she?"

"Easy there, Strawberry," Jack said.

"Her twin, Shawnee, delivered one of Gerald's notes to Grandpa," Marianne said. She pointed an accusing finger at the realtor. "How dare you do this to an elderly man!"

"How dare you insult my family with accusations!" Just Babs came out of her chair with a threatening look.

Jack grabbed the hem of Marianne's jacket, pulling her away from the desk.

"We have an eyewitness," he said to the realtor. "You were seen leaving a note at the gate."

"I told you! I wasn't there!" Just Babs gave an incredulous laugh as she plopped back into her chair. "Where is all this coming from? I'm your realtor not this crazy person you're describing. Give me a break. Jeez!" She dropped the pen onto her desk. "Did miss-prissy here put you up to this? Attacking me with these accusations?"

"More like your pretty white tennis shoes gave you up. And you killed a crow," Marianne pointed out.

"That wasn't me." Too late and Just Babs realized she'd said enough.

A sound came from the back of the office where a short hallway led to a restroom door and the rear exit.

"Who else is here?" Jack asked.

"I have staff," Just Babs said.

"My guess is that Shawnee is back there." Marianne said, intending to investigate.

Jack held her back. "We're not getting anywhere," he said. Raising his voice, he added, "We'll let the sheriff handle this."

Suddenly the restroom door flew open. A woman wearing a black baseball hat pulled low over her boyishly, short blonde hair and wearing a black, shiny tracksuit and white Keds ran toward the back door.

"Let's get out of here while we still can!" yelled the woman with an exact body weight and frame of Just Babs. She pushed open the back door and sprinted away.

Struggling to recover from not only being caught in a lie, but being abandoned by her twin, the realtor was on her feet, eyes darting back and forth between her accusers and her cellphone. Although looking in a state of panic, her face was flushed a blotchy, angry red.

"You're a Bullock," she nearly spat out the name. Her anger was directed at them both. "Your grandfathers messed up a once-in-a-lifetime opportunity for my great uncle!" She lunged forward and snatched up the glass vase.

A strong arm hooked around Marianne's waist and pulled her out of the line of fire just in time. The vase shattered against the door and glass flew everywhere.

Just Babs and her worldly possessions were gone out the back.

"That was close." Jack said.

Marianne lifted her head from where he'd sheltered her against him. She could feel his heart beating beneath her hands. Jack felt through her hair for any fragments of glass.

He held her face between his hands. "You okay?" he said.

"Yes." Although she didn't feel okay. She was terrified for her sister.

She gave Jack the latest note.

He read it swiftly.

"Give me your keys," he said. "I'm driving."

***

Vehicles lined the road at Massacre Bay and along one of the private lanes to the beach. The tide was out and those in the search party gathered in groups or walked the shoreline.

Up ahead, Ian crossed the road from where his jeep sat parked on the shoulder.

Jack slowed the vehicle and rolled down his window as they came abreast of her brother who'd stopped to wait for them.

"I'll check if the sheriff has a boat he can spare," Ian said. "That may be our best bet catching up to Gerald."

"Good idea," Jack said. "We'll go on to the mansion and see what information we can get out of Gilly. However, if the necklace doesn't miraculously appear in the next hour, we're going to have to come up with a decoy. Chances are, he has someone watching for the drop."

"Exactly what I was thinking," Ian said.

Her brother jogged off toward the group on the beach and they proceeded on to Perrigo.

They parked just inside the gate. The engine was barely off and Jack was out of the vehicle and heading toward Gilly's house.

"Be careful of the cat," she warned.

He was out of earshot and around the lilac trees.

She had her own mission. She rushed in through the back door.

Her mysterious intruder seemed to favor the rooms on the main floor. Starting in the formal dining room, she removed oil paintings off their hooks. Finding no hidden safes behind the artwork, she began flipping back area rugs on the hardwood floor hoping to find a loose section. She worked fast and didn't bother putting anything back as she dumped out drawers from the sideboard and turned urns and vases upside down.

She'd moved on to the library and started pulling books off the bookshelf when she heard Jack in the hallway. He appeared in the doorway holding Gilly's shotgun.

He didn't look happy and he wasn't alone.

"Get in there and sit down," he said to Gilly. "We're going to have a chat away from that crazy cat."

"That's no way to talk to a relative." Gilly had her nose in the air as she sat down on the edge of the sofa. She wore the gray and black Native American sweater wrapped tight about her as if she were cold or trying to protect herself.

"There's no proof yet that we're related."

"Jack is waiting for proof beyond a doubt," Marianne dryly informed her neighbor.

"You wouldn't do the same in my shoes?" Jack had a red scratch on the back of his hand.

"You look very much like him if you're looking for that sort of proof," Gilly said gruffly. "And you have his crooked pinky finger that doesn't bend correctly." Her chin trembled and her eyes grew watery. "He's dead, isn't he?"

The shotgun was emptied and the shells went into Jack's pocket. A silence fell on the room as he sat on the edge of the desk staring down at his crooked pinky finger.

Marianne imagined this couldn't be easy for him, having such a simple piece of proof before him that pretty much nailed it home that Albert Bullock was his grandfather.

Finally, he looked up and at Marianne.

"I'm sorry," she mouthed to him.

He gave a brief nod of thanks.

To Gilly, he spoke in a somber voice, "I'm sorry I couldn't tell you under different circumstances."

"I'd figured something had happened," Gilly said. "He used to send me money. It stopped several years ago."

"That's about the time he became ill," Jack said.

Gilly worked to control her grief. Marianne had returned to pulling books from the shelves. This seemed to give her elderly neighbor the distraction that she needed. "Why do you keep moving things around in my house?" she demanded. "My mother's Venetian glass collection has been on this mantle for years. You've no right to go and move it to the sideboard."

Marianne stopped in her search. "How do you know I moved them to the dining room? Have you been in my house?"

"You mean my house. You two are noisy, by the way."

Her eyes shot to Jack as heat flooded her face. "That's breaking and entering, Gilly."

"Not when you leave the storm cellar door unlocked."

"Were you looking for the necklace?" Jack asked.

"We know it's in the house." Marianne sat on the arm of the sofa. "Grandpa said that you told him that your mother had hidden it somewhere in the mansion."

"Ed told you that?" She looked surprised then her shoulders sagged in defeat. "I never meant to bring so much trouble into his life. He's never forgiven me."

Jack looked across at Marianne. The expression on his face seemed to reflect what she was thinking, that the story was real, the stolen necklace existed.

"Can you remember where you hid the necklace?" Jack asked.

"He threatened me," Gilly said, abruptly.

"Who?" Marianne said.

Gilly didn't answer directly. "He was always bugging me to let him sell some of the antiques. I made the mistake of giving him the jeweled opera glasses to sell. I needed the money and I didn't think anyone would remember them after all these years. I didn't know he was related to Harold. After that, he wouldn't leave me alone. Harold must have told him that there was also a necklace."

"What did he threaten you with?" Jack asked.

"He said he'd turn me into the FBI and that I would rot in jail." Despite the fight still in her, she looked frail. "It was a stupid thing that I did, taking them all those years ago. I was young, foolish, and thinking it would impress someone. It didn't. It just changed everything for the worse." She wiped her eyes with her knuckles. "Both Ed and Albert tried to get me to return them that same night. Harold had other plans. His family was poor and he wanted to come home from the war with a means to help his family. He took the jewel set and ran."

Jack moved to sit on the coffee table facing Gilly. "What happened then?"

The look on the older woman's face held doubt, as if she debated whether she could trust him with what she held inside.

She continued slowly with her story, "When Albert caught up with Harold, they fought. Albert was bigger and got the jewel set away from him. He hid it in my luggage, saying we'd figure out what to do when we got home. Our parents found them." She looked nervous about saying anything further.

"Go on," Jack encouraged her.

"Then the FBI came knocking on the door. My father told them that a Bullock would never commit a crime and that they were wasting his time. Once they left, Albert confessed to our parents. Only he told them that he stole the jewels. You see, our father ruled with a heavy hand and we didn't know how he would react. Our father told Albert to leave and never return, that he'd disgraced the family name. They made me pretend I had polio to make sure the FBI and the newspaper people stayed away." She looked at Marianne. "Your grandfather and Harold were warned to keep quiet or my father swore he'd ruin their families."

"What happened to the jewels," Marianne asked.

"My father told Ed and Harold that he'd thrown them in the channel." She paused. "And I believed that's what became of them, until I found the opera glasses in my mother's wardrobe."

"Why did your parents leave the inn to Albert," Jack asked.

"Our mother did that. After our father passed away, she had a change-of-heart. It was too late, though. Albert had a hard time getting over the fact that they would cast him off like that. Our father went as far as to demand that Albert change his last name. He wanted no association with him, whatsoever. That's why Albert never came back."

Marianne had kept one eye on the clock. Time was running out. She made a gesture with her hands, hoping that Jack had a plan to get the information out of the only one who could help them find the jewels.

"I know this is a difficult time for you," Jack said, "but we need your help finding these jewels."

Gilly wrinkled her nose. "You both smell."

"It's smoke," Marianne said. "The inn burned down this morning.

"I knew that!" barked Gilly. "The fire truck woke me up." She looked at Jack. "Are you going to turn your aunt into the sheriff?"

"Not if you help us find the necklace. Right, Jack?" Marianne said.

"Did it sound like I was talking to you?"

As gruff as her bark was at Marianne, the sight of Jack pulling his cellphone from his pocket had the older woman changing her tune.

"Wait!" Gilly looked alarmed. "I don't know where the necklace is. Just because I found the opera glasses doesn't mean the necklace is hidden here as well."

"You told my grandpa that your mother hid it somewhere in the mansion," Marianne said for the second time. "That's why you've been in my house. You're searching for the necklace."

The look on Gilly's face was answer enough.

Tires locked up in gravel just inside the front gate.

Jack went to the window. "It's Ian."

Marianne hurried to open the door as her brother strode up the walk, his shoulders wet from the rain.

"A boat was stolen from the marina about the time that Grandpa saw Missy with Gerald," Ian said as he stepped inside. "I caught up with the sheriff and he put an APB out on the boat name and registration number."

"Any word on the other woman?" Jack said.

"They're still looking," Ian said. "The sheriff ran priors on Gerald," he added. "The guy's no stranger to trouble. He was released from jail last year due to overcrowding. He was in for armed robbery and, according to his parole officer, Gerald would rather not have been released. While he was in jail, he was out of reach of some bad guys he owed money to."

"There's his motive," Jack said. "He's trying to save his ass."

"What about Missy?" Marianne said.

"We believe that he has her close by because what he wants is still here." Ian looked directly at Gilly.

"She doesn't know where the necklace is," Jack said.

"Her mother may have hidden it somewhere all those years ago. It could be anywhere." Marianne paced the room. "What if we can't find it? Is Gerald crazy enough to really hurt Missy?"

"We're going to get her back," Jack said.

One of their cellphones started ringing.

Jack looked down at his caller ID. "It's the sheriff."

Their conversation was brief. Jack relayed the hopeful news.

"The stolen boat's been spotted at West Sound Marina."

"That's not far," Ian said. He headed for the door.

Jack crossed the room to where she stood next to the window. His dark eyes held concern. "It's safer if you stay here with Gilly, help her search the house. We'll keep you posted."

She followed Jack out to the foyer. Everything was happening so fast.

Impulsively, she reached out to stop him from leaving. She wanted to say something, to connect with him. 'Sorry about last night' sounded trite. 'Please come back to me' sounded too much like one of her romance novels and might possibly be the words that would send Jack heading for the ferry even sooner than planned.

The jeep started up at the gate. There was a flicker of emotion in Jack's eyes. Was it relief that she didn't unload her heart on the doorstep? The moment was gone and so was Jack.

Chapter 22

Jack and her brother had only been gone fifteen minutes. The wait was already agonizing. She wondered if it would be like this when Jack returned to hunting terrorist. A constant worry for his well-being. Even if they didn't stay in touch, she'd still think of him.

Gilly had clammed up about the necklace, telling Marianne that she was too stressed to think and that food might encourage the return of her memory of just where her mother may have hidden the jewels.

Torn between empathy for the older woman and suspicion that this was just a stall tactic, sympathy won out.

As she made hot tea and a sandwich for Gilly, another concern began to torment her. When Jack did return to his career in Special Ops, the chances were high that he would find someone out there that fit him better.

She imagined him with a woman who had a gun as big as his and knew how to use it. A woman who could keep up with him chasing bad guys, always on the go, never really having a place to call home, yet, they'd have each other.

She'd be happy for him, of course, because her life in comparison might possibly bore him. Her adventures happened on paper while she wrote in front of a fire waiting for her teakettle to boil.

Jack would become restless within a week if he stayed with her.

She sliced the sandwich in half, slapped it on a plate, and played hostess to the woman in her library.

Gilly sat staring off into the far corner of the room and was slow to notice the tray that was set before her.

"Here's the tea and sandwich you wanted," Marianne said.

The sandwich was inspected, sniffed at, then dropped back on the plate. "I'll pass."

The tea didn't even receive a glance.

Marianne stared at the top of the gray head and wondered if anyone had ever had warm and fuzzy feelings for this woman. Then she thought of the old photo. Maybe once upon a time.

Outside, rain pattered against the windows. The dark clouds made the day seem later than it was. She turned on the desk lamp. Then checked her cellphone for any messages or missed calls from Jack or Ian.

It felt too quiet, like they were cut off from the world. That world not only included her family, now it felt only natural to think of Jack and Royce as those close to her heart, as well.

She wanted to be out there helping to right her world. Instead, she was stuck here with a woman whose actions so many years ago had them all in this tough spot. And they were running out of time.

She sent Jack a text message.

It's almost 2pm.

She hadn't even set the cellphone down and Jack responded.

Keep looking for the necklace. I'll be back before the drop time.

The drop time was less than twenty minutes away.

Her sister's fate depended on what remained of the hour.

Marianne paced the room with her hands in the back pockets of her jeans. Jack had managed to bring out an unexpected side of Gilly. She'd cooperated for a short time, telling Jack what had happened so long ago. What were the chances Marianne would be so lucky?

"Where haven't you looked, Gilly?" Even as she asked this question, she tried to think of where all she herself hadn't looked.

"We were in love," Gilly said suddenly. She played with the big, gaudy ring on her finger.

"Can we talk about that later?"

She'd yet to look behind the seascape paintings in the foyer. It was quick work with still no hidden safe that would make this all easier. There were more paintings up the stairwell. Then there were the additional two floors above that she'd yet to search.

She began up the stairs. "What room was your mother's favorite?"

"He gave me this ring from an arcade game the day he came home from the war." Gilly held her hand up to the light coming in from the window.

"Who did?" Marianne said.

"Your grandfather. We were in love. He almost married me instead of your grandmother."

It was enough to bring Marianne back down the stairs and into the room. She could only hope that she hadn't heard Gilly correctly.

"Ah, what?" Was all she could say. She'd guessed already that Gilly and her grandfather were once an item. But marriage had been in the picture?

"We pretended this was the engagement ring."

"What ended the engagement?" Marianne asked after a moment of trying to absorb this shock.

The smile left the elderly woman's face. "He couldn't forgive me for taking the necklace."

Funny how fate worked. She had a flash of a thought that she and her siblings were here on this planet because Gilly had taken a necklace.

She attempted to harden herself against the sad nostalgic look on Gilly's face.

"That's all in the past," Marianne said. "Right now, we must find that necklace. Missy's life depends on it. Please, do you have any idea where it might be? You've been looking for it. Tell me what rooms you've looked in so that I don't duplicate your efforts."

"Pete," Gilly said suddenly. "Where is he?"

Marianne did a slow count to ten and only made it to five. "The cat is fine. I guess I'll do this without your help."

"Try the kitchen."

Finally, they were getting somewhere. "Where in the kitchen?"

The indifferent shrug was of no help. "My mother liked to bake. She was always in the kitchen." Gilly paused as if to think. "Try the pantry. My mother wallpapered in there to make the cupboard doors match the wall. I don't know why I never thought to look there. While you're in the kitchen, this tea needs reheating."

Feeling a glimmer of hope for her sister's return, she grabbed up the tray. "Good job, Gilly," she praised her. "You may have just saved Missy." She hurried down the hall to push through the swinging door.

Gerald was at the kitchen window trying to push it open.

The tray fell from her hands and crashed to the floor.

"Hello, Sweetcakes. Saw your men leave and it wasn't to deliver my necklace where you were supposed to put it." He pulled himself up to work his way through the window. "Now you've forced me to personally collect."

The broom next to the wood stove was the only weapon within reach. She charged the window, swinging it like a bat. The wide plastic base hit him square on the forehead. Gerald swore and lost his grip on the windowsill.

He came back angrier and more determined only to meet a spray of blue dishwashing liquid as Marianne squirted it directly into his face, not stopping until he stumbled back cursing and madly wiping at his eyes.

She fumbled for her cellphone, trying to pull it out of her jean pocket. Her hands were slippery from the dish liquid and the cellphone fell to the floor and skidded away. She was right after it. With a slippery grip on the cellphone, she grabbed up the flour bin and raced back to the library.

Gilly stood holding her shotgun, ready for war. "It's him, isn't it?"

She pulled Gilly back into the library. "I need you to lie down on the floor."

She guided her to what she hoped was a safe place between the sofa and the coffee table. Gilly had another plan. She braced the shotgun over the back of the sofa.

"Jack emptied your gun, remember? You're going to use my gun only if absolutely necessary."

She ripped the lid off the flour bin and dumped its contents onto the coffee table. The gun shone silver in the middle of the mountain of white flour.

"That puny thing?" Gilly looked incredulous.

"I imagine if you can load a shotgun, you can load this. Shoot him in the kneecaps if he finds you. I'm going to try to lead him away from here."

Marianne crawled over to pull the antique suitcase out from under the desk. She turned it upside down to dump out the contents. Silken gowns and pewter goblets spilled onto the carpet, along with fake-jeweled crowns and handfuls of costume jewelry.

"You're looking to make yourself pretty at a time like this?" Gilly said as she fumbled in loading the handgun.

"I have an idea." She dug around in the ropes of fake pearls and bejeweled gold chains until she found what she was looking for. She ripped from the satin gown a dark blue, velvet pouch from another era just as a crash came from the kitchen.

Seeing what she was doing, Gilly said, "You're not so dumb after all."

An angry yell came from the kitchen. She put her finger to her lips to caution Gilly.

"Stay out of sight."

Gilly nodded her understanding. "Don't turn your back to the sneaky bastard," she whispered as she gripped the flour-covered gun with both hands.

Marianne slipped into the hallway. She cautiously pushed open the swinging door as a rock spun to a stop at her feet. Gerald reached through the broken window pane and unlocked the door.

"You've pissed me off, Sweetcakes."

"You want the necklace?" She held up the velvet pouched weight down now with the costume jewelry.

He sauntered into the kitchen, tracking mud, and flipping his blue-soaked bangs out of his eyes. More of the dishwashing liquid soaked the front of his sweater.

"Show me that you're a smart girl and hand it over."

"Where's Missy?"

"She's fine." His smile sickened her.

"Any time she's with you, she's not fine." Marianne put the kitchen island between her and Gerald.

"You don't approve of me as her boyfriend?"

"Good God, no! You've only used her to get to our grandpa, haven't you?"

He tried to lunge across the island to grab her arm. With his attempt having failed, he tried again to strike like a snake. He shot around the island and she hurried to the opposite side.

The door was now at her back.

"Hand it over, Marianne." He looked like he was trying to remain in control, smoothing his bangs back and licking his lips like he'd just had dinner. "You know, if you think about it, that piece could fetch millions. I could make you very happy on a tropical island where no one would ever find us. In fact, I've got a boat waiting."

"Is Missy on the boat?"

He shrugged as if that were trivial. "Why would I take her with me when I want you?"

"I don't want you. Nor do I want you near my sister."

In his furry, he lunged for her. To her horror, he grabbed the knife she'd set in the sink. She could only imagine that this was what Missy had lived in fear of. Marianne nearly slipped on broken glass as she bolted for the open door.

Behind her, Gerald crashed to the floor and yelled in pain.

"I'll kill you," he bellowed.

She raced for the gate and had to leap over Pete who sat in the driveway cleaning himself. Just as she thought that she had a lead on Gerald, she caught a whiff of Shalimar perfume. In the next instant, she slammed into the tall woman with a cap of gleaming, black hair who had just walked around the lilac trees.

The impact sent Fiona back onto the hood of her dark, green jaguar that was parked in Gilly's driveway.

"God, Marianne!" Fiona exclaimed in irritation as she rubbed the backside of her leather pants. Then her eyes fell on Gerald limping around the corner of the house with bloody hands and wielding a large kitchen knife. Her jaw dropped open. "What the hell!"

Pete had remained in the middle of the driveway curiously watching Marianne and Fiona. Gerald's approach startled him and he leaped into the air, spinning around and hissing. So fierce was the battle growl coming from the cat that Gerald took a wide detour. This bought them a few precious seconds.

"I don't have time to explain!" Marianne grabbed the sleeve of her friend's fur coat. "Run!"

Their feet pounded down the dirt lane toward the main road.

Fiona looked back over her shoulder. "He's not running very fast," she gasped for breath. "Can we stop, please? Or at least flag down a car to help? Where did you find this lunatic, anyway?"

They came to a halt at the end of the lane, drawing alarmed looks from a line of passing cars. A glance behind them, and one could see that it was not the two women drawing attention. The armed Gerald limped toward them with a menacing look.

Another car came around the corner. As soon as it passed them, Marianne urged her friend across to the field on the opposite side.

"Why are we going this way?" Fiona asked as they leaped the drainage ditch between the road and the field. "Wouldn't there be people at the marina that could help us?"

"Massacre Bay is this way." Marianne looked back to see Gerald flipping off drivers that wouldn't slow down to let him cross the road. "That's where Jack and Ian are, and we need to move faster."

"You are so going to owe me for this!" Fiona said as they pushed through the knee-high, wet grass and into the grove of fir trees.

It was the same deer path that Marianne remembered as a young girl and it led down to the beach. Her plan was to lead Gerald right to Jack or Ian, or even better, the sheriff and a pair of handcuffs.

Once through the trees, it wasn't members of the search party that they saw when they slid down the dirt slope to the rocky beach.

Just off shore, its propeller churning and spitting water as it fought the incoming tide, was a small cabin cruiser with Harold Swan at the wheel, his tan windbreaker rippling in the stiff wind. She knew then that they had followed the same path that Gerald had used to get to them.

Down the beach where it curved around the bay, the search party stood around in groups, too far away to be within shouting range. Boats were in the water with divers preparing to begin their search. There was more than one vessel out there that matched the description of the stolen boat. Gerald had cleverly blended in with the search party.

A rock fell to the beach behind them.

Fiona cried out in alarm and grabbed Marianne to pull her away from the slope.

Above on the incline, Gerald stopped to catch his breath, bent over with his hands on his knees.

"Run!" Marianne gave her friend a push.

"You're coming with me." Fiona pulled on her arm.

"Missy's on that boat. I can't leave her."

Gerald slid down the slope, making a small avalanche of dirt and rocks.

Fiona quickly picked up a length of driftwood as thick as her forearm. "Grab a stick. We can take him," she said.

Marianne tried again to get her friend away from the danger. "Go get help! The sheriff is with that search party." She pointed toward the curve of the bay.

"Just you and me again, Sweetcakes." Gerald walked toward her, breathing hard from exertion. A red swelling formed in the center of his forehead. "If you keep pissing me off, this isn't going to be as good for you as it could be."

"Help! Help!" Fiona screamed as she raced toward the search party, waving the makeshift weapon above her head.

Chapter 23

"Let's make a deal." She held up the velvet pouch. "You get Missy off that boat and this is yours."

"Sweeten the deal for me and we'll talk."

Caroline's warning the night of the party that Gerald was intelligent in a scary way was proving to be true. He looked in control, his eyes calculating as they shifted from her to the boat like this was all going according to his plan.

Without Fiona, she was even more terrified of Gerald. With her sister on that boat, she wasn't going anywhere.

"Tell your uncle to bring the boat closer to shore or I'm throwing this necklace in the water and you'll never have it." She moved toward wet sand and the tide that slapped ashore.

She could hear Fiona continuing to cry for help, her voice growing fainter as she drew closer to the search party.

"What's taking so long?" Even at his old age, Harold's voice was strong in his determination to finally have what he felt was his due.

"Bring the boat closer, old man," Gerald said as he moved toward the water's edge, his eyes darting down the beach toward the search party. Whatever he saw, took the sick smile off his face. "You want to do business?" He abruptly faced Marianne. "Bring it here."

"Show me my sister. I want to see that she's okay."

"Can't. She's kind of tied up."

"I swear, Gerald. I'll throw this so far you'll never find it." She stepped into the water. The cold of the water seeped right through her boots.

Gerald took a menacing step toward her, the knife clenched at his side.

"That's far enough," Jack said from the line of trees.

She turned in surprise.

"Marianne!" Jack called out a warning.

Gerald grabbed her arm and spun her around. He now had one arm painfully tight across her chest and the other held the knife to her throat.

Fiona had turned at the warning cry. She began to run back, screaming Marianne's name. Behind her two figures broke away from the search party. She recognized the official green sheriff's jacket and the taller figure wearing a baseball cap. Both men began to run in their direction. Was it too soon to hope that between Jack and Ian, they could stop Gerald?

Her captor dragged her into hip-deep water as the boat approached. The sea bottom was littered with rocks and she stumbled. She slipped out from Gerald's grip and under a wave. He grabbed her by the hair and pulled her back up. Marianne coughed and spit out the salty water.

An angry and panicked heart beat against her shoulder blade. She could smell the fear on Gerald.

Completely soaked, she began to shiver, the icy temperature of the water sending her body temperature diving so fast that her legs were going numb. To keep his hold on her, he twisted his fist into her hair so painfully that she could barely move her head.

Blinking water from her eyes, she saw Jack on the shoreline and he was armed. A cry drew her attention to see Fiona racing toward them. Her trajectory would have her running straight into the water and into the line of fire. She looked fierce with her driftwood weapon held high.

Sheriff Bradshaw was faster. He caught up to Fiona and swept an arm around her waist, swinging her around and out of harm's way.

Ian joined Jack where the tide nipped at the toes of their boots. There were now two guns trained at them.

"Let her go," Ian said in a deadly tone.

"There's nothing that would make my day better than to shoot you between the eyes," Jack said.

"Nice try," Gerald said. "Yet, you won't. You wouldn't risk hurting your pretty lady."

The boat was within arm's reach. Her boots stumbled over rocks and she had to grab hold of the arm across her chest to keep from going under, again. The drawstring of the jewelry bag was looped over her wrist. The waves tugged at the weighted bag.

"You all back away," Gerald said.

"You heard him." Harold had one hand on the wheel and another held a rifle. "Sheriff, I've been lied to and denied opportunity by this man's family. If you were in my shoes, you'd understand my actions." He'd used the barrel of his rifle to point toward Jack.

"I'm afraid I wouldn't," said Sheriff Bradshaw as he kept Fiona tucked behind him. "Tell your nephew to let Marianne go. Then you're going to release Missy. That's the only outcome of this situation."

"Don't listen to him!" Gerald shouted to his uncle.

The frigid water was now hitting under her chin. She spat out water, coughing and struggling to keep her face averted from another mouthful. Marianne could barely feel her legs or arms. Her hair was plastered to her head, an iron press of ice against her temples.

The side of the boat bumped into them.

"Keep your gun on them," Gerald instructed his uncle, his voice no longer as confident sounding as it was before. He tossed the knife into the boat then pulled Marianne around to the swim step.

He took hold of the swim ladder and a fistful of the back of her sweater. "Get up there."

She dragged herself up the ladder and over the stern of the boat. Another push sent her sliding face first over the back seating to the floor of the boat.

Below in the cabin, she caught a glimpse of two women lying on the bunk in the bow, their wrists and ankles were bound and duct tape covered their mouths.

"Missy!" Marianne said through chattering teeth as she tried to get to her knees.

Her sister's dark head came up at the sound of her voice.

"Take the jewels and let us go." Her fingers were too frozen to pull the bag from her wrist.

"I'll get those from you soon enough," Gerald said.

The engine sputtered as Harold put the throttle in reverse. The craft rocked wildly as the operator struggled to maintain enough engine power to fight the incoming tide and keep the boat off the shore.

"Why aren't we moving?" Gerald yelled at his uncle, taking his eyes momentarily off the shoreline.

Marianne's brain wasn't working right. She could have sworn there were now only two men on shore with Fiona. Who had abandoned them?

Harold fumbled with the controls. "Something's not right. I'm losing power." The engine sputtered and the boat rocked.

"Move out of my way." Gerald pulled his uncle away from the console. "Keep your gun on them."

Marianne was numb all over. She slumped against the side of the boat, her entire body feeling like ice.

"No!" Gerald slammed his hand down onto the consol. He pushed the throttle forward and the engine sputtered.

"Please, just let us go," Marianne begged. She had her eyes closed so she didn't see Gerald turn with his arm raised. The movement of the boat sent him off balance, lessoning what could have been a heavier blow that caught her shoulder. Still, it was enough to knock her over.

Missy's cry of protest was muffled by the tape across her mouth.

Afraid that Gerald might stomp on her, she pulled herself up and backed against the side of the boat.

Suddenly, the boat rocked hard and Ian came over the stern with water cascading off him, and a gun in his hand. In that same instant, a dark head, as sleek as a seal, surged out of the water behind her and an arm whipped around her waist and pulled her over the side.

***

It was over so fast. Jack carried her to shore and handed her over to Fiona.

He returned to the frigid water just as a deputy came running up to the scene with volunteers from the search party right on his heels.

There were plenty of hands to pull the boat to shore.

There was no discussion on how to get Gerald off the boat. Ian roughly grabbed him and threw him over the stern.

Jack received the goods by reaching beneath the waves and pulling a sputtering Gerald to his feet by the back of the neck.

Sheriff Bradshaw waded into the water with handcuffs to assist. Jack had other plans for the sleaze-ball.

He pushed Gerald back under the waves and held him there.

"Jack, I'll take it from here," said Sheriff Bradshaw as he kept an eye on the arms and legs thrashing the water.

A deputy awaited the handoff of Harold Swan who was helped down the swim step ladder. The older man looked alarmed as if he expected to receive a dunking as well.

"Jack," the sheriff said again.

Another two seconds went by before Gerald was released to stand on his own in the waist-high waves. He gasped for breath, his eyes wide with alarm.

"Sorry about that," Jack said as he handed Gerald over to the sheriff. "The gimp's knee gave out."

Ian carried Missy off the boat and two volunteers helped the missing mail carrier to shore.

Fiona had removed the velvet pouch from Marianne's wrist where the cord had twisted tightly.

Gerald took one look at what Fiona held. "That should be mine!" he shouted through chattering teeth.

By the look on her friend's face, Marianne should have anticipated what happened next.

"You get nothing, you son-of-a-bitch!" Fiona swung the pouch over her head like a lasso and it flew from her hands.

Sheriff Bradshaw ducked. Gerald wasn't so quick. The heavy pouch caught him hard on the ear, snapping his head to the side. The velvet bag busted open and the contents fell to the sand.

Gerald and his uncle stared down in stunned silence at the mix of costume jewelry.

***

A volunteer drove Jack and Marianne back to the mansion.

Jack carried her up the walk where Gilly peeked through the window with the nose of the handgun pressed to the glass.

"Stand down," Jack called out to her.

The door was opened and Pete shot out past their legs.

"Did you catch the bastard?" Gilly demanded.

"It's all over." Jack headed up the stairs with her still in his arms. "Aunt Gilly, can you make us some hot tea? Preferably spiked."

"You just called her your aunt," Marianne said through chattering teeth. "That's sweet."

In the bathroom, he set her on her feet.

"Thank you. I've got it from here," she said, and began to work at removing her sopping wet sweater. But chilled fingers were uncooperative.

Two strong hands grabbed the hem and whipped the sweater over her head. A second later she was sitting on the edge of the bathtub. The man in equally wet clothes knelt to pull off her boots and socks. The jeans felt like cardboard as he tugged those down and she wiggled out of them using his shoulders as support.

That left only her bra and panties between her and Jack. She grabbed the shower curtain for cover.

Jack shrugged out of his jacket and it dropped heavily to the floor. When he reached around her to turn on the shower, his wet T-shirt and chilled skin brushed against her. Goosebumps stood out on his tanned forearms and along his neck.

Jack was strong, but the rescue had taken a toll on his knee. He stood with most of his weight on the good leg.

"I can't thank you enough for what you did today," she said.

"Don't mention it," he said.

"I mean it, Jack. Even with Ian here, I don't know what we would have done without you." She reached up to brush away a grain of sand along his jaw. He covered her hand with his and held it.

"You keep looking at me like that and you're going to find trouble," he said. He tugged on the shower curtain and it slipped from her fingers.

Steam began to fill the small bathroom.

"In you go," he said, holding the shower curtain aside.

In she went, still in bra and panties. The hot spray of water had an immediate effect of warming her chilled body and stopping the shivering.

As Jack pulled the shower curtain across, she put her hand on his to stop him. This could be the last time they would be alone.

"There's room in here for two," she said.

There was a serious debate going on behind those eyes that considered her offer.

She turned her back to him and reached for the bar of soap.

A moment later, she was gently nudged aside as the now bare-assed man she'd invited in put his face under the hot spray. Water coursed over his shoulders and down his muscled back.

On their own accord, her hands began to rub the bar of soap across his back, working up a lather. Jack didn't move as she massaged away the chill. With a mind of their own, her hands worked the soap down to his lower back and over his muscled buttocks.

"Careful, Dunaway," he warned.

He braced his hands to the tiled wall of the shower and bent his head under the hot spray.

"Why the locked door last night?" he asked.

Perhaps it was the scare she'd received today, with the thought of losing her sister, and having to deal with those who held no value for the lives of others. Then seeing the actions of those who did and how far they'd go to help. What did she have to lose in being completely honest with this man?

She stopped with the soap massage. "You're leaving. I shouldn't get any more involved with you because it's going to be hard enough when you go."

He slowly turned around. His eyes were hooded, making it hard to read what he might be feeling. He was hard to read anyway.

"And, yet, we're naked in a shower."

"We are." She nudged Jack out of the way and stepped back under the hot shower.

The warmth of him was at her back, sending a sensual shiver along her spine. She felt the slight tug as her bra and panties were removed, then the soap was taken from her hand.

A silky soap massage began along her curves, working its way up from hip to ribcage. The bar of soap slipped from his hand just as it swept across her belly.

Jack pulled her back against him. His lips glided along her neck as his hand slowly traced a path across the flat of her stomach.

Someone pounded on the bathroom door, startling Marianne out of the moment.

Jack lifted his head and wiped the water from his face. "Shit. I forgot we weren't alone."

Marianne put a hand over his mouth. "Shhh."

"The tea is ready," said a gravelly voice from the other side of the door.

"Thank you, Gilly," she called out. "I'll be down, shortly. I don't know where Jack is."

"Yeah, right."

After a moment, when no other intrusion came from the other side of the door, Jack pulled her hand off his mouth, kissing the palm as he did.

"I'm actually surprised she made tea and didn't just tell us to fix it ourselves," Marianne said.

"She may have been worried about you."

"Gilly?" She laughed. "She likes her cat and her shotgun, and that's about it."

Jack circled his arms around her waist and pulled her closer.

She put the palms of her hands flat to his chest.

"We need to get out. The others should be coming back to the house, soon."

"How soon?" He lowered his mouth to hers and walked them back under the shower.

Chapter 24

All conversation stopped when Marianne came down the stairs. She had a library full of guests helping themselves to her bourbon.

"Get warmed up?" Fiona asked innocently from where she sat next to the sheriff on the sofa.

Marianne had dried her hair and wore a pair of old jeans with a hole in the knee, a pale blue shirt, and a thick cardigan sweater that was more like a robe.

Missy was in the leather armchair. She had a bandage above her eye and her wrist was wrapped and resting on an ice pack. Ian stood from adding a log to the fire. He tried to hide a smile.

"Hello, everyone," Marianne said. She immediately walked over to kneel beside her sister's chair. "Hey." She smiled and gingerly placed her hand over Missy's and hoped for the best.

Missy smiled. "Hey, back."

It was their old code that they'd used when they were kids. Ian reached out and tousled his youngest sister's hair.

"Okay, you guys. Enough love for now." Even with her discomfort at the attention, Missy's face flushed pink with pleasure.

Marianne moved to sit on the ottoman beside her sister's feet as Jack came into the room, his hair still wet from the shower. He wore a clean pair of jeans and a black T-shirt. He carried his boots and set them by the fire to dry.

"Did *you* get all warmed up?" Fiona tried again.

Jack just smiled. His eyes fell on the large tray that sat on the desk. It held a teapot, mugs, glassware, a plate of tuna-fish sandwiches, and the bourbon. He poured hot tea into a mug and added a shot of bourbon. He brought the mug over to Marianne. She smiled her thanks.

Jack made a drink for himself and glanced around the room as he did so. "Is my aunt in the kitchen?" he said.

Fiona looked up. "I haven't seen her. But there was a tea tray all made up. I added sandwiches and such."

"Maybe she went home," Marianne said.

"Speaking of Gilly," the sheriff said, "I should go have a talk with her. We've yet to see these jewels come out of hiding."

"Supposedly, they're here," Marianne said. "They could be under the floorboards for all we know."

Fiona clapped her hands together. "Should we have a treasure hunt?"

Jack moved past Marianne to stand in front of the fireplace next to Ian. As he did, he sent her a private smile.

287

"Tell her she's welcome to come back over here," Marianne said. "I feel like we should celebrate now that you're safe," she said to Missy.

"I'm not really feeling like a party," her sister replied. "I guess I'm not believing just yet that he's out of my life, finally."

"I won't let him back on this island," the sheriff said.

"He's not coming near you again, trust me," Ian said as he sipped at his drink.

Missy smiled her appreciation, although, it didn't quite reach her eyes. "I don't want to stay at my place," she said. "His presence is still there."

"Move in with me," Marianne said.

"I thought you said that you were back only temporarily," her sister replied.

"The dare required that you only stay ninety days," Fiona said.

"What dare?" A trio of voices asked.

Her siblings waited for her response and so did Jack.

Fiona wasn't of any help where she sat looking cozy beside the sheriff.

Marianne explained as briefly as she could, watching her sister's reaction.

"You came back because of a stupid dare?" She glared at Marianne.

It hit Marianne, then, that, no, she hadn't. She was back home without realizing that that had been her intention all along.

Her friend found the words for her. "She moved back because this island feels like home to her," Fiona said. "She bought this big house. That's not what someone does who's only a short-timer." She smiled at

Missy. "I think your sister secretly wanted to have a place where she can be close to family. It's the best of both worlds. Keep your place in Seattle so that you can enjoy the city and visit with me. Keep this place, too. It's the perfect get-a-way for me." Her friend smiled and her gold bangles jingled.

Missy relaxed a little. "If you're going to keep this place, it really is too big, for just you."

"I heartily agree," Marianne said.

The back door slammed and boots thumped along the hall. Royce appeared in the doorway. His eyes fell on the sheriff.

"Is it true? You arrested Gerald?"

Sheriff Bradshaw stood. "That's correct. He and his uncle are on their way over to the county jail. We have them both on kidnapping and Eleanor is prepared to testify against Gerald on charges of arson. She saw Gerald toss a can of gasoline in through the window of the inn. Unfortunately for her, he saw her, too. Other than suffering through the ordeal, she's going to be fine. As for the twins, they opened up and confessed their part." He turned to address Jack and Ian. "I want to thank the two of you. Can't say I've ever closed a case in this manner before. I'd work with either one of you again. That's a fact." He set his empty mug on the tray, pulling a wad of gum from the side first to pop back into his mouth. "Time to go have a chat with Gilly. I'll also need to speak with Ed," he said to the Dunaways in the room. "I'll hold off doing that until one of you can be there with him."

"What's going to happen to Gilly and Grandpa?" Marianne asked.

"Well," the sheriff chewed thoughtfully on his gum, "first we have to find that necklace. Until then, it's just rumor as far as I'm concerned. How do I know that Sal didn't make all this up just to help his book along?"

Fiona walked the sheriff out to his vehicle. She returned carrying her suitcase from the car, her cheeks flushed and a sparkle in her eye. "I invited him to dinner tomorrow," she said. "Don't worry, I'll do the cooking." She nearly floated up the stairs.

"I should go check on Grandpa," Ian said. "Want to come with?" he said to Missy.

The door barely closed behind them when Jack pulled his cellphone from his back pocket.

"I'd better take this," he said. He went down the hall to the kitchen.

Royce finished off the last of the sandwiches on the tray.

With his mouth full, he said, "Do you think that's the call he's been waiting for?"

"I don't know," Marianne said, even though her instincts told her that the chances were pretty good that what Jack wanted was about to happen. She steeled herself against what the next hours would bring and tried to think of anything other than Jack telling her goodbye. "Royce," she said on impulse, "if your plan is to stay on Orcas, and it's okay with your dad, you're welcome to live here."

His face lit up. "Seriously? This is such a sick house."

"You can attend the high school and graduate next year. I'm guessing you're either a junior or senior?"

"I'd be a junior if I hadn't dropped out," he said, dejectedly. "You don't need to ask my dad's permission. I don't even know where he is."

"Do you have any other relatives?"

"My mom left before I could even walk. I had a grandma, but she died. Mrs. Johnson said she was going to talk to someone about a legal guardian." He set down an unfinished sandwich. "If I could pick one, I'd want Jack. But if Mrs. Johnson wants to be my guardian, that's okay, too, since Jack's leaving." He wiped his hands off on his jeans as what truly bothered the teenager came to the surface. "Everyone leaves." He picked up his backpack. "Thank you for the sandwiches. I'll be in my room."

***

There was no sign of Jack in the kitchen. Fiona stood in front of the sink with a screwdriver in her hand.

"What are you doing?" Marianne asked in puzzlement.

Her friend turned wearing a smile of satisfaction. "I fixed the window for you."

Sure enough, the window was closed. "Wow! I'm impressed. Did you ruin your manicure?"

"Very funny. I'll have you know that I can fix a lot of things."

"I had no idea you were so talented," Marianne said.

"My dad was a handyman. I used to help him. I carry a small tool set in my big bag. A girl's got to know how to fix things." She surprised Marianne by adding, "In fact, there's a lot of projects I could take on around this place for you. How about I do that in return for letting me keep a room for my frequent visits?"

"Would those frequent visits have anything to do with the handsome sheriff?"

Her friend blushed. "Possibly." She then quickly changed the subject. "While I was cleaning up the flour all over your coffee table, I discovered my Lady Derringer quite covered with the stuff."

From outside, Jack's deep voice carried into the kitchen.

"I can explain about the flour," Marianne said as she kept one eye on the door.

"Forget about that," Fiona replied. "What do you think that's all about?" She, too, had heard Jack's voice. "It sounds serious." Fiona was the second person to inform her that Jack had a serious phone call.

"Yes, it does." Marianne bit down on her bottom lip. Something close to panic beat at her heart. "Fiona, I don't think I can say goodbye to him." She felt tears burn her eyes. "I'm going for a drive." She picked up her handbag and jacket. Fiona stopped her as she tried to escape down the hall to the front door.

"Hold on there," Fiona said. "There is something special between you and Jack. Who couldn't feel it when you two are in a room together? You put your butt in that chair and you wait and see what he has to say, about whatever's going on. If he has to leave, then he has to leave. Doesn't mean that whatever has begun between you two is over. Ever heard of a long-distance relationship? Nowadays it's so much easier with technology. You two can instant message."

She really didn't want to have this out with her friend while the subject of their conversation could walk in the door at any moment and probably figure out that they were talking about him just by the looks on their faces.

"He said from the beginning that he was a short-timer. Maybe this thing between us is just like spring break for him."

"He doesn't seem like that type. Look how attached he and Royce have become. And I've seen the way that Jack looks at you." Fiona began putting her tools back in the small tool bag. "You're a big girl. Toughen up and see where this goes."

The back door opened. Jack wasn't alone when he stepped inside. The sheriff carried a paper grocery sack. Concern knit his brow.

Fiona put a hand to her hair. "Is something wrong?" she said to the somber sheriff.

Whatever his phone conversation had entailed, Jack gave nothing away. Other than his eyes found her in the room, he now seemed more interested in any news the sheriff had brought.

"Gilly is gone," the sheriff announced.

There was a startled silence in the room.

"Gone as in dead?" Fiona asked.

"No. Gone as in pack a bag, gone." He set the paper sack on the kitchen island. "I'm assuming she took her cat with her as there was no sign of Pete, either."

"Where would she go and how?" Marianne asked. "She doesn't drive."

"She does. Just not very well. I made her park her car in the garage last year," the sheriff said. "She was last seen driving off the ferry in Anacortes."

"Why would she leave like that?" Fiona asked.

"I believe the answer is in this bag." The sheriff reached in and pulled out several large pieces of what remained of the antique ginger jar.

"That's mine!" Marianne exclaimed. She picked up the piece that still had the lid cemented to the neck. "She busted open a perfectly good antique."

"I'm guessing that what was in here is now in Gilly's possession."

"The necklace," Jack said.

"It was in the ginger jar all this time. Right under our noses," Marianne said. "And she knew it while she sat on my sofa and flat-out lied to all of us that she didn't know where the necklace was."

"Now what?" Fiona asked.

"I have a call in to the FBI field office in Seattle. Not sure what we can do because none of us know what the necklace looks like and I have no proof that the necklace was in this jar. She could have just dropped the ginger jar and it broke."

"She may get completely off the hook for this crime," Marianne said.

"I'd say that, unless the FBI come up with something, or the necklace makes an appearance as proof that it exists, yes, she just may get off the hook," said the sheriff.

"It's like the crime never existed," Fiona said.

***

Fiona walked the sheriff out to his car, leaving Marianne alone in the kitchen with Jack.

"Did you get all your arrangements made?" she asked.

"What arrangements would those be?"

She had to take a deep breath for bravery before she could go on. "Royce believes that you received orders to return to active duty."

A smile worked at the corner of his mouth. "I did receive a phone call that was something along those lines."

Her heart dropped. "He went up to his room, if you're looking to say goodbye."

"Is that what he thinks, that I'm leaving?"

"It's the impression you've been giving everyone."

"True," he said. He stood on the opposite side of the kitchen island as he looked steadily at her. "I had two phone conversations. One was from my mom. It wasn't easy telling her about my grandfather."

"I'm sure it wasn't. How did she take the news?"

"Surprisingly, she wasn't too shocked. She said that she's long suspected that her parents kept a secret from her. They kept to themselves, rarely socialized and didn't like their photo taken."

"And your other phone call?" she asked, bracing herself for the news.

He hesitated as if searching for words. "Can you wait right here?" he suddenly said. "I need to have a word with Royce."

As soon as Jack went through the swinging door to the hallway, Marianne grabbed up her jacket and purse and bolted from the kitchen.

Fiona stopped her at her vehicle. "Where are you going? I've been freezing out here giving you and Jack some alone time."

"He's upstairs saying goodbye to Royce." She struggled not to cry.

"Oh, hon' I'm so sorry. Is he really leaving, then?" Fiona walked swiftly over to give her a hug.

"I'm assuming he is because he had to go talk to Royce. I know he wouldn't leave without saying something to him."

"Okay," Fiona looked puzzled, "what did you two talk about?"

"He had to tell his mom that his grandfather wasn't who she thought he was."

"Anything else?"

She avoided her friend's direct gaze. "I don't need to hear anything else. I can't do this, Fiona. I don't want to hear him tell me that he's leaving and not returning, which would basically mean that he doesn't feel the same way."

In another instant, her friend had her by the arm and marched her across the muddy yard to the back door.

"What are you doing?" Marianne tried to free her arm.

"You go in that house and you tell that man that you're in love with him."

"Are you crazy? I'm not putting myself out there like that. And how do I know this is love?"

"Does your heart feel light when you're near him and would you miss him if he went away?"

"Yes, but isn't that the same feeling when you have a crush?"

Fiona nodded her head in reluctant agreement. Then she brightened. "Would you let him have the last bite of your favorite ice cream knowing that the recipe was destroyed and they could never make it again?"

"Fiona, be serious."

Her friend threw her hands up in frustration. "You're overthinking this, Marianne. Do you like him enough to want to pal around with him as a friend and also have wild, crazy sex with him?"

That wasn't hard to answer. "Yes."

"There you go, then. I'd say you're off to a good start towards the l-o-v-e business."

Marianne sent a hesitant look toward the back door. Could she do this? Tell Jack the direction her feelings were heading at the risk of being turned down again?

"For God's sake, Marianne, for a romance writer, you're crappy at getting your own love life off the ground," Fiona said.

The kitchen door suddenly opened. Jack stood there. "I've been looking for you," he said. He noticed that she held her car keys and purse. "Where are you going?"

Before Marianne could think of a believable reply, her best friend in the whole world pushed her inside.

Alone in the kitchen with Jack. Emotions were churning inside and her hands felt like ice. The man she was crazy about just stood there with his hands in his jean pockets and a warm look in his eyes.

"You like your handbag that much?" he said.

She realized that she fiercely hugged her handbag as if it were her security blanket and she was afraid someone might rip it from her. The handbag went on the kitchen table. Fiona was right, she was a big girl.

She noticed that Jack now wore a braided rope bracelet. "What's that?" she said.

Jack smiled as he played with it. "Royce gave me one of his friendship bracelets."

"That's sweet."

"Yeah."

Her nervousness returned.

"Jack," she began.

"I'm not leaving," he said.

She stared up at him. "You're not?"

"Nope. I'm kinda' getting to like this rock," he said with a smile, "and I was hoping you could extend my use of a guestroom. I know you're filling up quickly, but I'd have to find a place to rent anyway. It would only be until I rebuild on my property."

"What about the army?"

"I took my friend's advice and I'm not challenging the medical discharge. It's time for me to try something new." He pulled a business card from his back pocket. "Your brother gave me this. I have an interview with his captain next week."

"At the FBI field office in Seattle?" She wasn't sure she'd heard correctly.

"Yup. Seems I might be useful on domestic soil hunting bad guys."

She didn't know what to say. Her head was spinning and her heart beating overtime.

"I told Royce that he could stay for as long as he liked. That is, if whoever is appointed as his legal guardian approves," she said.

His smile widened just as Royce burst into the kitchen heading straight for the refrigerator. "Did you tell her?" he said to Jack.

"Tell me what?" Marianne said, her heart lifting.

"Jack's going to see if he can be my guardian. That's so rad! A terrorist hunter for my guardian."

"Former, terrorist hunter," Jack said. "And this will all depend on a judge."

"It's gonna be so dope," Royce said with his head inside the refrigerator.

"I can't think of a better person for the job," she said, smiling at Jack. She caught a glimpse of Fiona shivering outside. She knew that any moment her friend could come in and say the words for her. "Jack, there's something I need to say."

The man she needed to talk to was a little distracted, watching Royce examine the contents of the refrigerator.

"I should get to the store and fill that refrigerator up, or he's going to eat you out of house and home," Jack said.

Butterflies were flittering all over the place in her stomach. She nervously licked her lips. The door opened behind her and cold wind stirred her hair. Fiona came inside shivering so badly that her teeth rattled.

"Oh, for heaven's sake, girlfriend," she said. "A girl could turn into an ice cube waiting for you to tell this man—"

"Did you tell her that you're crazy about her?" Royce stood behind Jack holding a carton of milk and an apple.

There was total silence in the kitchen.

"No, Royce, I hadn't quite gotten there yet."

Unfazed by Jack's dangerous look, Royce bit into the apple.

Both Marianne and Fiona stared open-mouth at Jack who ran his hand through his hair.

The silence in the kitchen eventually pushed Fiona's patience to the limit. She pulled a bottle of red wine from the counter wine rack and pushed it into Jack's unresisting arms.

"You two desperately need to open this bottle."

Blushing, Marianne said, "Fiona, we don't need help in that department."

"Don't we all know that." Her friend teased. "I think that you two grownups can figure out on your own that a bottle of wine is good for many things." She took Royce by the arm. "Let's leave these two alone. How about I buy you a burger in town?"

"Cool," said Royce. "But we can't be gone too long. Jack and I are having a ceremony later to bury the crow. You're all invited."

The door closed behind the two.

"You know what's going to happen when I open this?" Jack set the wine on the counter and reached for her.

She took that last step toward him and slid her arms around his neck. "I'm hoping it means we're going to start something."

"Damn straight."

Jack lowered his mouth to hers and his hands began to roam over his new territory. It was the sweetest kiss as sunlight spilled through the window, warming this place that now felt like home.

The End

Acknowledgements

I cannot thank enough my family and friends who have each, in one way or the other, encouraged me toward publication. Whether they have kicked my butt, proofread, fun read, had a drink with me, shared writing, and publishing information, laughed with me, just plain believed in me, or flat-out said, "Just get it done!" Thank you a thousand times.

About the Author

Carmine Valentine is an award-winning novelist. She lives in the Seattle area.

All Fired Up is her first published novel in the Barefoot by Moonlight Mystery Series, and certainly not her last. This series takes place in the Pacific Northwest and some of the secondary characters you'll meet in one story will have their own mystery-romance in a following book. Keep abreast of what's next by visiting her website and blog at: www.carminevalentine.com

Made in the USA
Las Vegas, NV
30 April 2021